# BROKEN

a novel

## OBED OLIVARRÍA

# OTHER TITLES BY OBED OLIVARRÍA

## PSYCHOLOGICAL SUSPENSE NOVELS
*The Flight of the Butterfly*

*Scars*

*Dilated Pupils*

## NON-FICTION
*Divine Masterpiece*

*The Threefold Love*

BROKEN
Copyright © 2024 by Obed Olivarría.



Names: Olivarría, Obed, author.
Title: Broken / Obed Olivarría
Description: Metamorphosis Publishers
Subjects: LCSH: Kidnapping–Fiction. | Child-Slavery–Fiction. | Prostitution–Fiction. | Criminal-Rings–Fiction. | Immigration–Fiction. | Fatherhood–Fiction. | Divorce–Fiction. | Forgiveness–Fiction. | Identity–Fiction. | Restoration–Fiction. | Mixed-Marriages–Fiction. | Teens-Fiction. BISAC: FICTION / Psychological. | FICTION / Thrillers. | GSAFD: Mystery Fiction | Suspense Fiction



Print ISBN: 979-8-9913504-8-8
eBook ISBN: 979-8-9913504-9-5
Library of Congress Control Number: 2024922951

First Edition

Book and Cover design by Obed Olivarria

Printed in the United States

For Ojani.


Thank you for being so cool, dude.

This story is for you.

**Content Warning:**
This story includes graphic content that some readers may find distressing or triggering. Topics covered include extreme violence, hate crimes, sexual assault, rape, graphic homicide, and instances of suicide ideation.

**Author's Note:**
The inclusion of these challenging topics is intentional and aims to shed light on the harsh realities of human trafficking, modern-day slavery, and the exploitation of vulnerable individuals, including minors. These issues, often hidden from daily view, demand awareness and understanding. My goal in writing is not to sensationalize, but to bring these truths into the open, fostering a deeper consciousness about the struggles faced by victims around the world. Please take care while reading, and know that these scenes are crafted with the intent to drive awareness and empathy.

# CHAPTER ONE | 1

MY NAME IS PETRA LEÓN, and this is my story. However, you won't hear from me much throughout—only here and there, whenever necessary. That is because I am not around to recount it all. Don't worry; you can trust the narrator. Besides, it is important to learn about my loved ones and how my disappearance affected each of them. If you start to feel like it's been too long since you've heard from me, you are not alone—so did they.

# BROKEN

# CHAPTER TWO | 2

STILL A FEW MILES AWAY FROM HIS DESTINATION, Joel flew past the red light. He kept glancing at his watch furiously, willing time to slow down. He had rushed out of his office after realizing he had allowed the day to slip away; time had a way of playing with him. Now, he was desperate to get there on time.

Right behind his white Range Rover, flashing red and blue lights told him that someone had noticed his disregard.

*Where did you come from?* Joel was in no mood for this right now. What waited for him was more significant.

His work had taken the best of his day, having drowned himself in getting a deal done, which happened much later than he had envisioned. This was all that he had thought about for the past week. Getting this deal closed was his next big mission, taking him countless sleepless nights of planning and structuring.

Joel was a dedicated man, one of the best civil engineers in the state of Arizona, and a savvy businessman. The problem was his priorities. His work was his life, and he performed it to his best, even at the expense of any other person or thing. Including family.

*Family...*

The painful reminder of what he was to attend had dawned on him as he sat through the late meeting with his clients, roughing through the deals and required documents to make the deal a done one. Securing that construction deal for the new shopping center would be great financially, and God knew he needed that break. The *whoop-whoop* of the police car's siren jostled him back to reality.

"Ugh, cut me some slack!" Joel cursed underneath his breath as he realized that there was no option but for him to pull over. He didn't want things to escalate more than they should. He had no time for that.

Joel pulled over by the shopping center on the right, watching the dark blue and white police car come to a halt behind him. The officer eased out of the car, massive in frame, intimidating as he could be. Straight out of an action movie. The robust officer knocked gently on the side window for him to roll it down.

"Good evening, sir. Can I see your license and registration please?" The bright smile painted on his face screamed politeness, despite the actions occurred.

Joel handed over the documents and returned his hands to the steering wheel.

"I have been asking you to pull over for a couple of blocks. Why didn't you stop as soon as you went past the red light over on Greenway Road?" he asked.

"I am so sorry, officer. I am already really late for an important function, which I quite frankly need to be at right now," he explained. "It wasn't my intention to try to get away. I was simply absentminded."

The officer looked at the license and registration that he had in hand as Joel white-knuckled the wheel. His mind was racing, matching his impatient breathing.

"I am going to give you a ticket now, Mr. León," he said, staring at Joel with one brow raised, waiting for a response.

"I understand, sir." *Please, make it quick; I really need to be somewhere important right now.*

Joel looked at his watch impatiently; he was most likely too late now anyway.

This wouldn't be the first time, either.

It was a special night for me. Prior to my performance, I basked in the glory of the crowd gathered at the hall. The Spring Valley Christian Academy Auditorium was filled to the max. The people here, mostly friends and family of the student performers, would be the witnesses to the first public presentation of my own composition. And being the last performer of the student talent show was both an honor and a cause for anxiety. The moment of truth was finally here. This is how dreams began. Tonight I'd conquer this community in Scottsdale, Arizona, but in the near future it would be packed arenas from all around the world.

I walked across the stage, my heels echoing on the wooden floor, and sat at the piano. The lights were bright on my face and the silence pressed in like a weather front. Nerve racking, to say the least.

"You've got this, Petra!" I could hear Mateo's scream from the audience loud and clear, followed by random chuckles and applauses from throughout the large hall.

I smiled, and the uneasiness left. *I've got this.*

And so I played and sang my heart out. As my fingers caressed the ivory keys, my soul flowed through my hands. I sang with eyes closed, hearing the reverb of the room. Goosebumps on my skin, my heart bumping to the rhythm of the song.

And then I played the last note, a low C, finishing my piece. Cheers and applause erupted, bringing me back to the real world.

My brother James always told me that I am full of myself, and perhaps there might be some truth to that—although I never admitted such to him. But I knew I'd killed it. My playing was remarkable. Of course, this beautiful grand piano helped. My voice didn't crack at all this time, and I was thankful for that. And from the audience's response, I knew they'd liked it.

*Yes! Thank you, Jesus. All the countless hours of practice paid off.*

I took a bow, blushing, as the room filled with a standing ovation. As I finished thanking them for such gesture, I peered past the bright lights to scan the crowd. I noted the presence of important personalities from the school's staff and board of trustees, countless students from the high school, and also my family members, sitting right in the middle of the auditorium. They came to support me, and I smiled again.

But then, I also noticed his absence. Of course. What did I expect? I should've known that he wouldn't make it. And my father's absence delivered an all too familiar feeling of disappointment.

I got off the stage, and my family and friends rushed over to hug me and congratulate me, diverting my mind temporarily away from the annoyance rising within. My dad always had a way of quickly turning joy into gloom.

My mother, Katherine, and Brett, her fiancé, were the first to get to me, engulfing me in a warm embrace and giving me congratulatory kisses and a bouquet of beautiful roses. I could feel my mom's proudness dousing me.

"We are really proud of you, darling!" Brett said with a smile. "You did wonderfully well tonight."

"Thank you. It means so much that you came to support me."

I blushed as I saw Mateo close in. Mateo was James's best friend. In the recent months, however, he had become something more than that to me as well.

"You were smoking hot, P. I swear, if you had played on any longer, I was ready to come on stage and take you away," Mateo whispered in my ear.

I smiled, speechless, chills running through my body.

"No, but for reals, though. Great job, homie. Also... you look... ho... *very good* in that dress. I mean, wow!" Mateo never knew when to stop.

James came over; I am sure he heard Mateo. "Hey, dumbass, leave her alone. She is my baby sister," he growled, walking in between us just as Mateo took my hand in his.

Mateo heaved a sigh and let me go.

"Oh, my gosh. Mind your own business, Jimmy!" I shot back. I hated when he acted all cool and overprotective.

James looked at me, surprised. He turned around to walk away and simply mumbled, "You know what... whatever, fools."

It's like he found the entire ordeal between Mateo and I nauseating. In all honesty, I just think he was jealous—although I am not sure if he was jealous of his little sister or of his best friend.

James had told me days before that he couldn't understand what exactly his friends saw in me, since I was "just an annoying scrawny freshman girl" and that they didn't know me like he did. Of course, I couldn't be more furious at this. He just hated all the attention that I was suddenly getting from his friends. I, however, welcomed it.

I basked in every bit of the attention that the boys showered upon me. I was becoming a lady. A pretty one, evidently.

Mateo said that my long, straight, shiny black hair and my tanned complexion contrasted with my profound emerald eyes. I had the same eyes as my mother. Mateo also said that he loved how my thin frame distinguished my growing female curves. Ha! He even complimented my lips and how they gave way to beautiful bright teeth. That was compliments of two recent painful years of braces, but they suddenly felt worth the pain. He also said that he liked my toned legs. That was thanks to a decade of ballet and gymnastics. He constantly called me smart and talented. "A total package," he would say.

And, of course, I loved his compliments. At first it was weird. It was all happening too soon. Not to mention the fact that we had grown up together. I always found him cute. But it was beyond that now. He made me feel good about myself. He made me feel pretty. I used to be self-conscious of my freckled face and big lips. I felt skinny compared to James's friends. But suddenly, time was doing me a solid, and I couldn't complain.

While becoming a teenager and getting to high school hadn't been a plus for some of my friends, for me it had been a blessing. I was no longer the ugly duckling with glasses and braces. And I would savor every moment.

About fifteen minutes after the show ended, outside the auditorium, I saw my brother with his soccer friends. They appeared to be on a mission.

"Hey, Jimmy! Where are you guys going?" I asked, never one to miss an opportunity.

"We are off to get some food. Do you wanna come with us?"

"Uh, duh! I would love to!" I instantly replied with a big smile across my freckled cheeks.

See, I had accepted, not because I was entirely hungry, but for the sight of Mateo, whom I would be going along with. I invited some of my class friends to tag along as well.

A few paces ahead, just by James's car, the sight of my father rushing in set an entirely different tone of unpleasantness. He beelined to me, and I lowered my head in disappointment and resentment. I had truly wanted him to be there while I performed, and his absence had hurt me. He had promised me that he would be there! But being a "daddy's girl" for most of my young life, I could not be entirely displeased with seeing him.

I already knew that it would be the same story about some late work task that needed to be carried out, or some excuse about meeting up with a client over some important issue, as he wore a sad face while approaching me, clearly having found out that the performance had ended before he arrived.

He was always working.

"I am so sorry, *mi amor*! Please forgive me. I was this close to making it over on time," he tried to explain to me, most likely hoping that I would forgive his lateness—again. "But I got stopped by a cop..."

*Mi amor.* I used to love it when my Mexican father talked to us in Spanish. It was sweet then. Now, though, it only irritated me, since I knew well that he was trying to sound sweet.

Before responding, I saw James at a distance, simply watching, as if unwilling to get involved with the episode unraveling. Knowing him well, I figured he would choose to remain with his friends, at a distance. I knew of his own disappointment for our father, as he was also usually late, if he even made it, to his soccer games. Apparently, James had learned to brush it off, and it was now my own turn to learn the sad reality of who our father was.

A disappointment.

Once again, my dad's work had come between family time, and this was his cross to bear. So, I would let him have it. "Honestly, *Papi*, I wasn't even expecting you to show up tonight," I said softly, looking down. I raised her eyes to meet his, this time surer, and I snapped. "I mean, I wanted you to. So badly! But, you now what? I figured that this would happen."

I knew that my words had done more hurt than a bullet ever could.

The clicking sound of heels against the cement brought our focus to the presence of my mom and Brett, who had drawn nearer. I knew this would be good. She would let him have it, too. And he deserved it. Except, I was not really interested in witnessing an altercation between my parents. I hoped it wouldn't be too bad.

With an insincere smile, Mom showed her displeasure, "Wow! Look who decided to show up. Looks like the cat finally dragged you out of your office." She held Brett's hand in firm grip, almost in a show to make Dad jealous, or at the very least, provoke a response from him.

Dad simply bowed his head, refusing to say anything in response to his obviously pissed-off ex-wife. To be honest, I was impressed with his display of maturity.

But Mom wasn't done. "Oh, so now you have nothing to say, you piece of crap?"

I gasped. "Mom!"

She ignored me and continued advancing on him. "Of course you show up late, Joel. You always have. Even when you knew how long and hard she practiced for this! She wanted you to be here," she yelled as she poked him hard on his chest.

"Get off me, bitch!" Dad shouted, causing my heart to palpitate.

The scene threatened to get uglier, and I started to walk back, scared. I'd seen this before. I turned toward James and his friends, who were watching it all. This was embarrassing.

Brett came forward to calm things down. He got in between my parents, aiming to prevent any form of altercation ensuing—or getting worse, seeing that it had already begun. Brett grabbed Dad to calm him down. "Calm down, Joel. This is not the place—"

Provoked beyond walking away, Dad shoved Brett aside. "What do you think you are doing?" he asked, turning back to my mom. "Do you think that I would intentionally want to come late to my daughter's musical performance? She is my baby! I made her go into music in the first place, you melodramatic bitch! I was stopped by a cop—"

"You narcissistic, irresponsible bastard. We got a divorce because of this! Don't you remember? We ended the relationship because *you* were just too selfish to put aside your work for what mattered."

From a few feet away, I tried to calm them down. "Please, stop. Both of you! This is embarrassing." I couldn't stop the tears streaming down my burning cheeks.

"I am sorry, baby girl. It's just that your mother is such a... well, you know. And I know that she is just trying to bad-mouth me in front of "Yeah, you think you too good for me because you got some younger dude getting into your pants now."

"Dad!"

Brett jumped in. "Inappropriate, Joel. Your kids are here."

"And my friends too!" I said, fully crying now.

"Screw you, Joel!" Mom responded.

"Mom! You, too. Stop it!" I said, pointless as it was.

Brett stepped in once again to clear the air and bring peace. "Don't do this, guys. Both of you, please stop. Joel, just go home and let it all go, man."

"Get your filthy hands off from me, *pendejo*!" Dad yelled back, kicking Brett in his crotch hard and then shoving him. Brett doubled in on himself and fell to the ground.

I yelped. Mom gasped. James and his friends were also stunned.

"Stay away from *my* family's business, you piece of crap, or I'll drop you," Dad screamed at his fallen adversary, who simply crouched on the asphalt in pain.

I could not comprehend my father's rage. I was ashamed, but also worried by his actions. Some of our closest friends were there. I was sure that, even from a distance, a couple of other parents had witnessed the atrocious encounter. This was a show, and my parents were the entertainment. A bad-taste performance. Someone would most likely call the cops soon.

James and I had experienced our father's explosive episodes before, as well as Mom's melodramatic antics and bursts of anger. But this incident terrified me down to my guts. Our friends hadn't witnessed anything like this. And they simply stared in shock at the madness that Mr. León, their friends' dad, had displayed. They were looking at a different beast emerging from him. I was sure they were wondering what happened to the cool, collected, and fun Mr. León that they had interacted with throughout the years. The one that used to take them all bowling and to the movies. The one who would have them all over for a pool party, movie, and pizza in our home.

Dad seemed to suddenly notice the audience. "I am sorry, everyone. That escalated quickly, and it wasn't my intention. How about I take you guys all out to grab something to eat?" he asked to the group of teenagers gathered in the distance. I am sure he was hoping it'd do well enough to bribe them. "I know a very cool place not far from here, and all you can eat is on me," he added, sweetening the deal some more.

But not one soul responded to his offer. They were still shocked. Terrified of him. As was I.

Mom was on the ground, her bare knees painfully scraping the concrete as she tended to Brett.

"Come on, kids. What do you say? I mean, it's Saturday night, after all, and you're allowed to have as much fun as you want."

I was astonished.

James was the one brave enough to break the awkward silence. "Sorry, *Papi*. But we already had plans to go to the mall before you came," he said with a shrug. "Besides, Brett already promised to take us to the new laser tag place afterwards," he elaborated, showing his allegiance to Brett.

"Yes, Dad. Sorry," I added.

The others followed suit, and we all got in our cars, leaving my father behind.

Joel had finally emerged from his rage and realized that he had made a scene and embarrassed himself in the process, with his kids and their friends watching. Luckily, no one had called the cops on him.

No one had said a word after James had refused his offer. Joel just watched them get into the van with Brett and drive away. He felt his heart hurt, with the sour taste of defeat in his mouth.

Joel wasn't going to give up just yet. These were *his* babies! And he wasn't going to give Brett the satisfaction of letting him take over his family, like a new and improved replacement.

Standing there, all by himself, Joel ground his teeth until they ached. He clenched his fists, feeling rather alone, cheated. He could not fathom why his ex-wife would stick with someone in Brett's mold, or why his own kids wouldn't accept his invitation to treat them to dinner.

He really was trying. He truly wanted to make things right. But Joel León just didn't know how.

As he heaved a sigh in frustration and emptiness, Joel headed back to his Range Rover, violently unlocking the door, before slamming it hard once he climbed inside. He was a mess. A hot one.

This wasn't fair.

Rubbing his hand hard against his temple, almost questioning his choices, he began to ponder. "What have you done, Joel? You messed up... again."

He recounted the entire occurrence over in his head. How did it get to this? He never intended to hit Brett or anyone else, but Brett's interference had upset him. He understood too well that his presence there was the poison which had made things erupt into the scene it had.

Picking up his phone, he dialed Kathy's phone. He waited for her to pick up from her end. He badly needed to speak with her.

Things just couldn't end like this.

# CHAPTER THREE | 3

KATHY HAD JUST TAKEN A BITE of juicy steak when she heard her phone buzz inside her handbag. She got it out, grimacing at seeing Joel's name spread across the screen.

"Why don't you answer, honey?" Brett asked, noticing his fiancée had returned the phone back into her bag.

"It's nothing, dear. I just don't want to interrupt this delicious meal," she replied casually, taking a new bite of her food.

The phone buzzed on and on for the next few minutes, and Kathy continued to ignore it. She was absolutely not in the mood to speak with him.

"How is your steak, Jimmy?" Brett asked James, while watching the kids chatting on the other side of the table.

"It's freaking amazing!" James responded with a thumb-up to Brett.

Kathy's phone began buzzing differently, this time with multiple text messages coming in a rush.

*I really need to speak with you about something important.*

*It's urgent!*

*Please answer the phone.*

Kathy could no longer ignore the messages, as she worried that something might be wrong with Joel. She dialed his phone back, with her palms sweaty and her heart racing. She listened to the phone ring for a split second before his voice patched through.

"Hi, Katherine. Look, I am sorry for my behavior earlier. I have no idea what came over me," he apologized.

It sounded sincere. Then again, he usually was.

Kathy stood up from the table and excused herself. A few steps away from her family, she finally responded. "It's okay, Joel. I've gotten over it," Kathy replied, feeling glad at heart that he was fine. "Besides, I know that I pushed your buttons too. I was just sad for your daughter. She loves you, Joel. But you are going to have to apologize to the kids and Brett for what you did. They are the ones that are hurt the most."

He sighed. "I know. But you must understand that his presence there brought out the worst in me. There is just *something* about that guy that spooks me. And I don't trust him around my family, Kathy," Joel explained from his end.

"Brett is a really sweet guy, Joel. And you must accept that and find a way to deal with that reality. He is *not* going anywhere." Kathy was not about to let her ex-husband poison her relationship with a genuinely good guy.

"I am telling you, something doesn't feel right about him. I don't know what it is, though. Come on, Kathy; don't be blinded by infatuation. Think about it. Why would you marry a guy that you barely know or even know anything about?" Joel pressed, trying to discourage her.

Kathy's resolve was stone hard, and she was willing to stand by Brett. "Now you're starting to sound pathetic, Joel. Listen to yourself rant on! Jealousy doesn't look good on a man your age. Grow up."

Kathy and Joel had gotten on a similar argument regarding Brett two weeks prior. Joel was upset that she was moving "too fast" with him, saying that she barely even knew the guy. But she knew well that Joel was only mad because she had mentioned that Brett was the opposite of him, better in every way. Brett Miller was an upgrade from Joel. And while she meant what she said, she immediately regretted voicing it out loud.

Mindful of how poorly that went, she resolved to be more tactful this time and not rub it in. "Look, Joel, the truth is that the kids adore him. And I think that this fact scares you very much."

She knew the words would only fuel Joel's dislike for Brett even further, but she needed to state her truth. "They feel closer, more secure, comfortable, and loved by him. Most importantly, he gives them the time of day! When was the last time *you* did that? All you do is push them away. And me too. Now, I'm not going to spend any more time on this with you. I have a family dinner I don't want to miss." With those words, she hung up the phone pressed her hand to her burning cheeks.

She turned toward her family, who were enjoying their meals and having a few laughs. She took another deep breath to ease her tension and walked back to them, plastering a fake smile on her face and taking her seat at the table.

Slowly, Brett stretched his hand across the table, holding hers tightly. She fixated her eyes on his in response. Her smile now a sincere one. This man was marvelous.

"What's going on, babe? Tell me what is bothering you," Brett asked.

Kathy wasn't quick to respond, feeling the burden of Joel's endless rant and insinuations about her beloved Brett. She could feel her heart weigh heavy, and her bank of thoughts overflowing. She looked down into their embracing hands, then up into Brett's blue eyes, wondering how someone could see such a good and loving soul as evil. She couldn't comprehend the madness behind Joel's behavior. She couldn't believe that this was the man that at some point in her life she had believed she would be with until death. Now, she couldn't trust him.

"There is nothing to worry about, Brett," she finally said. "Everything is just fine." She aided her lies with an equally deceptive smile as she let go of him.

Brett nodded back, alluding his understanding in silence.

She could tell that her soon-to-be-husband had more to say, with his head now bowed to the floor and his fingers curled into a ball. And the only means by which their conversation would go well was with the kids away. She directed her focus toward the kids, who had finished their meals and seemed aching to head off to the laser tag.

"So, who's ready for some laser tag?" she asked them.

"Heck, yeah! Brett, can we head off to the laser tag now?" James asked Brett, instead of directing his permission seeking to his own mother.

"Yeah, sure. You guys go have fun!" Brett nodded them in the direction of the laser tag.

Kathy smiled, knowing that her own son was growing quite fond of the man she loved. She watched them as they exited the restaurant, teasing and elbowing each other, eager to have some fun.

She permitted a few more seconds to pass by before turning to Brett. "I can tell that something is bothering you, my love."

"Look, babe. I know that you are upset. But you can talk to me whenever you are ready. I don't want you to feel pressure to share things with me before you are ready."

Kathy wondered if he was playing a guilty card, but he spoke in a calm and loving tone that spelled sincerity and understanding.

"It's Joel," she finally explained. "He just seems so stubborn and unwilling to move on. I don't know what's gotten into him lately. It's worrying me."

"I just think that he's a hurt man wishing to be with his family, that's all." He spoke with kind words, even when referring to someone who had assaulted him.

"That's sweet of you, but I doubt that's what it is. He seems hurt and jealous about the fact that you and I are together, to the point that it's making him lose his senses."

Brett listened as he stretched both his hands out on the table to connect with hers once again. His warm hands engulfed her cold pair, as he brought them closer to his face to plant a gentle kiss on the backside of her hands. She loved how passionate he was. He always understood when she hurt and when she needed him to listen. He knew instinctively how to help her through the rough times.

"He used to be so sweet, you know? He would care for the kids, he was such a loving father, and never hurt anybody," she explained.

She paused briefly, deep in thought.

"Well... that would be the old Joel, at least. Now, I can hardly recognize him. It is almost as if his jealousy is driving him mad, making him into an entirely different being. It shocks me."

"Babe, I am sure that he will come around eventually. He probably just needs some time to adjust."

Kathy couldn't understand why Brett was defending him.

"I doubt it. I really don't know if I know him anymore," Kathy confessed, deep in sorrow. "He is a different person from the one that I married." Her tone expressed sincere concern. "To be honest... I am really scared of him right now." The last part she whispered, as if though he could hear her talk about him that way.

She looked around.

Brett squeezed hard on her hands, as if trying his best to keep her calm. She could read the hurt in his eyes. But the truth was that everything about Joel León right now spooked her, and all she wanted to hear was that he would keep her and the kids safe.

"I understand what you mean, dear. Believe me, I can relate with everything you've said," he said, "But don't worry; I'll be here with you guys, and nothing will happen to any of you. I promise."

This was one of the features that Kathy loved the most about Brett, the fact that he would listen and always come up with soothing words to help calm her nerves when she had things bothering her. It was as if innately knew the right words to say and the right time to say them. His strength was his ability to bridge the gap between a saddened heart and happiness. He had the magic words, touch, and expressions to get Kathy through the most difficult moments and to a place of peace.

"I am here for you, my love. Whenever and every time that you need me," he consoled. "You can trust that I would protect you to my last living breath!" It was a promise that spoke of violence she couldn't even contemplate, but he spilled it in such loving words that seemed to melt away her worries.

"Aw! You always know just what I need to hear, babe."

Brett leaned over from the other side of the table and pressed his lips to hers, kissing her lovingly.

"I love the fact that you are patient and understanding with me," she confessed. "I also like the fact that you are great with the kids and that they seem to accept, respect, and love you. They look up to you, and that says a lot."

Kathy knew that compliments overwhelmed Brett, and he always had a tendency to play it cool and not smile. But this time he lost the battle, with a bright smile taking over his face from ear to ear.

"Thank you." This was all that he could say as he kissed her again.

Over at the laser tag place, Petra, James, and their friends were having a great time. Time trickled by and neither of them realized it. In the middle of a battle, Petra and Mateo had vanished. James wondered where his teammates had gone. He looked around, finding neither of them.

He approached his sister's best friend. "Sorry, Amanda, I didn't mean to scare you. I'm not here to shoot you, either. I just have a question. Have you seen my sister?"

Amanda remained low, not wanting to be discovered in the middle of a battle, and simply whispered, "No."

"What about Mateo?"

Amanda gave the same answer by shaking her head and running away to a different part of the cavernous, dark room.

Nobody seemed to have known when or where they had headed off.

*Where the hell are you two?*

He walked away from the scene, wandering around until he came across a secluded and darker area on a corner of the premises. And there they were, Mateo and Petra, their bodies locked together in an intimate kiss. Mateo's hand was moving down, making its way onto her thigh under her skirt. Petra's hands were around his waist, enjoying and welcoming Mateo's movements on her body.

James threw his laser blaster on the ground, rage rising from within, and barreled their way. "What the hell? What do you think you're doing with my sister?" he demanded, feeling disgusted and betrayed by his friend's actions.

"Chill out, bro! We're just having fun," Mateo responded, far to casually for James's taste. "Besides, you do the same thing with other girls and even brag about it. It's not a big deal."

"Say that when you see *my* hand on your sister's ass, you piece of shit!" James snapped, infuriated by the comparison. He then turned to his sister. "And you! What the hell, Petra? What would Mom say if she saw you doing this? Last week you are embarrassed by my friends' flirting, and today you are doing *this*?"

He was disappointed by her decision to welcome Mateo's groping. And he was surprised.

Petra wasn't interested in his opinions on her behavior, though. "Back the hell off, James. I'm not a baby. I have a life, and it doesn't concern you!" she yelled at him.

James stood still, struck hard in the chest by the words. He parted his lips, but nothing came past them. He was in disbelief in her tone and choice of words, not knowing how to react.

But his little sister wasn't done. "I don't need a babysitter. You need to chill out, or you'll burst a blood vessel," she continued, this time without making eye contact with him.

"Don't you see what you're doing is disgusting?" James finally said to her, wondering where she had dumped her morality.

She had always been the good one, the one with higher morals. His baby sister. Who was this girl he was seeing now? Where had *that* innocent baby sister gone? She was growing up way to fast, and he didn't like it. She was only fifteen, for crying out loud. And he wanted to keep her safe and innocent for as long as possible.

James turned to his friend, but Mateo was silent, clearly unwilling to get involved in this sibling spat.

"You are acting just like Dad," Petra said as she grabbed Mateo's arm and tugged him to come along with her back to the game.

James felt the words pierce through his chest, striking his heart dearly, and rendering him further speechless. The comparison Petra had made of him being like their father hurt him more than she could have realized. She had compared him to the one person they never intended to be like when they grew up. It hurt.

It stung so much that James refused to move from the spot where he stood.

# CHAPTER FOUR | 4

I REMAINED QUIET through the journey back home, pensive. There had been highlights and dark valleys in my night. The drive felt particularly long tonight. My mind was simply occupied, and my thoughts littered every field on my consciousness. I just couldn't come to comprehend how things had turn out the way they had. Too much had happened. But, either everyone seemed to have forgotten about the night's incident back at the school's parking lot, or they were all ignoring it, choosing to focus on happier topics as we headed back home.

Mom chatted cheerfully with her new-found love up front. I was happy for her. And her joy brought a smile to my face. We talked about the show, about my performance and my song, and about the food at the restaurant. But nothing else.

We finally arrived home after the seemingly endless drive, after they had dropped off our friends at their respective homes, not very far from our own. Good thing we all lived close by. I watched Mom head out of the van with Brett, while James did the same. I, however, took my time, reflecting on everything—my performance in the school's talent show, but also the altercation between my parents, and the embarrassment that it caused. Then there was also Mateo. Were things moving too fast? I certainly liked it, and my body craved him, but my conscience told me to slow down.

I let out a heavy sigh, eventually summoning enough courage to leave the van, heading straight upstairs for bed. I slammed the door hard behind me, hoping to remain undisturbed for the night, especially by James, who had a habit of coming over to nag about something. Lately, he came over to complain about my late phone calls with friends, which supposedly he could hear through the hardly soundproof wall that we shared.

"Shut up already, Petra. I am trying to get some sleep; I have practice in the morning," he told me on more than one occasion.

Lately, he was upset that I would talk a lot on the phone with *his* friends. He was upset that the boys were more interested in me than him. I would simply ignore him most of the times.

I crawled into bed, glancing at my phone, wondering if Dad would call. He was the only man that I wanted to hear from tonight, even if I still couldn't believe his behavior this evening.

As the dreams took over my thoughts, my phone slid off gently from my hand. I began to venture into a world without performances, worries, boys, or daddy issues. I hadn't even changed from my talent show dress. I needed the rest and hoped that it would all go away by morning.

But I was wrong.

I rubbed my eyes open while still in bed and stretched my rested limbs. As I sat on the side of my bed, my eyes met a framed picture that I had taken with Dad sometime back. The smile across my younger face was priceless, the genuine feel of happiness was evident, and unwavering, and so was my father's.

It was a great time then, unlike how things were now.

I felt a headache settling in. Depression began to weigh my mind down. I blinked intermittently at the frame, biting my lip in hurt.

*When did it all begin to fall apart? How did it all come to be like this?*

Perhaps I was asking the wrong question, seeing as everything revolved around Dad. It began with him, and now circled all around him. The change had been the epitome of it all —the feather that came crashing and broke our camel's back.

He was never like that before, though. I wasn't familiar with this man who hurt people and called my mother names.

*What happened to you, Papi? What happened to us?*

With a weighty sigh, heaved from a worried and heavy heart, I went further down memory lane, recalling how much of a daddy's girl I had always been growing up. I remembered the old days. These were the times when Dad and I were inseparable. He was my father, guardian angel, best friend, and mentor in every aspect. But now, things were different.

With a tearful, nostalgic smile, still staring at the picture in front of me, I felt the urge to see more of them. I pulled open the top drawer to grab my scrapbooks. Some of the pictures seemed like from another lifetime, in a world that no longer existed. I flipped through the pages, noting the progressive smile from my father's face from the time that I was born, while he held me, to the time that we began spending lots of time together. *Papi and mija.*

A third flip of the pages brought with it a picture of a vacation at my father's hometown in Mexico. San Carlos, Sonora. Back in the day, we visited often, and James and I loved every moment there. The beach, the food, the fun, Grandma. The nostalgia brought another wave of sadness. The photographic evidence of how happy we were made me wish the picture could somehow transmit the happiness into my present life.

"Why did everything change?" I murmured, flipping through the album some more before dumping it back into the drawer.

All I felt now was pain and hurt. Dad had always been the rock behind most of my decisions and actions. He had understood me from an early age so well. I believed he would stick with and for me through thick and thin, no matter what. He always found a way to encourage me to do the things that I wanted to do, even if others saw no meaning in it whatsoever. Things like music.

He had encouraged me to write my first songs, and stood firmly in support of me, when everyone else grew frustrated by the countless and repetitive practice sessions. Granted, I knew that I was in no way worthy to be classified as being any good back then, but Dad seemed to see nothing but endless potential in me. It was as if my noises were music to his ears. My persistence was pride and joy to his soul. I was the apple of his eye, and everything that I produced was somehow beautiful to him.

James would groan in dismay every time that I would practice, unwilling to go through the torture of having to listen to me plunking out the same notes, over and over, especially during the first couple of years of learning.

In those days, if anyone could make a good song sound bad, or as though they should never have been written, it was me. Still, without fail, I always had an audience of one – Dad. He remained the one person who would painstakingly sit through my so-called concerts at home, cheering on, no matter how bad it was.

The situation differed now, however. My parents' divorce couldn't be labeled as the epitome of it all, remembering that they still had a healthy relationship after they had split. Dad still acted like himself, even after, including his unchangeable habit of always coming late to important things due to work.

Things had begun getting bad after Mom found Brett. My dad just couldn't handle it. The introduction of Brett Miller into the picture had brought with it unimaginable issues and turmoil. Granted, Mom had found new joy, seeming happier with him than she ever had been with Dad, at least in the latter years.

Brett's introduction into the picture had not only affected Dad. James simply retreated into his own world. He used to be very close with Dad, too, and they often played soccer together in the backyard or at the park. But Brett had taken Dad's mentor role with my brother as well.

I was grateful for Brett and that Mom had met him. He was a sweet man, with such a nice personality. Still, I missed my biological father. I just wanted my family back the way that it was and used to be, when we were all close. But the fact that Dad was getting worse perplexed me. He just wasn't the man that he used to be. And I refused to accept that it could be just jealousy. There had to be another reason or cause to this. Perhaps it was work. Or something else.

I grabbed my phone, with the desire to call my father. But it was dead, as I hadn't charged it before I passed out last night. Bummer.

I plugged it in and decided to take a much-needed shower. I would try to call him later.

As I got into the shower to get ready for the day, I recalled the day it all began to go sour. It began with Mom introducing us to Brett at a family barbeque. He was funny and charming. And handsome. That helped too. Again, I was happy for Mom. Her joy overflowed.

"Hey kids, this is Brett. You're going to be seeing a lot of him around now," Mom had said with a wink. Mom sure knew how make bigger deals of something small, but she also minimized major things.

Would this man be Dad's replacement? That was no small thing, and some warning would have been nice. I was skeptical of him at first. But he walked over to me, held out his hand, and cracked a smile. "I'm Brett. You must be the lovely Petra!" he said enthusiastically. "I've heard so much about you from your mother," he explained.

James got a similar introduction, but he seemed more eager to let his wall down. He began a friendship relationship with Brett almost instantly once they spoke at length about European Soccer that same afternoon over hot dogs.

Mom met Brett at the park, during one of her usual morning jogs. He approached her and they hit it off well from the beginning. He wasn't like Dad. He enjoyed romantic comedies, he didn't argue about politics, and most importantly, he was always present.

Brett was a gentleman who would offer to help us through whatever it was that we needed. He dropped James off at soccer practice and picked him up when he was done— before Dad bought James his

Audi A4. At times he would even sit through the practice sessions, watching him play and giving him advice. He had nicknamed James "Jimbo" from the beginning. The family was used to calling him Jimmy, but Jimbo had a nice ring to it. And James didn't seem to mind.

Occasionally, Brett would also assist me with things that I needed help with. He won all of us over soon enough.

James believed Brett was with us for the long haul. "I think Mom is in love again."

I heard him, but chose to ignore his theories, until I walked into the kitchen to see them kissing passionately. It was a sight impossible to burn from my brain. Yeah, I guess James was right.

The news of their engagement came not long afterward, like a bombshell. It was dropped during another barbeque in which Brett had brought along a friend of his, Floyd Smith, and his wife, Martha. Floyd was a co-worker of Brett, and a nice fellow as well.

I felt that a grave mistake was made on that day, as my dad was also present during the barbeque, which was apparently only organized to share the good news with those she cared about. I had already begun digging through my meal when the bombshell dropped, halting my chew as I looked up to Mom, whose hand was extended to show off the engagement ring that Brett had gotten her.

"We're engaged!" Mom shouted, like an excited schoolgirl, while everyone else gaped in surprise.

James turned to me, giving me the "I told you so" look and smirk before casually returning to his meal. I guess we were both fine with it. We had gotten to know Brett well and had no issues with him.

One person would beg to differ though – my father.

After the shower, I decided not to call Dad. If he wanted to see me, or apologize for his behavior, he would make an effort. So I waited. And waited.

# BROKEN

# CHAPTER FIVE | 5

JOEL HAD ALSO BEEN THINKING about that fateful day when Kathy announced her engagement. He waited for the perfect opportunity that afternoon before pulling Kathy to the side, away from prying eyes.

"Are you really sure this is a good move?" he asked her in a whisper, watching Kathy's face fold into a frown.

"Obviously I do or I wouldn't have said yes. This is *my* decision, Joel, and you have to respect it," she shot back at him before heading off back to the party, irritated.

He was hurt. He barely knew the guy, and felt like Kathy barely knew him as well. He decided to reach out to someone whom he knew could help. He walked back to his seat, distant as ever, while sweeping a scornful look and stare all over Brett's body. Joel left the party a few minutes later, dialing his phone as he pulled out of the driveway.

It wasn't jealousy. It was... something else. Disgust. Mistrust. Doubt. He called it a hunch. Or was it jealousy, masquerading as something else?

"Hello, Ricky. I need you to find out everything about someone for me. And I mean *everything* that you can lay your hands on, fast." He spit out the facts he had like a machine gun. "His name is Brett Miller, supposedly from Little Rock, Arkansas. Blond hair, blue eyes. About 5'9". That is all I know. Call me back."

A few days later, Joel got the news that he waited for, but not what he had expected or wanted. He wanted something fishy about Brett that he could air to his ex-wife and kids, but he got nothing. Brett Miller had no record whatsoever, and nothing about him could be found.

It drove Joel nuts.

Now, he was even more disturbed by the mysterious guy. He decided that he needed to warn his kids about him. He needed them to be careful.

One afternoon, after school, James and Petra walked out of school to the sight of their father waiting for them.

"Hey, kids! How was school today?" he asked them, waving their friends away before opening the car door for them to get into it. "I thought I'd drop you guys off today," he said in a jovial tone.

"What are you doing here, Dad?" Petra asked, looking at her brother for support.

"I came to ask you guys for a favor. Is that okay?" Joel said, going straight to the point.

He looked at his watch, knowing he didn't have much time to spend with them, since he had a work meeting waiting for him within the hour. The distance between school and the house should be sufficient to get his children on board with his plan.

"What kind of favor?" James asked, looking wary.

"It is about Brett, you mom's new boy toy," he replied without looking at him, focused on his driving. "I need you both to be very careful and watchful of him. Something about him doesn't sit right with me, and he spooks me out. I need you both to trust me on this. Okay?"

He waited for their response, eyeing Petra through the mirror in the back seat.

"Brett is a really nice guy, Dad. And you have nothing to worry about," James informed his father after a few silent seconds, watching his sister back him up with a nod in acknowledgment of what he had said.

"He seems really normal," Petra voiced out in addition.

"All I ask is that you guys be careful around him. That is all. But please, don't say anything about this to anyone," Joel said.

They both nodded, and then looked at each other, as if wondering what exactly their father was talking about. Joel drove them home, expecting them to keep his secret and keep an eye on things at home.

When he found out they had immediately told their mother, Joel felt betrayed.

Two weeks later, he bought James a car, in an effort to win him over. As thankful and excited as his son was, however, the effort had failed.

Over the next few days, Kathy grew increasingly preoccupied with how to save her forthcoming marriage from her ex-husband's undermining. She needed help, and she sought it from her church friends, who were rather vocal in their disdain of Joel and his behavior.

"You need to change the locks on your door," one suggested.

"Simply file for a restraining order against him," another of her friends added.

The advices kept pouring in from lips that had tasted marriage woes and emotional torment from men alike. Kathy listened to them all, sifting through the needed ones and neglecting the ones brought on by vitriol. At times, they all seemed like a good idea; at other times, they all sounded like an overreaction. In spite of everything, Joel wasn't as bad as *their* ex-husbands, or at least how they made them sound.

Kathy hadn't truly planned to go ahead with any of them, but the thought of Brett and what he would have to go through with Joel forced her into deciding that she needed a firm grip on things.

She took both pieces of advice, changing the locks all around the house before heading off to the police station to file a restraining order against Joel. Unfortunately, it was deemed impossible by the police, due to the fact Joel hadn't threatened or dealt her any act of violence. And he did have partial custody. She believed that the incident in the school's parking lot with Brett would be enough, but that wasn't the case.

Kathy's heart sank at the news. Who knew what Joel was capable of doing, blinded by rage and jealousy?

# BROKEN

# CHAPTER SIX | 6

MY FRIENDS AND I GATHERED AROUND a picnic table in school, mostly gossiping about rumors swirling about a couple of seniors found in a compromising situation on school premises.

We were all so absorbed in our chat that we remained unaware of a fellow classmate, Toby, who lurking nearby, hidden by a large bush.

"I heard he turned her around against the wall..." my best friend Amanda elaborated on about the couple caught.

As Amanda went on, the scene reminded me about an erotic movie that I had seen one night when Mom was gone with Brett. It was so hot, and I imagined myself with Mateo then.

Toby had made a habit of spying on me, following me until he was caught and yelled at by all of my friends. In the past year, I had become his obsession, and he could not seem to get over me. I felt objectified. Embarrassed. And I hated him for that.

Repeatedly, other kids had scolded him, even calling him "Creeper Toby" due to his odd nature and lurking. He was a loner. He was a creep. I felt bad for him, too, though. He had no friends. But stalking me didn't help.

This time, Amanda was the first to notice the weird boy doing his thing again. "Look, Petra! It's your shadow, Toby. There he goes, stalking you again!" she said, followed by an outburst of rude laughter, as the other girls joined in. "I bet you that he masturbates every day with your picture at home. Perv!"

I was red-faced with embarrassment and angry that he wouldn't leave me alone. I had had enough of his behavior. I had tried to talk to him about it, and when that didn't work, I was blatantly rude to him, but it only made him more obsessed. And as much as I felt bad for the kid, I was done. Enough was enough.

I fumed, as I listened to my friends continue their ribbing. And though I knew that the jokes weren't meant to make *me* feel bad, but were rather directed at the peeping tom, I felt terrible humiliation. I just wished I could make Toby disappear. Or blow his brains out.

The last thought scared me. Where had that come from?

The laughter of mockery from my friends simmered down, with a more serious and concerned look now across their faces. They knew too well that stalkers could eventually resort to other means if watching them stopped satisfying their urges.

Toby's persistence remained the baffling case for us all. It had gotten out of hand. People had seen him following me at the mall, and

I had caught him in my neighborhood more than once. He even managed to show up at church!

"What kind of pervert is that guy?" Amanda finally voiced her concern. "He is so weird!"

The other girls nodded in agreement. They fixed their gaze on him, hoping it'd deter him, but he appeared unfazed.

Another group of girls walked past, someone making a crack about Toby and his stalker ways. It was becoming a known fact around school, and not just for the freshmen class.

I fumed in anger, wishing I could do something about it. I needed a solution, but my friends weren't helpful in that front.

"I bet if I reported him to the principal, he'd stop his watching me everywhere I go," I said hotly.

Amanda shook her head and sighed. "It's not as if Mrs. Clarke could prevent him from doing it outside of school. And he could just deny it, even if we reported him." The other girls nodded in agreement.

The solution soon came walking by in form of my brother and his buddies, who were headed for their soccer practice. I perked up. Maybe I could use James's obnoxiously overprotective urges to my advantage.

"Jimmy! James, I need to talk to you," I called out to him.

I eyed Toby, watching him disappear almost immediately from the corner of the building, like a scared gopher going deep into his tunnel at the sight of a threat.

I ran toward James, who waited impatiently for me.

"I have practice in a few minutes, Petra. What do you want?"

I chose to ignore my brother's petulant tone, since I was about to ask him for a favor. "I know. Sorry, but it has something to do with *a boy*," I replied, nodding my head to where Toby had disappeared. I waited a few seconds, but he didn't reemerge. "It has to do with Toby."

"You mean the weird kid from your class with the funny haircut?" James asked.

"Yes, him. Toby Adams. He has been stalking me around school, and lately he's been showing up other places. He is creeping me out, Jimmy! I didn't want to say anything, because I felt kind of sorry for him, but it's getting out of hand. Can you do something about it, please?" I begged, hands steepled in prayer.

James looked around for Toby, but he was long gone. He then looked over to his impatient friends. One pointed to his watch, indicating it was almost time for practice. Mateo simply smiled at me, patiently waiting for James, and winked.

I returned his smile and played with my hair.

"Okay, I'll figure something out," James said with a sigh. I gave him a baleful look in response to his reluctance, and he dropped his soccer ball and placed both his hands on my shoulders. "I promise!" he said.

"Thank you!" I beamed in relief and gave him a quick hug before pushing him off to his friends. In spite of our constant arguments, I knew that he truly cared for my wellbeing. I was his baby sister, after all.

I watched James leave and knew the exact moment he told Mateo what was up, because his handsome face darkened as James spoke to him.

I re-joined Amanda and the other girls with a skip in my step. Problem solved.

# BROKEN

# CHAPTER SEVEN | 7

AFTER SOCCER PRACTICE, James and his teammates awaited Toby just outside the school grounds.

"Toby, wait up!" James called out to him, with Mateo following closely, as well as a few other boys from the soccer team.

Toby watched with wary eyes, before suddenly making a run for it, but to no avail. James and the boys caught up to him just around a corner not far off from the school.

"Petra said you've been stalking her," Mateo said first as if seeking confirmation.

Toby didn't have the chance to reply, as Mateo's sucker punch to the face was solid, sending Toby to the ground. James joined Mateo in kicking Toby on the ground, while the younger boy pleaded for them to stop. Encouraged, the others then joined in as well.

"I'm sorry... I am sorry guys! Please stop!" Toby begged amidst obvious profuse pain.

But James wasn't in any mood to let him go, though, as he continued to kick the poor boy on the ground. One kick followed by another.

A car swerved by them abruptly, bringing their shameful act to a forceful end.

"Leave him be!" a female voice echoed from behind the wheel.

Stunned, James turned and recognized her as another student's mother.

"You are hurting him. I am going to call the cops!" she shouted, while taking a quick picture with her phone. She leaped from the car, helping the beat up kid and pushing James and his teammates aside.

"Let's go!" James said to the group, making a run for it. "I'm sure the perv learned his lesson." With that, they all ran away.

Mateo laughed. A few feet away, James turned and saw that the concerned woman helped Toby up and made a phone call.

"You are all suspended for your actions against Tobias Adams," Mrs. Clarke announced. "There are pictures of each of you assaulting Mr. Adams while he is lying on the ground."

"We can't be suspended right now. Please, Mrs. Clarke! We have to play in the championship game on Thursday night!" James pleaded, with Mateo and the two other boys backing him up, ignoring what she had said about the victim.

"James is one of our best players, Mrs. Clarke," Mateo said. "The rest of us can sit out, but the team can't afford to not have Jimmy!"

"If I were you, Mr. García, I would rather be concerned about my own self, than others," replied Principal Clarke. "Be grateful you aren't expelled."

James, Mateo, and the other boys were kicked off the team due to their suspension. Spring Valley Christian lost the match. It was a devastating result for James and Mateo, who had thought of nothing else but finally winning state ever since the date had been fixed. They had been working hard for this since their freshman year, and as seniors, they would not have the opportunity come again.

*Thanks for nothing, Petra. Thanks for ruining my life... again.*

# BROKEN

# CHAPTER EIGHT | 8

IT WAS SUNDAY MORNING, and with it came the obligatory visit to church. I got ready, as usual, taking my time, almost as though I didn't want the dressing session to come to an end. You see, I had to wear a uniform every day of the week, so this was my favorite part of going to church. I didn't have to hold back on Sundays.

My collection of clothes was endless. And I especially loved my dresses. I owned them all – formal, casual, sun dresses, halter tops, cocktail, bright, dark, long, short, midi, maxi, sheath. And I loved them all. I could open my own boutique store.

Then there were the shoes. Oh, so many shoes to choose from!

Maybe James was right, and I was vain. But this was my time, and I didn't care. I took my time in front of the mirror, recalling how I caused a stir a few Sundays before by wearing a long skirt but with an extended slit. I had no problem showing off some skin, but Mom had not been very fond of the idea.

"There is a time and place for everything," Mom would say.

She was right. I got scolded, but the deed was done. And I looked good.

*Humbleness, Petra! Don't be vain.* I sighed.

"This should be good," I said to myself out loud, having one final glance at my shape in the mirror before James's bellow from the front door for me to hurry up.

I knew that he wasn't thrilled to be having to drive me to church or school, but that was the price to pay for having his own car now. And Mom had to be at church early, since she was involved with the greeting ministries. So, having his own car had its benefits, but it also came with certain annoying responsibilities, like being my personal chauffeur in times of need. I, on the other hand, enjoyed it.

"Get your ass down here now, Petra, or I will leave you behind!" he cried out again, but this time from the car outside while honking.

I knew well that he wouldn't leave me, or he would get in trouble. I took my time to walk down the stairs, stopping once again on the mirror by the door to check myself out. Yeah, I looked good. Just making sure.

*There it is again, Petra. You're being too vain. Ugh! Whatever.*

I finally made it out of the house to an annoyed Jimmy. I grinned, seeing how red in face he was. As much as we loved each other, James and I enjoyed annoying each other like good old siblings. But nobody better mess with one of us, or we'd destroy them! Only we could do it to each other. Jimmy was upset with the suspension thing after the whole Creeper Toby fiasco. But I was thankful for his help.

Today, it was my turn to annoy him.

I knew that James hated being late to things. And while church was only a few miles away from our Scottsdale home, James argued that thanks to the streetlights on Scottsdale Road, it would take forever to reach Bell Road, where the church was located.

As soon as I got in the car, James booked floored it, trying to beat time. Of course, I knew he most likely just wanted to see Cindy and his buddies.

I wondered how long the sermon would be today, already thinking of securing the best place to sit in which I could take a nap without being spotted. The senior pastor could be really long-winded sometimes. But then I remembered that it was Youth Day, so we would stay at the side chapel with the youth pastor. He and his wife were nice. Their two-year old daughter, Jessica, was so cute.

"Calm your jets, Jimmy. We are gonna crash, you fool. I had to get dressed. Unlike you, I have standards on how I must look every day," I informed him with a cheeky smile to break the silence on the drive.

"Ugh. You are so dumb. It's just church, you know?" James reminded me. Rather than waiting for a response, he continued. "Most girls your age are not going through the ceremonial process that you dwell in every Sunday morning, which quite frankly doesn't make a difference," he said before stopping at a red light. "No matter what, fool, *estás fea!*" Then he laughed.

I punched him on the shoulder for calling me ugly and laughed with him. "Punk."

"Fix your makeup, at least," he added.

I instantly whipped out a small mirror from my purse to check my face. Of course he was kidding. My makeup was fine. I made duck lips and tilted my head, assuming every annoying position possible to irk James some more.

"You are just mad because everybody likes me," I confidently stated, meaning to taunt him. "Even your friends like me more than you now, fool!"

"Haha. You are so funny!" James sarcastically said. "All joking aside, though, you do know that nobody likes a narcissist, right? You can be so full of yourself sometimes, Petra, and that's not cute," he said as he gripped the steering wheel in a tight clench. When the light turned green, he gunned it without turning to look at me.

His change in demeanor made me think. "I know. I'm trying, Jimmy."

He didn't say anything the rest of the drive.

Once parked in the expansive lot of the nondenominational mega-church, we went our separate ways without saying a word. James went straight to the youth room to find his friends; I chose to do the same with Amanda and some of the other girls on the foyer.

The praise music was, of course, my favorite part of church. Some college-aged young adults lead it, and they were good. How I wished that I could jam and sing with them. Maybe someday.

The message began shortly after an ice-breaker. The young pastor, John Meyers, was constantly funny. He had been here for about two years, and his sermons were usually short and to the point, but always good. I never really had any real interaction with him, but he was always polite and seemed interested in everyone's lives and families.

James and his friends loved him. He was cool and played sports with them on open gym nights. All the high school girls adored him, too. He had long, blond hair—a California surfer type. But he cleaned up well. And Sandra, his wife, was so sweet. She always brought baked treats to youth class.

Unexpectedly, I didn't find the need to help myself to a nap after all.

Pastor John began his preaching about a topic we all found interesting to listen to, as well as connectable. He had begun speaking about the tender subject of sex and marriage.

*Ugh… what a cliché,* I thought at first.

But to my surprise, the message was interesting. Many of the teenagers started to pull out notepads, and the scratching from pencils could be heard. Pastor John spoke with maturity, depicting his level of insight and understanding of the subject, while still remaining practical, relevant, and funny at the same time.

*Wow, this guy is pretty good!*

Pastor John's words stoked my interest, and I found myself joining in the group of those jotting down the high points. I lent my ears to the teachings coming from the young pastor's lips throughout the entire message.

After his sermon, there was a time for discussion, and I wanted to ask questions, but found it difficult to do so, since I wasn't certain on how best to express my feelings without being judged or made fun of by my friends. I didn't want to make a fool of myself.

Finding his teaching irresistibly insightful and also in sync with what I was battling through, I decided to seek him out after church, while everyone went about meeting up with friends.

"Pastor John, can I speak with you for a moment, please?" I called out to him as he finished up talking with a group of kids.

The handsome pastor turned around. "Hi... Petra?"

I was glad he remembered my name.

"Yes! Hi." I smiled nervously as I twirled my hair.

*Keep it together!*

"What can I do for you?" he asked with his hands folded behind his back. It was a habit of his, I had noticed.

I felt my breath quicken, wondering how I could spill my gut to him without being judged. Guilt stung me, holding back my words. But I needed to open up to him with regard to everything that troubled me so much.

"Um... I need your help. But I am not exactly sure on how to say it without feeling horrible and... sinful," I said to him, looking down.

"I see. How about you walk back into the chapel with me, away from the crowd here in the lobby. My wife is there picking up some stuff, so maybe we can chat for a few minutes before she's ready to go." He was already walking back inside the large room, and we settled not too far from where I had sat for the youth service.

"I am struggling with some personal things, and they make me feel rather... dirty, I guess." I whispered the last part, feeling the words weigh past my lips.

The young pastor listened without giving any signs of discomfort or judgment on his part. I appreciated it, and it made me feel a little more comfortable.

"We all feel dirty at one point in time in our lives," he explained, helping me remain calm and obviously understanding my discomfort. "I have had troubling and challenging times myself, which required God's assistance and guidance to pull me through."

"Yeah, I guess that is true. It's just that lately I've been very lustful. I can't stop these immoral thoughts that I am constantly bombarded with. I see some of my brother's friends and I want to do... things... with them. To them. If you know what I mean. Sometimes when I am by myself in my room I see things that I shouldn't on my phone."

I waited for him to rebuke me or judge me. He didn't.

I continued, "At first it was simply curiosity, after talking about this with some friends. But then it became a habit. But it's not just that."

He simply nodded, prompting me to go on.

"When I go out, I like to dress u —to get attention. Especially from the older guys. It's like, I want them to stare. My brother swears I am full of myself, and maybe I am. I know. I don't want to be narcissistic. It's just that... ugh, I don't know how to explain it."

"Just tell me how you feel."

"Feeling pretty and desired is the only way that I feel good about myself." Tears trickled out as I explained my struggles to him, his face never betraying any disgust or disappointment. I tried my best to describe how my hormones were killing me from the inside out, and I didn't know how to stop. "I've never told this to anyone. But for some reason, after hearing your talk, I felt like I had to get it out. Please don't judge me or think any less of me."

"Petra, first of all, I don't judge you. I am no one to do so, so don't worry about that. And most importantly, I want you to know that God doesn't expect you to focus on your failures. The Bible says that we have all fallen short of the glory of God, but the good news is that we are justified and made whole again freely through His grace. God wants you to ask for forgiveness and to look up to Him for help. We can't fix ourselves; only He can do that. And trust me, I know what it means to be young and have certain... desires too, Petra."

"You do?"

Pastor John let out a chuckle. "Of course! We all struggle with sin differently, but many times it is more similar than we realize. Living a self-controlled life in our hyper-sexualized culture is no small thing. We live in an era in which the idea of restraint, of reining in our sexual desire for some higher purpose, seems old-fashioned. Lust has no easy or quick fix. But I do believe that progress is possible with God's help and with some accountability. Conquering lust is a journey. But you are not alone."

My chest felt light and less burdened from knowing that I was not alone. He was such a professional with his method and words. Nonjudgmental. Just, awesome!

"Can I pray with you, Petra?" he asked as he put one hand on my shoulder.

I nodded silently.

He prayed for me and my struggles. He also prayed for my family. After the amen, I wiped my tears, thankful for this man.

"How is your dad, by the way?" Pastor John asked me after the prayer, as if to relieve some tension. "I used to see him come to worship with us, even after your parents split," he pointed out. "But I haven't seen him at the open gyms in some time. He was a fun guy to play with."

I know that his question had been intended as a simple inquiry, but it ended up piercing through my emotions, bringing forth a new stream of tears that came rolling down my cheeks. I was a mess, and I was embarrassed. The question about my dad was another aspect of my life that I was struggling with, and I didn't know exactly how to deal with it. Maybe all my problems were related.

Seeing that I could not hold back the tears, Pastor John lent me his shoulder to cry on. I held him in a hug.

"I miss him so much… I really do, every day!" I confessed, feeling my words break out. "I wish our family was still together. I wish that all this wasn't happening. But there is nothing I can do about it," I said with a sigh.

"Everything will be okay, Petra," he assured me with soft, warm strokes on my back. "If you need me in any way, please know that I am here for you."

I knew that he meant what he said. I had never felt so at ease in my life, feeling my hurt wash away slowly.

At that moment, James walked into the room. "Petra, where have you been? Let's go! I've been looking for you."

I looked at the young pastor and gave him one last hug, before detaching and walking out with my brother.

Getting into the car, James asked me, "What the heck was *that* all about?"

"That's between me and God," I retorted.

He shot me a quizzical look, but chose to remain silent. I kept quiet, staring out the window the rest of the way home.

The next few days would see a blossoming of my newly found relationship with Pastor John, who seemed to always have time to indulge me. He frequently visited the Spring Valley Christian Academy campus, which was adjacent to the church, and was a regular speaker at our chapels. He was a bag of talent, with the ability to play various musical instruments and sing wonderfully. I found him fascinating.

*Why didn't I get close to him before?*

After hearing me sing and play the piano at school, Pastor John invited me to be a part of the praise band, something that I had wanted to do for quite some time. And from there on, I spent the hours after school with him, practicing at the church. He would be at the guitar while I was at the piano. We both sang. He was a good coach, and I was a quick learner. It was great.

I began to feel new emotions gather strength for him, too. This was new. I knew that Pastor John had a beautiful wife and the cutest two-year-old daughter at home waiting for him. But I just couldn't help myself, as the desire grew stronger each day. And soon, the one person who was helping me deal with my lust issues became the cause of them.

I hadn't given Mateo much time either, spurning his calls and blowing him off when he asked to see me. Now, my attention was somewhere else.

Pastor John became my dangerous desire.

# CHAPTER NINE | 9

MATEO WAS WORRIED AND CURIOUS about why Petra had grown distant after such a promising start to their relationship. Seeking an answer from her one evening, while waiting for her outside her house, he had finally decided to confront her.

"Hey, Petra, can I speak with you?" he called out to her as she walked outside toward the van.

She turned to him and reluctantly went over while answering, "What do you want, Mateo? I am late for a meeting at the church, and my mom is about to take me. Have you been just hanging out here?"

"Um, I was gonna knock."

"Jimmy is inside. You can go chill with him."

"Actually, I am here for you."

She sighed. "Look, Mateo, I don't have much to say to you right now. And like I said, I'm leaving. My mom is about to walk out, so I suggest you either leave or go with Jimmy. But I'm out."

Mateo was struck by her sudden change in attitude toward him and others, watching her walk away and got inside the van. He was disappointed. Hurt. He had felt the distance growing, but hadn't expected it to be that glaring to his face.

Mrs. León walked out and said hi to him. Then they left.

Mateo decided he needed to understand what was going on with her, so he went home, borrowed his mom's car, and drove himself to church.

He watched Ms. León leave as he drove into the parking lot. He watched Petra walk into the church, with Pastor John's car parked just outside, indicating that he was the one she had come to see. He parked, his level of fury and jealousy skyrocketing. He had heard murmurs about Petra spending a lot of time with the pastor, but he hadn't really connected it to her attitude toward him. Now, he was witnessing it for himself. And her mom was even bringing her!

A few minutes later, other young adults showed up. That was a relief; at least they wouldn't be there alone. He waited in the parking lot for their practice to be done, hoping on having some words with her upon her exit.

Petra exited the church building an hour and a half later, glowing with a happiness that Mateo had not seen for a while.

"So, that is who you're into right now, huh?" he called out to her from the dark where he rested against a column.

Petra turned around, startled, as Mateo walked out of the shadows.

"What are you doing here, Mateo? Don't be such a creep!" Petra asked him, wondering if he had been watching her. "Or should I call you *Toby*?"

Mateo ignored her comment. "*You* should tell me what you're really doing here, seeing as I followed you and it's like I've been hearing, that you are into Pastor John now."

"Oh, my goodness! Are you freaking kidding me? I come here for music practice, you idiot!" Petra shot back. "You should get a life, loser." She turned around and started to walk away. "My mom should be here any minute now. Go home. Go jump off a bridge. Whatever. I don't give a crap anymore about you anyway. It's not like we were ever official."

"What do you mean?" Mateo demanded, his anger rising.

Petra's words pierced his ego. They hurt his soul. And the thought of Petra spending so much time with the talented, funny, good-looking pastor did nothing but enrage him further. He knew that he was no match compared to Meyers.

"You're so dumb, Mateo. Just leave, please."

As some of the other young adults emerged from the building, Mateo walked back to his car, defeated. He kicked continuously at every innocent stone or piece of wood in his path, picturing every horribly wrong scenario that could be going on behind the church doors.

His jealousy had begun getting the better of him. He couldn't help the gut-wrenching feeling fueling his rage as he watched her walk away the opposite direction, unfazed by her meeting with him, singing a tune.

*Ugh!*

Even with her self-absorbed attitude, she was stunning. She might be only be a *quinceañera*, but she could easily pass for nineteen instead of fifteen.

*Why does she have to be so hot?*

Mateo sped away, agitated. He had always seen Petra as his, and his alone, until now. He had no idea what to do, but he was certain that he wouldn't stand for it. Maybe he didn't know how to show her, but he really loved her. It was more than a physical attraction to the girl. And now, he worried for her.

He decided that he would try to find out if she was actually getting involved with their youth pastor. If so, he would bring them both down. It was for her own good. He felt better after coming to this conclusion, and as he drove away from the church, plans were already forming in his mind.

# CHAPTER TEN | 10

J OEL SAT IN HIS LIVING ROOM, with a half-empty bottle of
scotch in hand and an ocean of depressed feelings at heart. He
wasn't much of a drinker. He drank socially back in college, and in
the past decade he would indulge in an occasional glass of wine while
on lunch or dinner meetings with clients or potential clients. But this
depression had gotten the worst of him. He had been drinking for the
past hour, and by the sight of the empty bottles dead on the floor, he
could tell that he had done justice to them all well enough.

He had gotten stuck in his head, on how things used to be, the
way they ought to be, and the way they currently were. Things were
falling apart around him, and he was lonely. As Joel drank to the past,
he relived the times when he had it all, from a great paying job—which
he still had, but quite frankly didn't seem to like it anymore—to the
family that he was once loved by, and he equally adored. Thoughts of

his family constantly floated to the surface of his mind, hurting him. Piercing him.

For the most part, Joel still spent time with them, and had lunch, dinners, and even an occasional barbeque back at what was once his home. Even though things weren't all that perfect, they were still good and healthy... until *he* appeared. Things had been okay until Brett Miller came into the picture, and it made Joel's life miserable.

He sorely missed the times that he spent with his kids, which now looked like a distant time. The added hurt of Kathy trying to get a restraining order against him made him take some more gulps from his bottle.

"That bitch thought that she could prevent me from seeing my kids!" he shouted, although he knew well that seeing them would be hard now even without a restraining order.
The thought of how well Brett and Kathy had poisoned his kids' minds against him caused a physical ache in his chest.

"They only think that I am a bad person because of that bastard!" he muttered, picturing Brett. "That home-wrecking bastard is the cause of all this," he continued, in slurred but perfectly spiteful words.

Joel had no idea what to do next. Confusion begin to set in, along with the sadness and hurt. The fact that he was being depicted as a horrible person wounded his soul. He wished to show them they were wrong, but he just couldn't stand the presence of Mr. Do-Good Brett, who seemed to be loved by everyone for his almost-perfect nature.

The fact that nothing about him could be obtained from Joel's investigations irked him; it also worried him. Richard "Ricky" Matul was good at finding out stuff about anyone, but this was not the case with Brett. He cursed the day that Brett walked into their lives, making things messy from the very first day. Nothing had been the same since.

"I need to take action," Joel told himself with a bogus sense of courage. "I need to do something about it soon." He tried convincing himself in words that got drowned by every bit of alcohol he downed.

He searched and surfed through his thoughts bank, wondering what his next line of action should be. It was obvious that he couldn't walk over to Kathy's house demanding to see the kids, as that would only further sour things. Plus, he was certain that the thorn in his flesh, Brett, would also be there, which would only bring out his inner demon.

Joel was at a crossroad. His temples throbbed, and he rubbed them, pondering on how little help the bottles of alcohol had been.

*Why did I even do this, again?*

The migraine started to settle in.

Still, his thoughts refused to bring forth a solution. His sense of reasoning was at an all-time low.

He glanced around his living room, looking at the pictures of his kids during the happy times. He wasn't the man that they expected him to be, nor the father he ought to be for them. This realization brought forth a deep sadness. His regret was almost tangible, it so consumed him.

*I need to speak with Kathy. She must listen to what I have to say.*

He started digging through his pocket for his phone.

He dialed her number, which had always been on his speed dial, waiting for her to pick up. No answer. More frustration came. He tried again, and again.

"Come on, Kathy. Answer your phone!" he yelled, hearing his voice echo around the empty home.

Paranoia began to take root, as his fingers started doing the talking for him. He poured out his heart into sending the words he felt through a text message. No introduction or courteous salute needed.

*Kathy, I don't like this, and it isn't fair at all. I don't trust that Brett guy, if that is even his name. And I need you to believe my instincts, because I'm certain that they are right. I am sure that there is something that he isn't being entirely honest about. I need you to be careful, please.*

He looked at the message and felt satisfied that he had poured out a good sum of his thoughts, so he sent it. He waited, with hope of getting a read receipt, at least. Ten minutes passed. No receipt. No reply.

Joel couldn't understand why Kathy hadn't answered. He tasted bile. Agitated, he tried again. He was punching his keypad violently this time, getting more aggressive and less subtle than he had been with his first message.

The fact that he had been ignored, and fears that the two of them were reading his messages and ridiculing him, brought out his darker side. His frustration did the typing, while his moral sense hid away.

*What the hell, Kathy? You are choosing not to reply my messages because of that punk ass you're with, huh? I need to see my kids, and I demand to see them. I don't want them around that idiot that you brought home. In fact, I'm coming to get them right now. I am gonna come get my kids, whether you like it or not.*

He clicked the send button, watching the confirmation of delivery come through. A few minutes went by. Still, no response. He clenched his fists and cursed out loud. Loud enough for the neighbors to be concerned.

Joel hurled his phone hard against the opposite wall, knocking the half-empty bottle to the floor, sending a cascade of broken glass across the floor and spraying amber liquid around the living room. Some found its way on his jeans.

Joel's rage escalated, further drowning his sense of reason, and his eyes landed on the flat-screen television hung on the adjacent wall. He yanked it off the wall mount and slammed it against the floor, then cast about, looking for other things to vent his anger and frustration. He wished there was something he could do to hurt Brett and make things right again.

Joel could feel his hate and disdain for Brett rise with every passing second. The thought of the man being with *his* family—being loved, while he remained an outcast, and being a father to *his* kids and making love to his ex-wife—wasn't something that he could cope with anymore.

Something snapped within him, and he was unrecognizable even to himself.

"I need to see my kids!" Joel said as he sat down on a pile of broken glass on his couch, tears of anger cascading down his face. "That bitch and that bastard cannot and will not keep them away from me. I am their rightful father, and I have the right to see them whenever I want to," he continued, almost as though he had an audience in front of him instead of a destroyed living room.

Joel wanted things the way they were, before the strange man came crawling from wherever pit he came from. Brett was a threat that needed neutralizing. And this threat was all that Joel could think about—while he slept, ate, or showered. This obsession had entirely consumed him. It had begun to mess with his work as well, and this was the last straw.

*There is no way that I'm backing down without a fight*, Joel thought "If you think that I am going to roll over like a little bitch then you must have me mistaken for someone else!" he voiced.

Joel knew himself to be a driven kind of man, provided he put his mind into wanting to get something done. He had applied it into building his company by himself from the ground up. And that was no small feat, considering the obstacles that he had to hurdle past, including sacrificing his family time.

Brett would be a small fry for him to deal with, he thought to himself. He felt alone, with his family getting more distant as the days went by. And he wasn't going to put up to it any longer. Joel had to do something soon.

Soon, as in now.

With the blood hot in his veins, he got up, grabbed his keys, and left.

Kathy went on an all-day outing to Theodore Roosevelt Lake with the greeting ministry from church. Brett accompanied her. The group rented a houseboat, and a couple from church had brought their twelve-passenger pulling boat as well as a towable banana boat. It was a fun day.

The cell reception was poor, warranting Kathy to do away with her phone all throughout the trip. Besides, she was occupied by other things, like cooking in the boat while some of the others were out on the lake. There were also her meddlesome friends, who seemed unable to keep their eyes off of Brett.

It wasn't poaching; most of them were married. But they wondered how it was possible for Kathy to bag such handsome men. First, Joel. He was a looker. Tall, dark, and handsome. His Latino accent made him even more desirable. And now, Brett. He was also pleasant to the eyes. And he was nice, handy, had great taste, dressed well, and above all, he had a fantastic sense of humor. Joel was great. But Kathy had upgraded.

"He is so sweet!" one had whispered to the other, wondering if Brett had heard, as he let off a thin smile.

Kathy loved the fact that he was the talk of the trip, and she stuck close to him, unwilling to let him be alone with any of these piranhas. It was a fun day. They spent the entire time laughing and joking.

Brett shared fun memories of growing up in the Ozarks and moving stories from his time in the military. Kathy basked in the warm tone of his voice, wondering how in the world she had been so lucky. He was perfect in every measurable way.

As their fun trip came to an end, Brett and Kathy were the first to bid their friends goodbye. They still had to make it back home before it was late, and they had a two-hour journey to make.

About fifty minutes into the road, right before reaching Highway 87, Kathy finally had reception. She surfed through her phone, finally seeing the messages that Joel had sent her. She read them through, feeling a pang of anxiety and anger rush through her from the audacity and harshness of Joel's words. She couldn't trust him any longer and wasn't sure that she or her family were even safe around him anymore. She watched Brett drive, reluctant to let him in on the hateful texts that her ex-husband had sent to her.

She felt her heart sink with worry and her soul in pain for Joel. She wondered what had come over him, to make him so unlike the man that she had fallen in love with and married. She read the messages once more and was all the more certain that she had to be careful of Joel. She needed her kids to be careful and safe as well.

Keeping an eye on Brett, who seemed rather carried away by the song playing on the radio, she texted James and Petra.

*You father is losing it, and I need you both to be very careful if or when you see him. Don't give him an audience whatsoever, and don't let him into the house if you see him at the door. Don't even think about accompanying him anywhere. Stay together at all times.*

Kathy sent it to her kids' phones, watching it get delivered, but, remained uneasy.

*What does he mean that I cannot keep him away from his kids? What does he intend to do?*

She was hit with weariness, going from the high of spending a day on the water with friends to the shock of Joel's threats. She considered telling Brett, but was afraid her ex-husband's behavior would scare him off, especially after their recent altercation.

She realized that she had forgotten to ask her kids to inform the police, should her ex-husband come calling. She knew they were out at a festival now, but hopefully they were together and safe.

*If he comes near you, do not hesitate to call the cops immediately.*

She sent the second message, feeling a little bit relieved that she had given them tips on how to stay safe until she got home. The relieved feeling only lasted a few minutes before Brett turned to her, sensing something was up.

"Are you okay, Kathy?" Brett asked her in his usual gentle voice. "You don't look so good."

Kathy remained silent for a long moment, wondering what she had to tell him. She loved him very much and didn't want her past marriage ruining what they had now. She didn't want Brett suffering for her sins, as she found herself caught in the head-aching position of protecting her soon-to-be-husband and her kids who were back in Phoenix.

She made her pick immediately.

"We need to get home fast, Brett," she said to a startled Brett.

"Are you okay? What is wrong?" Brett asked again, but this time with a hint of alarm.

"I have a feeling that something horrible is about to happen to the kids. I cannot tell what, exactly, but it is there right in my gut. I just have a bad feeling," she replied. "Call it a maternal instinct."

Brett needed her to say no more, as if understanding that she needed him to take her home fast. He accelerated but still maneuvered carefully for their safety. Kathy was glad that Brett was with her, as she watched him drive like his life depended on it.

Her mind wasn't at ease, though. She had given everything up for Joel while he worked his butt off without caring about spending some quality time with his family. He had focused on being a provider so much that he forgot the most important things – quality time with his family. She had given up her career as a CPA to be a stay-at-home mother and parent the kids in his absence. Joel would simply disappear, going AWOL for days at times, all in the name of work. He would always bring back gifts and kisses for each of them, as though that would work to fix things. But nothing would bring back the missed time.

She had given him more than enough years to mend his ways, but he just wouldn't change. It had become tiring for her. The idea of getting divorced was so that she could have a life.

But it didn't seem like it would ever happen, even after he was well out of the picture. He was vengeful and determined to bring everything down with him because of his jealousy. And there was no way that she would give him such joy and satisfaction. She would take care of her kids and protect them as best as she could without letting him have his way.

*You will not win this time, Joel.*

# BROKEN

# CHAPTER ELEVEN | 11

EARLIER THAT MORNING, with their mother away with Brett on their lake trip, Petra had popped out of bed and began her morning routine quickly. It was an anomaly that stunned James. He had never seen his sister get ready for anything as fast as she had done for the youth event they had at the church-school grounds. He, on the other hand, had taken his sweet time getting ready, wanting to put her through the same amount of crap that she dealt him whenever he tried hurrying her for an outing. He draped on his shirt slowly, watching Petra eye him in annoyance.

It was a beautiful day outside their home, the sky beaming with the ever-present Arizona sun rays. He felt good, a little less worried, since they had gone about their lives without any additional incidents with their father and his newly found rage and temper.

James had been shocked upon witnessing it that evening. He wondered if Petra had experienced the same emotion, but simply shelved it away as best as she could, since she hadn't mention anything about it since.

James hadn't considered it much either, but since Petra was there staring him down like a piece of meat that she wanted to give to the dogs because he was wasting her time, he thought it would be best to converse with her about the current situation in their family.

"Do you think that Dad is ever going to be himself again with us?" he asked while putting on his socks.

He awaited her response, but Petra wasn't paying any attention, now glancing at her phone.

"Did you hear what I just asked, Petra?" he questioned, wondering why she was so suddenly absentminded. "And why are you so eager to go to the Fall Fest anyway?" he added to his list of questions. He awaited some form of response from his little sister, who remained focused on her phone.

"Honestly, I just don't want to think about Dad and Mom right now," Petra confessed. "I don't know exactly what is going on with Dad, but I am sure that Mom is trying to protect us from him. Even though I think she might be overreacting."

James had gotten one answer. He awaited another, which he could tell his sister was willing to ignore. He wasn't letting it go that easy, though. He needed some explanation regarding why she was in such a hurry to go to this event, which quite frankly wasn't in any way normal for her.

"And the other question I asked?" he reminded her, watching Petra get up and walk toward his room window, which faced the front street.

She stared out into the street, watching other neighborhood families leaving home. "Stop your interrogation, James. We need to go. Other people are leaving already. We are going to be late," she snapped at him. "If I have to leave you here with your stupid questions, then I will. I can probably just get a ride."

James could tell that something was up with her. But he also understood one thing about Petra, and it was that things would always come to reveal themselves when the time was due. Silently, he put on his shoes, searching for his new car key, before finding it next to his smart tablet on a small corner table.

"By the way, when did you last see Mateo?" James asked.

Petra turned around in a rather worrying pace. Her lips were curled as though she wanted to spill something, but was holding it in. She opened them and clamped them shut again almost immediately. "It's been a while... Um, I don't remember," she finally answered.

"Hm. That's weird. I haven't heard from him for days, and he hasn't reached out to me. He is also not answering, which is unusual for him," James explained, leading them both out of his room. James wondered if something bad had happened between them.

Petra remained silent until they got to the car. "We need to hurry, James. Stop being a douche! I know you're taking your sweet time on purpose," she snapped again. "Can't you tell we're already late?"

she reminded him, pointing to the time on the car's electronic dashboard.

James chuckled, enjoying every bit of the payback. He simply looked at himself in the mirror, making sure he was presentable. He was dressed way more informally than his sister, with shorts and a T-shirt; he couldn't understand why his sister insisted on overdressing for any occasion. He had waited a long time to get back at her, and was enjoying every moment. This was payback for all of those times that she had messed up his plans with her nonchalant attitude toward commitments and for taking forever to get ready.

Revenge was a sweet thing.

The fact it was an all-day youth event had made James certain that they didn't need to go that early. They wouldn't miss much anyway. He would rather get there when the real fun had begun and when his friends would be there for sure.

Their mother, Kathy, had gone away for the day, knowing they would be busy until nighttime. It was an annual Fall Festival, held on the church's and school's adjacent parking lots. There were fair rides, animals, games, food, entertainment booths, and other fun stuff. They always had a great time there with their friends.

James finally reversed the car out of the driveway, blasting the stereo and basking in his moment of payback. He could still see Petra's face blush red with anger, but remaining as quiet as she could be. James could be a prick at times, and this was one of the moments when he enjoyed aggravating her. James drove at a snail's pace. He normally loved to push his A4, but he could swear that a tortoise would race them to church today and beat them. He loved it.

"You are going to get pulled over for driving below the speed limit, Jimbo!" she lashed out at him.

"How does it taste? How does it *feel*?" he asked her, staring her in the face as he drove, laughing.

"How does *what* taste?" she replied with her own confused question.

"Well, having your time wasted!" James responded, happy to provide her with the answer to his taunting question.

She ignored him, facing outward instead.

They finally arrived, and Petra leaped out of the car the moment it came to a halt, even before he turned the engine off. James knew that she couldn't wait to get out and about, but didn't know why.

James got out of the car and took out his phone, searching for his friends as well. He looked around, with his other hand in his pocket. He was looking for one person in particular. Where in the world was Cindy?

# CHAPTER TWELVE | 12

THE SIGHT OF HAYRIDES, HORSES, and fair games gladdened my heart. I had been yearning for some fun for a while, although this wasn't necessarily the reason why I had come to the fair with so much enthusiasm.

The church had gone all out this time too, inviting the entire local community to the fair. Hundreds, if not thousands, of people were littered everywhere, some in pairs, some in groups, and a few with their siblings. It was the time of the year when young people, like me, paired up and got themselves hooked with someone they liked. It was also an avenue for those who were shy to find the courage to speak with someone that they had been admiring from the shadows for a very long time.

I left Jimmy behind and scanned the grounds, looking for my friends, as well as for the one person that mattered, whom I had come to the fair to see specifically.

"Petra! Over here!" Amanda waved me over to a game booth, where she and some other friends had gathered.

My crazy night, the one that changed everything, was about to begin. I just didn't know it yet.

# CHAPTER THIRTEEN | 13

JAMES' FRIENDS PULLED IN, the stereo booming in their car, piquing the attention of the closer crowds. James loved the fact that things were never dull with them around. They were the cool kids from school, and everyone knew that.

He approached them, exchanging handshakes and brotherly hugs. He watched Petra chat and laugh away with Amanda, with some boys eyeing them both like a piece of meat. James couldn't help but notice Mateo's absence there, though. He wondered where he was, until he found him sitting at some patio tables in the distance, all by himself with his face pale with worry and his eyes barely moving around in their sockets. He was just playing on his phone.

James whistled, calling for Mateo to come and join them, but he waved back telling him later. James and the group went about their own business. It was unusual for Mateo to remain alone, especially when the opportunity was in hand to make advances to girls their age seeking cool guys and their attention.

Something was wrong.

Mateo had his eyes fixated into the distance, with his view falling on Petra, who had now walked over to a group of older boys, with whom she was flirting. The sight of Petra flipping her hair and smiling at the boys kept on eating at him, and his rancor grew. She really had a problem. She was an attention whore. He clenched his fists, as his breath got heavier and his headache increased.

But wow, did she look hot. That was an understatement. Mateo was obsessed.

She eventually walked away from the guys, who eyed her absurdly short dress and heels with hunger. He suddenly felt underdressed.

He watched as Petra wandered around, frequently scanning the crowd as if looking for someone in particular. She stopped and stared. Mateo continued to do the same—at her.

# CHAPTER FOURTEEN | 14

I HADN'T SEEN HIM SINCE I ARRIVED, and it gave me a strange sense of letdown. But then, I saw him, tangled in the midst of some young ladies who were playing with his daughter. He chatted on, smiling, revealing his perfect set of white teeth in the process.

*There you are, Pastor John! Oh, man, you look good.*

I tossed my straight, dark hair playfully as I made my way toward him, my entire demeanor screaming feminine interest. I wet my lips. The man was... delicious. Desirable. I found no fault on him. And I figured that the fact that Pastor John had an arsenal of talent within him was a turn-on for other women at the church as well, with his sporty physique and great personality. But I would eventually figure out a way to get rid of competition.

John Meyers coming to our church had been the best thing that could have ever happened to our upscale suburban community.

As I made my way to the handsome pastor, his equally young, pretty wife came over to his side, dampening my mood almost immediately. I stopped. The sight of Sandra Meyers holding her husband's hand nauseated me. I tried desperately to hide my jealousy and disdain for the woman, but I just could not do it.

*Ugh… Why does she have to be so pretty and so perfect too?*

I couldn't help but resent the sweet young mother, whom other girls liked very much. But I wasn't like other girls.

At least the blond man was into brunette Latinas. I was half Latino, and I was brunette as well, just like Sandra. Plus, I was also pretty. Well, at least everyone else seemed to think so. So, maybe John would look at me the way he looked at Sandra.

Maybe…

Consumed by jealousy, I turned around and walked back toward the booths to find comfort in Amanda. Hopefully, some sound advice would come in from my well-grounded, astute friend.

I had only made the walk halfway to where Amanda stood when, suddenly, the unlikeliest of persons approached me. I froze, wondering what had given Creeper Toby the courage to come near enough for me to smell his excessive cologne.

Toby looked at me, his face placid, not appearing angry, despite what my brother, Mateo, and the other guys had done to him.

I held my hands behind my back, trying desperately to remain calm, while Toby seemed to be struggling to get words out of his mouth.

Amanda turned around and noticed the encounter. Her eyes widened in alarm and she left her entourage of boys behind and began to walk toward us. But before Amanda arrived, Toby finally spoke.

"Hello, Petra. How are you doing?" he asked with newly found confidence.

I didn't really know what to say. "Um... Hi, Toby. I am fine, thank you," I replied, exchanging a wide-eyed glance with Amanda, who had made it to her side already.

"Hello, Amanda," Toby greeted her. "Well, I am sure that you are surprised to see me here, talking to you."

"Um... yeah. Kinda..."

Amanda grabbed my arm without saying a word.

"I understand," Toby said. "The thing is, I just needed to apologize for my past actions."

It was a sincere-sounding apology. Had he been coached? Where were the cameras?

I stared at him still, trying to fathom if he truly meant it or if he was up to something again. I had always found it difficult reading him, and his motives were not exactly clear. He was a weird boy from school who kept to himself and didn't seem to have friends. Toby lacked social skills. But everyone knew that he was obsessed with me, and had been for quite some time. Even before all the other guys started noticing me, I had been Toby's object of admiration.

The fact that he came seeking peace with me wasn't something that I could just ignore, though. His sincere apology melted my worries away, and I let out a short smile. "Thank you. I have to apologize to you as well, Toby. I am very sorry for what my brother and his friends did to you."

"It's okay. You have nothing to apologize about," Toby replied, sounding more confident by the second. "I had it coming, I guess. But yeah, I actually came here to apologize, but also to ask and see if we can make peace with each other after what happened that day. What do you say? Can we begin anew?"

I looked at Amanda, hoping for some supportive words or ideas from her, but she was equally dumbstruck by Toby's words and kept her mouth shut. She had nothing. It was my bridge to cross on my own, I guess. I frowned at her as she shrugged, mute.

Then I turned to Toby. "Sure. I accept your peace offering. And I'd like that very much as well," I said with a smile. I extended my hand to him. "Friends?"

"Friends," Toby said with a bright smile.

Mateo had been watching Petra like an eagle all along, wondering what the entire episode had been all about. He found it weird that she would indulge Toby, the boy who had stalked her and gotten them into so much trouble for beating him up. His rage heightened, and he waited for the perfect time to confront Petra. The moment would come once Tobias left.

"What the hell is wrong with you?" he rehearsed in his head, knowing exactly what he was going to say to her.

"I am glad that I could clear this up with you, Petra. I feel better now," Toby confessed. "By the way, I promise not to be a creep anymore."

"That would be lovely," I responded, shaking his hand.

Toby walked away with a light smile on his face.

Amanda and I exchanged one more look and giggled uncontrollably, wondering what in the world had just happened. Our giggles were abruptly interrupted as Mateo came into view.

"What the hell was he doing talking with you?" he asked me, without preamble. "Why was Toby here with you just now?" He was staring down at me, one hand on his hip.

"How is that any of your business, Mateo?" I shot right back. "Why are you grilling me about my life all of a sudden?"

"Just answer my question and stop being so difficult already!"

"Like I said before, and I will say it again"—I took a brief pause—"it is *none* of *your* freaking *business!*" I accentuated the words in the sentence, making sure that he got the message loud and clear.

Mateo could tell that something about Petra had changed. He could see it right there in her eyes and could smell the arrogance and vanity seep out of her very being. It was ugly. It was sad.

"You've changed, Petra," he informed her, leaving the thoughts of her conceit and heightened ego to himself. "You've really changed..."

"Is that so? Or is the change that I'm not begging for your time and attention anymore? You should stop following me around, by the way. Get a life. Please, do yourself that favor. I wonder what Toby would think if he knew that you are now what he used to be...?"

Mateo had never been so humiliated in his life. He could tell that she meant every single word that she had uttered; He just wasn't sure that he wanted to accept it. He liked her too much to let go without a fight.

He loved the girl. That's why he was ready to defend her from the stalker, and also why he worried about her relationship with their youth pastor. Something felt wrong in all of this. And he would do almost anything for her.

But her newly found ego was too much for him to bear. He shook his head in dismay and walked away, without saying another word, obviously disappointed in the teenaged girl.

I assumed that Mateo's worry and rage about whom I talked to was simply jealousy. It was just like Dad. Same show, different monkey. Why did all the men in my life have to act so absurdly whenever jealousy got the best of them? It baffled me.

I hadn't paid much attention to Mateo lately, since my admiration had shifted to Pastor John, and it clearly upset him. His feelings about my life were not my problem, though. If he thought I was a bitch, then I would act as one to him.

I looked at Amanda, whose tongue seemed to have been knotted, once again, preventing her from saying a word all through the entire episodes with both Toby *and* Mateo. "Let go find something fun to do," I said to her, pulling her along. "Men. Can't live with them; can't live without them."

Amanda just laughed as she held on to my arm and walked beside me.

# BROKEN

# CHAPTER FIFTEEN | 15

JAMES WAS HALFWAY THROUGH his second larger-than-life burrito when he received a text message. He ignored it, needing both hands to grip the overstuffed tortilla. Then another message came through. Surprised, he gently laid his food down to view it, hoping it was from Cindy. Instead he saw it was from his mother.

He read the words over and over again, wondering what exactly was going on. His friends had taken note of his furrowed brows, prompting one of them to inquire what was going on. "Jimmy, is everything okay?"

James gave him no reply, focusing on the texts once more, confirming that his mother had asked them not to allow their biological father entrance into their home and to call the police on him if he showed up. James couldn't imagine what had happened to cause this concern, but it worried him.

*I need to find Petra*, he thought for the first time since they had arrived and parted ways.

He excused himself from his friends and searched around for his younger sister, who seemed rather put out by something once he found her. She wore a frown on her face, her hand trembling as she stared at her phone. James didn't need anybody to tell him that she had also seen the same text messages that he had.

"Petra, did you get Mom's text messages?"

She nodded while staring at her phone, but remained quiet.

"Do you have any idea what this is all about?" he asked.

He awaited some response from his obviously shocked sister, who simply scrolled through her phone continuously. In silence. Clearly she was no more aware of the circumstances that he was.

"What does she mean that we should stay together at all times?" Petra finally asked, knowing it was a highly unusual request. "Is she just being dramatic?"

In all honesty, James had no interest in being at Petra's side the rest of the evening. Besides, he already had plans. "I don't know, but I don't like it."

"Yeah, I honestly have no idea what's going on either. But it's starting to suck big time!" she complained.

"Whatever is going on with those two, I'm sure not getting involved in it. And I am definitely not babysitting a grown-ass girl like you!" he informed her. "I don't want you ruining my plans for tonight."

"What do you mean with *your plans for tonight*? You're going to ditch me when Mom clearly just stated that we remain together?"

James could tell that the text message would bring more harm than good for him, even without their father showing up to make things difficult for them. But he couldn't let Petra in on his true intent for the evening and needed a good lie to keep her from following him around like a lost puppy.

James had a special date planned with Cindy, his girlfriend. Cindy Gifford was the class hottie, and she was finally his. Her parents were going out of town, and she would be alone overnight. Jimmy and Cindy had been texting back and forth all throughout the evening, and he was waiting for her text to give him the all-clear. Things would only get awkward for them both without the privacy that he intended to have, if he had Petra tagging along with him. He couldn't let it happen. This night was going to be his lucky night, and his sister was not going to spoil that for him.

"The guys and I are planning on going to Cindy's house for a little get-together, and you cannot come with us," he informed her point blank. "Are you happy now?"

Petra clinched her fists in protest. "What is the big deal with me going to Cindy's house too? I know that Cindy is your *special friend*, even though you aren't public about it. But why can't I go, since your friends are going too? I am down for a party. I promise that you won't even have to worry about me. Besides, Cindy likes me, and your friends do, too!"

"You can dream on all you want, Petra. But you aren't coming with us, and I mean it," James reiterated. "You can go somewhere with Amanda, paint your toenails, I don't care. But you are not coming with me."

"You can't be serious right now!" she replied. "What has gotten into you? You want to leave me here *alone*, even after what Mom just said? Not cool, Jimmy. What is wrong with you?"

Amanda had walked over during their argument, her ears perking up at the mention of a party. "Come on, James! We would love to go and have fun too," she whined. "The fair is kinda getting boring now anyway."

James simply shook his head in refusal, watching both girls pout at his unwavering stance.

"You're being unfair, and you know it," Amanda informed him with a frown.

"I don't care what you girls think. I'm leaving, and you are not coming with me. Petra, you can stay here until Mom gets back... or not. Your choice. Besides, Amanda, your parents are manning a booth. They'll probably flip if they find out that I took you somewhere away."

James turned around and walked away, not wanting or needing to hear anything from them anymore. There was no way that he was going to allow them to tag along and ruin the personal time he hoped to have with Cindy. He had everything planned, and none of those plans included Amanda and his infuriating little sister. He couldn't wait. And

Cindy's text had finally come as he was talking to his sister. He was ready to leave immediately, hormones skyrocketing.

James, however, was not ready to be queried by his mother afterward about going to Cindy's place, which he was certain that Petra was going to mention. If this happened, he knew it would mean trouble.

James tried his best to shelve his worries. He needed his game face on; he was about to go meet his girl. And she was waiting eagerly for him. Alone.

There was no party. No other friend was coming with him to Cindy's place. That was a lie. And he couldn't wait to get there. He wondered what she would be wearing.

# CHAPTER SIXTEEN | 16

I KNEW THAT there was no changing Jimmy's mind once he had decided on something. His stubbornness made me resentful. I didn't want to be alone right now, and I certainly did not want to wait by myself for Mom. No telling what time she would be coming back from the lake, anyway.

I ached to know what was going on, even though I could tell that it wasn't something that I would be glad to find out.

I grumbled some disagreements, then hissing, before returning to my attention to Amanda. "Let that idiot go, Amanda. It's fine. Whatever. We will be fine all by ourselves," I said, not sure if I was trying to comfort her or myself.

We walked back to where we were formerly seated with some other friends, but our food was cold and unpalatable.

"What else is going on with you, Petra? Are you sure it's just about your brother not taking you to that party?"

I really didn't want to tell Amanda about my mom's texts regarding Dad. "No, that's it. I'm fine," I lied.

"Have you seen the way that Mateo has been looking at you?" Amanda asked. "I don't think he took your rejection well. Honestly, it's kinda scary."

I heard her, but I was not fully listening. I was still upset that Jimmy had left me alone. I was worried about my parents. And I was also pissed about missing an opportunity to have time with Pastor John.

*Aw, Pastor John. An angel. My angel.* I finally smiled.

I looked around, wondering where he was. From a distance, I saw him. And he saw me. He smiled and waved at me. My heart pumped. I smiled back and nervously waved back. Suddenly, Sandra Meyer came to his side, again, and gave him a kiss. He immediately turned to her, and I was forgotten. The day I had looked forward to all week was just one disappointment after another.

"Petra? Hello? What's wrong with you?" Amanda asked, evidently taking note of my demeanor. "Did you hear what I said?" she asked again, turning around looking in the direction where I was looking at and where I had just waved to someone.

"I'm fine. Yeah, sorry. It's just that... well, everything just sucks today!" I complained, thinking of my brother, mother, Sandra Meyer, and the other events that had marred my day so far.

Amanda made a frown. "I'm sorry, girl."

"I freaking hate this!" I screamed as a rush of anger swarmed my entire body. My fury was a physical thing, and before I even knew what I was doing, I hurled my phone to the asphalt at my feet.

Amanda and I both stared, wide-eyed, at the bits of plastic that exploded from the phone as it hit the pavement.

"What have I done?" I whispered, instantly contrite. "Oh, my gosh! I'm so dumb," I added, this time louder.

I tried gathering the few pieces that I could off the ground, but the glass screen was essentially gone, and what remained of the device wouldn't even turn on.

I was distraught, and Amanda did her best in trying to console me. Above all, though, I was dead worried about my mother's reaction to my stupidity. I had gotten the phone as a gift from her recently, and I knew it wasn't cheap. I also knew her fury would be triggered by not being able to reach me, especially when she was clearly already worried about my safety.

*Ugh! This sucks!*

I desperately needed it to work. This small thing was my life.

I held on tight to my broken device, unable to staunch the tears. This really wasn't my day.

Turns out, a broken phone was the least of my worries. And I had every reason to be scared.

# BROKEN

# CHAPTER SEVENTEEN | 17

"EVERYTHING WILL BE ALL RIGHT, DARLING," Brett consoled Kathy as he focused on the road. "I'm here for you."

"Thank you, babe. I know you are." Kathy put her hand on his thigh as he drove, passing most cars by, acting immediately, on just her gut feeling. "Let's just focus on getting there quick and safe."

Kathy cast her memory upon her times with Joel during the early days. They had spent enough time together to know each other well. He was a driven and determined person, especially when it came to his career. He had been a loving man, before his company began to grow, before he made his business his number one priority. There was always an excuse. New construction deals. A new shopping center here. A school expansion there. A freeway overpass. It never ended.

She couldn't help but wonder what had happened to the man she'd given her heart to so many years ago. The man she knew then would have never threatened anyone in any way, much less in front of his kids. Joel used to be the envy of her friends and a pillar of the church.

She bit her bottom lip, almost tasting the bitterness that this entire period had brought upon her and her family. Now, her kids' lives were being threatened, or so her gut told her deep within. The feeling of doom was almost intolerable.

"I'm sorry for putting you through this, Brett. This is not your fault," Kathy said. He just smiled and shook his head dismissively.

They had almost gotten to the city limits when Kathy decided to dial her daughter's phone once more. No answer. She tried it the second time, but got nothing once again. Her phone was going straight to voicemail.

"Oh, my God!" she exclaimed, worried sick that something terrible had happened to her baby girl. "What the hell is going on?"

She scrolled through her phone to call James. It connected, but he wouldn't pick up.

James had seen the call from his mom, but ignored it. He was with Cindy, having a good time, and wanting nothing to spoil their special moment.

"Why don't you answer, James?" Cindy had asked him after the third time his phone buzzed. "It's your mom. It might be important."

James knew exactly why she was calling, and there was no way that he was going to answer her call. At least not now. He knew that he would have to answer for his behavior. But later, it would have been worth it, and he would have gathered enough excuses to explain himself. He grabbed his phone, put it in do not disturb mode, and returned his attention to Cindy. His phone continued to light up with notifications, but it wasn't attracting Cindy's attention.

*Now, where was I…?*

Kathy could feel herself begin to hyperventilate. Her throat felt tight and it was hard to swallow. Her chest grew heavy, compressed with worries, and her heart raced fast, like a wild horse. She was panicking, and this would do her no good. She felt her hands begin to tremble as she tried calling Petra once more. The fact that Petra's phone wasn't even ringing scared her further. She wasn't just concerned; she was terrified.

*What if Joel has gone mad and hurt them both? No, he wouldn't dare! Would he…?* She was lost in wild, paranoid thoughts.

Kathy had watched an episode of a TV show where one member of a family snapped after getting divorced and took it out on their kids.

She was scared like she had never been before. Her babies could not be reached, and her husband's actions for the past weeks couldn't be trusted. Then there were the threatening texts that he had sent. What did they even mean? He seemed desperate. Irrational. And ready to do stupid stuff.

She tried not to imagine the worse possible case scenario, hoping and imploring that her children were safe.

"Drive as fast as you possibly can, Brett. Please," she pleaded with him.

Kathy knew that Brett needed no explanation. If something bothered her, it affected him too. His loyalty and commitment to her was communicated in the way he responded to her request. Kathy saw that Brett didn't care how fast he was going anymore, or if he was breaking several state rules; all he wanted was to help her ease the worry that she could no longer hide within.

"I got you, babe. We will be there soon. Do not fear."

"I know, my love. I'm just... concerned," she said, as looking for the right word. "I don't trust Joel, and I know that something is wrong."

*Please, Joel... Please don't do something stupid*, she begged inwardly, hoping that somehow it would reach him and touch his heart and bring him back to his senses.

Joel had finally calmed down from the raging state of mind that he was in earlier. He had emptied the bottles and tossed them out, then walked to a nearby park to clear his head. The evening Arizona autumn breeze swept past him in a welcomed sensation, caressing every inch of his body.

His mind felt sore, and his head ached badly. He picked his phone, going through the messages that he had sent earlier while under the influence of the alcohol. He had sent those messages of his clear will and not entirely because he was under the influence. He had meant every bit of it.

He rubbed his temple tenderly, wondering what to do next. He hadn't seen his kids in days, and it felt like years already. For all the failures that his marriage had brought with it, those two were absolute wins. They were enough. And he wasn't willing to let them go without a fight.

But then again, there still was the issue with the strange guy that his ex-wife had brought into their lives. The bastard had won the hearts of those around him, making them fall for his charm and dashing personality. Everyone. Except for Joel León, who just couldn't... wouldn't do so.

*I need to keep my kids safe*, he whispered into the air. *They need me, and nothing will stop me from keeping them away from that bastard. I'll do whatever it takes.*

Rage blinded him. He was determined.

Joel looked ahead into the night, sighing in frustration and tiredness from the course that things had taken. He could hardly focus while at work, and his life was becoming consumed with personal problems. He wished it all back: the period when he only got worried about his job and his young kids. He wanted the calmness of things as they used to be, and not the torment that he was passing through emotionally every day now.

He was alone and barely living what he could call a life. He missed the homemade meals, the laughter echoing through the living room from his family, even after he had split with his wife, and most importantly, the freedom to spend time with his kids on a regular basis without feeling threatened.

Joel's life had become chaos because of another man. He had become less than a man before his wife and kids all because of *this* other man. Joel had become nothing but a thorn to his family because of Brett.

*Fucking. Brett. Miller.*

As he fastened his thoughts around Brett and his family, he recalled the church's Fall Fest. He had marked the date on his calendar, remembering all the fun that his kids used to have there. Knowing that Kathy would most likely not be there since it was for teens, and also because he remembered how back in the day, they would use the opportunity to have some fun on their own, he decided that he would take the chance to stop by and see if they were there. He felt sober enough.

He hoped they would be there. He prayed they were.

Joel had missed his kids, and the church's Fall Festival would be the perfect avenue to meet with them. He glanced at his watch, noting there was still enough time to meet with them if they were there. He thought about calling Kathy to inform her of his intent, but discarded the idea quickly. He knew that she hardly ever answered his calls anymore. The fact that she hadn't replied any of his messages was proof to that.

*I guess I must take matters into my own hands. It might be the only way to go.*

The thought of Petra growing into a beautiful young lady made him proud. And James becoming such a mature and well-rounded young man brought a smile to his face. They were good kids. Despite the hardships in his marriage, they had done well raising them.

Joel headed back home. He wanted to look presentable to his kids so that he could spend some quality time with them. He took a quick shower, shaved, and carefully selected casual but expensive clothing from labels his kids would recognize.

He was beginning to feel excited about the night. He picked his car keys, stepped out of his condominium, and locked the door behind him. The evening breeze of fall remained, and would make the festival even nicer.

He would stop at Fashion Square Mall to get them something nice. It was on his way to the fair. He thought on what to get them. These kids were the living manifestation of stereotypical gender roles; she was a girly girl, and James was a man's man. But this made things easier for him. He wanted to be fair to both, so something similar and around the same dollar amount for each of them would be ideal.

Joel's main love language was gifts. Unfortunately for him, this was often misinterpreted as bribing, when in reality, that was never his intention. He simply wanted to show his love this way. His second love language was physical touch, but being absent so much made this one much harder to accomplish.

Joel glanced in the rearview mirror before switching lanes and noticed a car behind one—one that had been behind him since he left the condo. He didn't live in a busy area, and had crossed several major intersections on the way to the mall, so it caught his attention. He had no reason to be followed. He hadn't done anything wrong to anyone, except...

*Is that you, Brett? You want to play a game with me too, huh?*

Joel sped off, watching the car behind him do the same but keeping a cushion of distance between them. He drove like his life depended on it, hoping to lose the follower he had behind him.

*You can't catch up with me, idiot!* Joel smirked, feeling himself far ahead in his SUV. *I'm going to go see my kids.* He laughed aloud.

He had finally driven a good mile before realizing that he hadn't actually been followed. The only car behind him belonged to a random woman who was apparently just a bad driver. He would have never realized, had he not made a stop by the shopping mall. The car whizzed past, the lady inside paying little to no attention to him.

*I really need to stop drinking. Now I am just being paranoid,* he thought as he parked his car in the first available spot he found.

He walked into the mall, in search of the perfect gifts for his kids. He swept his eyes around the crowded mall, wondering when it was he had done this last. It had truly been a while. The thought made him sad. This showed just how much he had failed his kids. He surfed the first floor, hoping to find just the right thing, but nothing seemed to be coming in focus.

*Ugh. I'm getting too old for this crap.*

Joel wondered what Kathy would have gotten the kids, had she been the one coming to shop for them. And then, he thought of another way to get what he wanted—he was going to call the kids to do some detective work.

He rang James's phone first, hearing the ring back tone continue without end until the voicemail came in. He wasn't answering. This was unlike him.

*Maybe Kathy has gotten to him, too. Stupid bitch.*

He stood in front of a wristwatch rack. They were all beautiful. This could work; one for him and one for her. This would be a nice surprise.

James picked two beautiful, expensive wristwatches off the rack. One of them was made specifically for ladies, the other one a trendy, oversized masculine one. He felt proud of his choices, walking over to the counter to pay for them.

Upon arriving to the counter, he felt a tap on the back. Behind him he found the man that he had hired to help investigate and gather evidence and information about Brett. Ricky looked surprised to meet Joel there as well, giving him a friendly squeeze on the shoulder.

"What are you doing here, Joel?" he asked, holding his toddler daughter in hand.

"I came to get some gifts for my kids," he said, winking at the little girl.

"Oh, that's nice. It's really nice of you," the sleuth replied. "Have you been able to get anything else about the guy you asked me to run a check on?"

Joel hated the fact that thoughts of his one and only enemy at present were brought back into focus. He would rather not indulge in talking about this snake, but he found it impossible to resist. His hate for the man could not be hidden.

"No. Unfortunately, I haven't gotten absolutely anything about the son..." Ricky's eyes widened, remind him of the little girl's presence. "No. Nothing at all."

"Well, that's a shame. People like that scare the living crap out of me. You know, I was thinking, it is possible that he could be ex-military of some sort, with his records above my pay grade. And maybe that is the reason why his historical bio is classified, if even existent."

"Could *that* be it?" Joel asked, looking bothered that an ex-military man would be shacking up with his wife and rearing his kids. "What if that bastard has PTSD or something like that and snaps?"

"He *could* be. I am just saying that it is a possibility. But don't get carried away, Joel. Not all ex-military people have PTSD. Besides, there could be other explanations. He could also be someone with a past that he simply wouldn't want anyone knowing about and made sure no one would," he said with a shrug.

After a couple of minutes, Joel gave his farewell, heading back to his car with the wristwatches in hand and worry in his heart. He couldn't stop going over Brett's actions, physique, and behavior in his head, trying to make a link between them and being a high-rank military person. It was certainly possible.

But just in case, now, more than ever, he needed some proof to prove to his ex-wife and kids that he wasn't being overly jealous or insane. He wanted the upper hand against Brett, and he wasn't going to relent until he found it.

Joel drove off with his mind split between seeing his kids and foiling Brett. He checked occasionally to see if he was being followed, even though he knew he had been paranoid and simply imagining things the previous time.

He finally arrived at the festival, the sky dark and the parking lot half empty, scattered with trash. People were closing shop, cleaning up, or straight up leaving already. He wondered if he had gotten there too late. He drove slowly, with high hopes of spotting his kids.

After a right turn, going around one of the buses there, he saw them. He almost drove past Amanda and Petra, who were seated on the edge of the sidewalk.

He couldn't contain his excitement upon seeing his baby girl. He had truly missed her so much. He watched Amanda raise her head up first before nudging Petra to have a look at the person in front of them.

# CHAPTER EIGHTEEN | 18

I WAS LOOKING DOWN AT THE GROUND between my feet, too busy to notice Dad's white Range Rover. I felt terrible for breaking my phone, unsure of what punishment Mom would dole out over this, and I was still angry with James. I wanted nothing more than to be alone, and the sight of my father did absolutely nothing to ease my worries.

I stood up and walked toward the passenger side, without getting inside the car. Dad had lowered the window before stopping the car, engine still running.

"*Papi*? What are you doing here?" I asked, confused.

"Good evening, Mr. León!" Amanda greeted respectfully as she waved from the sidewalk, standing up, before Dad could answer me.

"Hi, Amanda. How are you doing? How are your parents, *mija*?" he asked, all smiles.

"Good. They're fine too, thank you," Amanda said, remaining a few feet from the car.

Dad turned his attention to me, but I remained wary. The air between us wasn't the usual one. Knowing him well, I knew that he would sense that something was up immediately. He would blame Mom's handwork in this, and I didn't want that.

"Hey, *mi amor*! How are you doing? I came to see you guys. I miss you so much," he said.

I was stuck in the dilemma of what to do. I wished James was around; he would have known what to do. But his absence only left me in a more confused state. Mom had painstakingly warned me, for some reason. She had warned us both about Dad, and it would seem disrespectful not to heed her warnings. But then, so would ignoring *him*. Right? He was my father, after all. And he was right in front of me.

The fact that Dad had made a special trip just to see us was another thing. I couldn't just ignore him. Besides, I missed my daddy.

"I'm okay," I said, shyly.

"Where is Jimmy? Didn't he come for the festival with you?" Dad asked, looking around for him.

"He left with some friends earlier. Pretty much everyone is gone by now. Amanda's parents are over there by the church, talking to the pastor, just waiting for me to be picked up," I replied.

I was feeling ignored and was partly glad that Dad was around, even though I was desperately trying not to show it.

"Okay, I guess I'll see him some other time, then. For some reason, he isn't answering any of my calls," he stated, clearly disappointed.

I wondered if he had tried calling *my* phone too. The thought worried me. "Yeah, I don't know what's up."

"I need to speak with you, Petra. Could you come into the car with me, please?"

I was stuck in the moral dilemma of heeding Mom's warnings—who wasn't here—and accepting Dad's offer, who *was* present. I was confused on what to do, wondering if I would or wouldn't get into trouble if I went with him. I could tell from his face that he was worried about something, even if his excitement about seeing me had masked it at first.

A cool breeze blew past, sending a slight shiver through me. My dress didn't cover much, after all, and I hadn't even brought a sweater. My open-toe wedges didn't help, and my feet felt cold. The dark clouds forming above were also a possible indication that it could start to rain at any time. A late monsoon appeared to threaten. I would rather have the shelter of Dad's car than remain outside, alone and cold, waiting for someone to pick me up. Besides, who even knew for how much longer I would have to wait for either for Jimmy or Mom.

I also didn't want to create a scene, should Dad take it personally if I refused to go with him. So, I decided to ignore Mom's warnings and opened the door to step into the car with Dad. I turned around to Amanda, who had been there for me through the night, and gave her a quick wave goodbye. Her parents oversaw and ran a food booth, so they would be staying behind even longer to supervise the cleanup.

I slipped into the car, feeling some warmth for the first time that night, and closed the door and window. I looked at Dad with a mix of joy and guilt. I wondered what Mom would come to think about my disobedience. I wanted to let daddy in on it, but stopped myself from doing so. I gave him a hug and a kiss.

"Are you okay, *pollita*? What is wrong?" he asked. "Is there something that you want to tell me?"

I adjusted myself properly in the seat, fixed my dress, put on the seatbelt, and looked up at him while smiling as hard as my face could lie and my body could act. I couldn't let him know about anything. I wasn't exactly ready to throw Dad under the bus, but I was certainly not going to backstab Mom either by telling him anything about those text messages.

"I am fine, *Papi*," I lied, playing with the purse on my lap.

I took one good and hard stare at him, feeling sorry for how things had turned out for him—from losing his wife through divorce, and now his kids through jealousy following his divorce. I wanted to know why he had come and to hear what he had to say, but I also wanted to be certain that I was safe. I reminded myself not to over say or overstep.

As he drove away, I wondered where we were going.

"You said that you have no idea where Jimmy went, right?" he asked one final time. "I was hoping we could pick him up so he can come with us too. It would be nice having both of you, even if for a short time."

"Yeah, I don't know. All I know is that he left with some friends about an hour ago," I replied truthfully, being that this was all I really knew about his whereabouts. He had mentioned Cindy's house, but who knew if he was even telling the truth. "Where are we going?"

"You'll see."

# BROKEN

# CHAPTER NINETEEN | 19

JOEL NODDED GENTLY, driving the car outside the parking lot, and wondering about the look on Kathy's face if she could see him with his daughter right now. This brought a smile to his face.

*In your face, bitch!*

He would have said that to her face if he could, if only to provoke her and let her know that she couldn't stop him or keep him from seeing or being with his kids. He felt a stream of relief wash through him gently, staring right back into Petra's beautiful emerald eyes.

Man, he had really missed his baby girl.

Joel thought that Petra was wearing something a little too revealing for his taste, but he stopped himself from saying anything to her that could potentially ruin this time together. He wanted quality time, and critiquing her at this time would not serve his purposes. She was his daughter, after all, and just like him, she would most likely respond negatively to criticism. He simply smiled as he changed gears.

"So... you said that you wanted to speak with me about something?" Petra asked, as if hoping it just wasn't a ruse to get her into the car with him. She looked back at the church and school premises as they pulled away.

"Yes, honey. We need to talk. It's important. But first things first. I got you a gift. I hope you like it," he said, pulling out the lovely chain wristwatch that he had gotten her from the center console. "I got your brother one as well."

Petra examined the wristwatch, realizing it was expensive and, indeed, very pretty. She couldn't hide her excitement. He always did buy the best gifts!

"Thank you, *Papi*!" she said in appreciation and gave him a kiss on the cheek as he drove.

"You are more than welcome, *mi amor*," an equally happy Joel replied, watching her try it on.

His baby girl was becoming such a beautiful woman. She was maturing physically, emotionally, and spiritually. He couldn't be prouder. And he loved being with her.

Things were about to take a turn for the best for the León family. He could sense it.

# CHAPTER TWENTY | 20

JUST IN CASE I FORGOT TO TELL YOU, my name means "rock." You know, like a stone. My father always wanted a daughter; and once they had me, he was adamant about naming me Petra, because he believed that I would be the solid foundation upon which our family would stand. With me around, he believed, our family was now complete. Solid.

Yeah, I know. It's stupid. I told him so more than once.

I never really liked my name. Petra Louise León just doesn't have a good ring to it. Louise, after my nana Louise, my mother's mom, which means resolute warrior. And Petra as a symbolic unshakable foundation.

Sheesh. Thanks Mom and Dad, no pressure.

# BROKEN

# CHAPTER TWENTY-ONE | 21

JOEL SAT BEHIND THE STEERING WHEEL OF HIS CAR, feeling guilty for everything that he had done. His outing with Petra had been marred by an occurrence that he blamed himself solely for. He hadn't been his intention at all, but it had come to be. She had smiled her way along for most of the trip with her to the restaurant up north, in Desert Ridge, not too far from where he and Kathy used to spend time away from the kids on holidays and weekends, if by miracle he wasn't working.

*It's all your fault, Joel!* he thought to himself, mounting the blame for their fallout.

Things had begun well enough, with Petra digging enthusiastically into her avocado sandwich and gulping the soda she'd ordered with it. Joel had basked in her joy, trying to commit every moment to memory. The truth was, he knew these times together would be less and less frequent.

He wondered how much better things would have turned out to be had James been with them too. He had always shared a special relationship and bond with Petra, somewhat making his relationship with James pale in comparison, but still equally of weight and importance to him. He loved them both. They were his everything. But Petra was his baby girl.

He gave her a few minutes to finish her meal, while she sipped her soda, before finally indulging in his purpose. It was the conversation that he had been dying to begin with her all through their ride in the car. Joel looked outside the restaurant, onto North Tatum Boulevard, casting his thoughts far and away before recollecting them into the right words to share with his daughter.

"Petra... how is your food?"

Quite frankly, Joel couldn't care less about the sandwich, at least at the point in time when he had other pressing worries at heart. He had counted time as it ticked away, while his daughter, for some reason, took a considerable amount of time finishing her meal.

"It was really good, *Papi*. Thank you," Petra replied with a hint of how good it had tasted by licking her fingers gently. "I wished you had tried some of it yourself."

Joel wasn't paying any attention to her regret, locking his fingers into one another as he awaited her to get through with her sentence, so as not to interrupt.

"Ok... I need your honest answer and opinion." Joel began.

"What exactly do you want to know?" she asked, a quizzical look on her lovely face.

"It's about Brett," Joel said.

Petra sighed in exhaustion, almost as though she had guessed that her father wouldn't be able to avoid the topic.

Joel had taken note of her expression, wondering if he had said something wrong. Her countenance had spoken without her mouth moving, as if she simply wasn't interested in indulging him about the subject matter anymore.

Unfortunately, Joel had chosen to press on.

"Baby, all I ask is that you answer me truthfully and listen to me," he pleaded.

"Dad, if it's about Brett, then I am not honestly sure that I want to discuss him with you. Not after what happened the last time you came to school."

"I... I know. I know, baby. I know that I messed up, bad. And I understand your frustration. But hear me out, at least. Please!" Joel pleaded, conceding to the fact that he had been horrible while handling Brett's presence the last time that they had seen each other. "What do you honestly think of Brett?" Joel genuinely wanted her truthful opinion, while also hoping for something negative, which would give him an opening to discuss his concerns.

Petra adjusted herself into a comfortable position before answering her father's question. She cleared her throat and took a sip of her orange soda. "Do you really want to hear the truth?"

Joel nodded affirmatively, encouraging her to be herself and to speak freely.

"Brett is a really nice guy, Dad. James and I don't really have a problem with him at all."

Joel felt the words hit his chest like bullets, his hopes crashing down hard in gravitational pull. He had hoped to hear something horrible, something that he could work with.

Petra wasn't done and had more to spill in Brett's defense, as if in hopes that he would come to his senses and rescind his witch hunt. "Mom is also very happy with him. He is good to us all. She has been on a good patch since they began dating, and we find that comforting. She wasn't always easy to deal with when you were gone all the time," Petra continued, without realizing that she was really doing more harm than good.

Her words hurt.

Joel tried his best to mask how he truly felt about the commendations that his daughter was giving Brett. He tried his best, tapping his feet underneath the table, trying to ease his nerves. He tried to keep his composure and not create a scene in the somewhat crowded restaurant they were dining in.

"I think you should spend some time with him, *Papi*. You should find out for yourself what kind of man he is," Petra suggested.

"I hear you, honey. But you need to listen to what I have to say," he implored. "I know you all see him as super nice and all, but I am sure that he isn't. Something within me just tells me that this guy is nothing but bad business."

"You need to drop this, *Pa*! You really need to let it go, for your own good," Petra encouraged him, stretching her hand across the table to hold his. She was scolding him, but still remaining sweet as an angel. Until she said the last part. "Brett has been wonderful to us. He has never harmed any of us, and never would. In fact, quite often, he goes out of his way to help us. Your jealousy is poisoning your opinion. And honestly, it's uncomfortable."

There it was. She had professed her loyalty to her own father's enemy once again.

"Baby, I am telling you that this guy is not right for your mother. Just trust me. There is something fishy about him."

"What makes you think this? Why exactly do you hate him so much?" Petra shook her head. "Brett doesn't deserve all these accusations and damage to his image simply because of your suspicions or insecurities."

Joel desperately wanted to share his investigations and defend his concerns, but he was wary of the consequences if his daughter labeled him a stalker for digging into Brett's past.

"Like I said, I just need you to trust me. Okay?" His emotions ratcheted up, as did his volume, and heads began to turn to where they sat.

Petra noticed. "You are creating a scene... again. Please don't embarrass me like this. I think you're having trouble letting Mom go."

Her words were the final straw, as Joel went into a rant that would draw the attention of the entire restaurant.

"Look, I need you to believe me when I say that this guy is bad business. And I don't want you or your brother going about thinking otherwise!" he yelled as he slammed his hand hard on the table.

Petra cringed.

Joel stood up, appalled by her words. "You think that I am jealous because I am trying to protect you and your mom? You think you know better than I do about that man wandering about, like he owns the house that *I* paid for with *my* hard-earned money while still married to your mother?" he asked his terrified daughter.

Teary eyed, Petra stood up and made her way to leave.

Joel slightly holding her arm to prevent her from walking away. "I am still talking to you, Petra!" he yelled in disgust that she was leaving.

"Please, let me go. You are hurting me!" she pleaded with him as his grip dug in tighter.

"Hey, let her go, man!" a college-aged guy who was sitting with his date not far from them interfered grasping Joel's shoulder.

The touch prompted Joel to let go of Petra's arm, before turning around and jamming his fist into the poor guy's jaw. He sent him crashing to the ground to the gasps of everyone present. His overly dressed date came running in his defense, yelling obscenities at Joel, asking him what his problem was.

"Mind your own business!" Joel said to the young man while he was down, ignoring the girlfriend.

His eyes were red, and his veins lined his neck, indicating how pissed off he was. He looked around, taking into sight the people in the room, without a care in the world about any of them, but one – his daughter, who had headed for the door in fear of her own safety.

Joel had succeeded in creating drama. Again. He watched Petra run out of the restaurant, while he followed her angrily as people watched on. A few of them recorded the entire episode on their phones as it went on. The young man's girlfriend was still screaming at him, while tending to her hurt boyfriend.

It was a scene, all right.

Joel had lost it, just as Petra had feared he would. And there was no going back.

He took out a crisp $100 bill and put it on their table. he knocked a tray of dirty dishes onto the floor and shoved a man who had the misfortune to be walking in. He ran toward the parking lot, catching up to his daughter by the car.

"Please, take me home. Please, Dad. I want to go home. And I... I don't think I want to see you again," she pleaded, crying, as she looked at her broken phone in her purse, as if wanting to call someone to come to her rescue. Her mom. Her brother. Brett. Mateo. Pastor John. A taxi. The cops. Anyone. "I am scared of you," she finally said to him from the other side of the car.

The words were acid on Joel's heart, her tears evidence of his stupidity. He knew that he had messed up, but was still unable to let go of the anger and sense of betrayal that his daughter's defense of Brett had sparked.

He let her in, without saying a word, and veered recklessly out of the parking lot and toward home.

Petra sobbed all through the journey.

Joel was in a brute mood and unwilling to apologize, feeling she didn't deserve it. This wouldn't end like this; he'd make sure of that.

A few blocks away from Petra's home, he made a wrong turn.

Back behind the wheel, where he recounted the horrible choices he had chosen for the night, Joel heard his phone ring, indicating he had gotten a message. It was from Kathy, and it was urgent.

He read it and his blood boiled. He needed to deal with this soon. But he wasn't in the best shape at the moment.

*I need to get home first*, he thought to himself. *I need to change, or it will be worse. She can't see me like this with all this blood on me.*

# CHAPTER TWENTY-TWO | 22

KATHY ARRIVED HOME WITH BRETT, rushing into their home, only to find it empty. She picked up her phone to ring her son, once again. She had noted that James's Audi wasn't in the driveway or garage, but she hoped that they were at least together.

James still wasn't picking up his calls. She waited on the other end of the line, but there was no response. Voicemail again.

"Take me back to the church, Brett. I think something happened," Kathy demanded.

Brett drove off immediately, arriving at the church and school premises in half the time that it would normally take.

"You go up into the church parking to search for them, while I search around the school," Kathy ordered Brett, who was more than willing to do whatever she asked.

They were both worried. This wasn't like the kids, not to communicate.

Kathy remained relentless in calling James's phone, seeing it was the only one going through. Petra's phone must have died at some point during the day. She dialed it for the umpteenth time before deciding to send him a text message.

*Where on earth are you and your sister? Why is her phone unreachable for the past hour? Why aren't you answering? I need to talk to you NOW!*

Kathy hit the send button immediately, watching the sent notification pop up on her phone. She needed to vent her desperation and worry out while she awaited Brett to come back bearing some good news, hopefully.

She took out her phone once more, tapping the screen as hard and as fast as her fingers could translate her innermost fears into written words. She felt the sting of sweat rolling into her eyes from her forehead. All she could think were horrible thoughts.

*James, I need you to answer your phone right this instant, or you will be in so much trouble, young man. Please pick up and bring your sister with you. I am at the church waiting for you guys. Where are you?*

She couldn't type much longer, as her fingers had begun trembling. She could feel something vile coming, but her heart wasn't ready to believe it. Her mouth tasted dry, and her throat threatened to clamp shut, starving her of air.

"Where are you? What have you done, Joel?" Kathy asked herself aloud, having a clear picture of her ex-husband's face, twisted in anger, in her mind.

She had never thought Joel capable of harming the kids, but his threats and actions for the last couple of months had given her cause to believe otherwise.

Kathy's phone rang, jolting her out of her dark thoughts. It was Brett. Feeling partly disappointed it wasn't her kids, but hoping he had some good news of their whereabouts, she scrambled to slide right the green button to answer.

"Hi, Brett. Please tell me that you found them. Please tell me that you've found my babies!"

With a breath into the receiver from his end depicting how equally frustrated and affected he was by the situation, he spilled the news to her as gently as he could. "They aren't here, Kat," he said, calling her by the pet name he used whenever things weren't going well, or when they had issues to sort out. "I've checked and asked around with the few people still left."

"They were here, Brett. They came to the Fall Fest; I am sure of it. My babies were here, and something has happened to them," Katy wailed. "I need to find them."

"Wait for me, sweetheart. I will back there soon," Brett assured her as he began jogging from where he stood.

Brett was on his way back to Kathy when he saw a familiar face among a group of family members. Brett had gone a few steps further before it hit him, and he quickly turned around and backtracked.

"Amanda... Amanda!" he called out.

"Mr. Brett?" Amanda said in a surprised tone. She let go of her mom's arm and shortened the distance between them as Brett came to a stop, breathing hard and loud.

"I'm sorry to disturb you, Amanda. But... have you seen Petra today at all?" he asked.

"Of course. We were together all afternoon. We had lots of fun."

Her parents had made their way to them at this point, clearly concerned about what the stranger was doing with their daughter. Brett ignored them for the moment, and continued interrogating the teenager.

"What about James?" Brett asked, just to be certain that he was there as well.

"Yes, he hung out with the guys, while Petra and I did our thing," she replied. "I hope they aren't in trouble? I can assure you we did nothing wrong all night," she clarified, looking worried.

"We can't find either of them. Petra's phone isn't even going through," Brett explained to the girl.

"Oh, Petra left with her father a few hours back," Amanda informed Brett. "He picked her up in his car. She seemed reluctant to go with him at first, but he said that he needed to talk to her, or something like that. James went with some friends to a party, I think. But that was like way before."

"Are you sure?"

"Well, yeah."

"Is there anything we can do?" Amanda's father asked.

Brett let out a long sigh. "Honestly, I don't know. At this point we are just trying to find them. But what Amanda has shared helps a lot." He then turned to Amanda once again. "Did anyone else see them leave together?" Brett asked. His phone began pulsing in his pocket. It was Kathy. Brett ignored it and turned to Amanda's parents. "Actually, I might need your help. Can you guys come with me?"

"Yes, of course," Amanda's father answered promptly. "Anything you need."

Amanda and her parents followed him.

On the way back to Kathy, Brett made another phone call, but not to Kathy. He spoke in a low tone, almost murmuring.

They made it over to Kathy who was unraveling. She was shivering from head to toe, and her face was wet from tears of desperation.

"Oh, no! What's wrong, babe?"

"James still isn't answering his phone," Kathy complained upon seeing them. "I just know Joel has a hand in this. Something is really wrong!"

"I am sorry, Kathy. I think you might be right, actually. Amanda said that she saw Petra leave with him in his car a while ago," Brett said. "James is still unaccounted for, and the reason why he isn't picking his phone remains unclear. But Amanda thinks he is at a party, which means they are not together."

"I need to call 911," she said and lifted her phone, but decided to call James one last time.

This time around, he answered, bringing some instant relief and also a fair amount of fury. He seemed perfectly fine and had obviously been ignoring her calls and texts.

"Where are you, Jimmy? Is your sister with you?" she asked, her questions firing back to back. "Her phone isn't working."

"Oh... um... Petra kind of dropped her phone and got it broken..." Amanda offered from where she stood. Her father had left to get their car from the other side of the campus. "That's why she hasn't answered."

Kathy nodded at her to acknowledge her statement, but she continued to talk to her son.

"I will be there soon, Mom," James promised her, "Don't worry. I'm super close by anyway."

Kathy wiped her eyes dry with the back of her hand, feeling slightly less hysteric since getting in touch with James and hearing about the broken phone. But now she needed to know for certain if Petra was with Joel, as Amanda mentioned. If this was true, that was bad news. She hoped for another possibility.

She walked over to Brett, who had been so helpful all through their search, leaning into his well-built frame for some hearty warmth against the cold she now felt. "Do you really think Joel took her?"

"I don't know. But don't worry. I am sure they are both be fine, Kat," he assured her. "I'm not sure what the deal is with Petra, and if she is with Joel or not, but I know for certain that it isn't going to help if you push yourself to a nervous breakdown."

James arrived sooner than expected, tearing into the parking lot far faster than his mother would have ever approved. As he parked, he went straight to Kathy, who was a mess in Brett's arms. He looked remorseful. He had his head slumped down, and his fingers tucked into each other as he approached his mother with a guilty and burdened heart. "I am so sorry, Mom! It's all my fault," he said as Kathy opened her arms to engulf him in a hug. "If I hadn't left her alone here, we would know where she is."

Kathy didn't want to hear anything, or at least, not yet, hugging him tightly to her chest. "What on earth happened, Jimmy?" she finally asked. "Do you know where your sister could be?"

James sniffed gently. "I don't know, Mom. I left her behind with Amanda, and then I went to a party with some friends," he said. He turned to Amanda to see if she had anything to add. She didn't speak a word, just simply stayed cuddled up with her mom, waiting for her dad to come back and pick them up.

"What about your friends? I mean the ones that Petra hangs out with often? Do you think she could be with Mateo?" Kathy suggested.

"No. They had a fight earlier today," Amanda chipped in before James could reply. "Like I already told you, the last time I saw her was with her father," Amanda reiterated.

Kathy wasn't ignoring Amanda. She simply couldn't come to terms with the idea of Petra going with her maniac of an ex-husband after she had explicitly warned them not to.

"Where did you see them together?" James asked Amanda.

"He came and picked her up some time after you left us for your party," Amanda replied. "That was the last time I saw her."

Amanda's father was back and waiting for her and his wife in the car.

"I think we need to get the police involved, Kat," Brett said. "I've changed my mind. I don't want any more of Joel's episodes to threaten the peace in this family."

Kathy, for all she had been through with Joel, wanted nothing else than to believe he wouldn't harm her daughter, their child. Joel adored her! Petra had been daddy's girl for so many years. She did not want to believe that she had been unknowingly married to a monster all those years.

*He wouldn't dare! Would he?*

"I need to call him," Kathy stated. "He needs to look me in the eyes and tell me where my daughter is," she continued, as she began dialing Joel's number.

"I'm with Brett," said James. "We should call the police."

"I'm calling your father first."

"What? Why? I don't think that's the best idea at this moment, Mom!"

Kathy could clearly read the disdain from his fame as her son fumed in anger. "I know what I am doing, Jimmy. I don't need more issues with you too right now."

James stomped off to his car to make a phone call of his own, but Brett followed him.

"You should at least wait and respect your mother's decision," he rebuked James, who was startled at the sight of Brett, who remained as calm as ever.

There seemed to be something about him which exuded strength and confidence, even in times of stress.

James responded defensively, "I wasn't planning on calling the police! Besides, who I call is my business, by the way. You're not my father."

Brett took a deep breath before responding. "I understand, Jimbo. All I want is for you to realize that your mom is under so much emotional strain right now. Put yourself in her shoes. She is considering the fact that Joel is your father and the years they spent together in harmony. She is giving him the benefit of the doubt, and perhaps you should do so too. He, after all, is *your* father." Brett responded with words of reason, facing James's unruly manner with maturity. "So please think about your mother here, and about the difficult situation she is in right now. That's all. If you still desire to call the police, then make certain you do it with some respect, at least, and only after your mother gives you permission to do so."

Brett ended his lecture and turned back, returning to where Kathy was, leaving James alone by his car.

James gently slid his finger off the dial button, with 911 on the phone screen waiting to be sent through with just a click. He erased the emergency number, dialing Mateo's contact instead, hoping he could shed some light on his sister's whereabouts, even though he was convinced that his father was with her, since he was last seen driving off with her.

Mateo didn't answer.

James turned on his engine and drove off, not before shouting out the window, "I'll be back soon. I'm going to Mateo's!"

He didn't give them a chance to say anything. He was determined to see if his friend knew anything. A few blocks from his house, he dialed again. This time, Mateo picked up, sounding groggy. Which was weird, given the early evening hour.

"Hey, fool! When did you last see my sister?" James went straight to the point, racing through the otherwise quiet, upscale neighborhood street.

"Huh? What? What are you talking about, Jimmy?" Mateo asked, his confusion apparent through the Bluetooth speakers of the car.

"Dude, my little sister is missing! When was the last time that you last saw her? Is she with you?" James cried into the mounted phone, threatening to burst Mateo's ear drums. "I'm on my way to your house right now!"

"Bro, chill out. We had a fight earlier in the day, but that's all. We never hung out. I went home right after she went with your dad in his car. I saw it from where I was watching her and Amanda at a distance," Mateo explained, supporting Amanda's claims. "What do you mean she is missing?"

James hung up without giving any further information to his friend. He turned around and drove straight back to his mother. He needed to inform them of Mateo's confirmation. He dialed her, but she didn't answer. His frustration boiled.

As he drove into the parking lot, James arrived just in time to witness some ruckus. His dad was on the scene and, as usual, making a scene.

"You are going to accuse me because of *that* idiot?" he was yelling, while gesturing toward Brett, who kept his cool and chose not to exchange words with him.

James couldn't figure out what was going on. His mother kept grabbing onto his father's shirt, demanding for him to bring Petra back from wherever he had taken her.

"You took her, Joel. We know it! You were seen driving away with our baby girl... *my* baby girl!" his mom screamed, tears flooding her face.

His dad was equally outraged, insisting on his innocence.

"I told you, I don't know where she is! I got here as quickly as I could after getting your call. And then, I get here, and as soon as I get out of my car, you walk right into me with your accusations? You shout at me and tell me to bring our daughter back? I'm not going to be bullied by you or your boy toy!" he responded by shoving Brett aside, who was trying his best to keep the peace between them. "I bet you he probably knows where she is!"

James was worried that his dad would snap and hit Brett again... or his mom. He wasn't sure what he was capable of doing under such conditions.

"Dad, calm down. Please! You're scaring us. We just want to know where Petra is. There have been two people who saw you leave with her. Please, just tell us where she is, that's all we want."

"You too, Jimmy? Did Brett turn you against me too? I see how it is."

"What are you talking about, Dad?"

He turned to his mom, ignoring his question. "What makes you think that I would ever harm my own daughter, or hide her from you? You people are crazy." He questioned their sanity once again. "*¡Están locos!*"

"No, *you* are the crazy one! You can't fool me," his mom snapped at him, dialing on her phone. "We'll see what the police have to say about this."

# BROKEN

# CHAPTER TWENTY-THREE | 23

THE BRUTAL COLD AWAKENS ME. I am naked, with only my underwear on. There is something covering my mouth and a bag over my head. My hands and feet are tightly tied with something. My wrists hurt.

I am terrified. I don't know where I am, or why I am being taken like this.

Then my fuzzy memory begins to come back. I was forced to go with him at gunpoint. I was drugged.

What did I ever do? Why is this happening to me? Why would *he* do this? I don't understand. This doesn't make any sense.

I wonder how long it has been. I can't see anything, but I can tell that I am now in the trunk of a car. I've been in one before, but that was only a game. This is real.

I begin yelling through the tape and banging my bound feet against the side of the car, but there's no response.

I wonder where he is taking me.

# BROKEN

# CHAPTER TWENTY-FOUR | 24

WHILE KATHY WAITED FOR THE POLICE, the situation escalated. Joel confronted Brett, who had finally found his voice to defend himself. "You brought this on yourself in the first place, Joel, so take responsibility and stop trying to make me the cause of your problems!" Brett shot back, tired of the accusations. "Be a man, for once!"

Joel lunged forward, swinging a fist at Brett, but Brett was able to easily dodge him.

"Trust me, Joel; you don't want to do this! It won't end like last time."

Joel smirked. "Oh, yeah? Well, we'll see about that." While Brett simply tried to block Joel's punches, Joel persisted with jabs and hooks. One of them finally connected with Brett's jaw, as Joel remembered his boxing days as a teen. His right fist connected well enough to send Brett stumbling backward, although not to the ground.

Brett was livid. "Oh, you've done it now, bro."

As Brett made his way to Joel, James yelled, "What is wrong with you guys?"

Both adults looked surprised.

Kathy ran back to them, yelling in frustration, just as a police car entered the parking lot. Brett put his arms down and took a step back, but Joel wasn't done. He pushed Brett once more.

One of the officers came running and grabbed Joel and hauled him to the squad car, giving him a shake and bellowing for him to stop before he cuffed him.

"You need to take him away, officer!" Kathy yelled. "And put him away for good." She was weeping now. "He kidnapped my daughter and refuses to tell us where she is or to let her go," she said through sobs.

"Ma'am, we're gonna need you to calm down," one of them said.

The other added, "We are going to need all of you to come with us to the precinct to give a statement," the other officer said while directing a still-struggling and screaming Joel into the back seat of his car.

Brett, Kathy, James, and Amanda's family followed behind in their respective cars. James's Audi and Joel's SUV remained at the church lot.

Their drive to the precinct on 56th Street was short, with Joel being hauled out of the car and into the station first, the others following accordingly. Joel was put in a holding room, and a brief interrogation was begun regarding the events that had led them all here.

"Why do you think they are accusing you of kidnapping your own daughter?" the officer in charge asked.

"Honestly, I don't know. They are crazy. I'll tell you one thing, officer, I'm innocent. I would never hurt my baby girl. And I bet you that this is all *Brett's* doing. He came into my family and messed everything up. But, somehow, I am now to take the blame?"

"Well, sir, they are saying that you were the last person with her."

"I don't know about that. Yes, I did take my daughter out for a meal; it's true. I don't deny that. She is my daughter, and I wanted some quality time. But after that, I dropped her off at her house, and I went home. This was before coming all the way back north to meet these people at the school after Kathy called me. And for the record, I live all the way south, in Mesa!" Joel explained, leaving out the part about them having an ugly scene at the restaurant. "I tried to explain that to them, but they just wouldn't listen."

Joel gave his statement and was finally allowed to leave, after assuring them that he was calm and wouldn't resort to violence anymore. He shot Brett a dark look as he left the station. He wasn't done with him. But for now, he was alone in all of this. They didn't trust him, and he didn't trust them. That much he knew.

On her own end, Kathy gave her testimony of the events of the day. "And what about my daughter? Can you help with that? Or do I have to wait twenty-four hours to report her missing?"

"No, ma'am. With regards to you daughter, you do not need to wait twenty-four hours to report her as missing. She's a minor. You can do that now. We'd love to have details on the clothes she had on, a good, detailed physical description, and any other helpful information that you can give us about her. Of course, recent pictures would be essential as well."

"You need to talk to Joel about this! I know he did it. Look at these text messages!" Kathy demanded.

She opened up the messages that Joel had sent her, scrolling through them, and showing them to the officer.

"This doesn't prove anything, though."

"I am telling you, I don't trust him."

"I understand that. We've talked to him, and he's told us what happened and where he last saw your daughter."

At that time, Joel passed by, on his way to the front door. "Why is he leaving? Why isn't he behind bars?"

"I'm sorry, ma'am, but there isn't much more that we can do at this point. He has given us his statement, and we will check it out and follow up. But for the time being, he is free to go."

Upset, Kathy moved forward. "My son James knows what she was wearing today. He can tell you more. I was away with my fiancée and some friends to the lake. But I have some pictures here of Petra…"

Outside the precinct, Joel waited for a cab. But he was surprised by his ex-wife, now calm, behind him. "I'm begging you, Joel. Please let my baby come home," she pleaded in sincere words, obviously distraught.

Joel looked from Kathy to Brett, and eventually from James and Amanda with her parents, all of them coming out of the precinct, behind her. He could tell that they all thought that he had something to do with Petra missing.

"I'm telling you, Kathy, if anything, *he* has something to do with all of this," Joel said, pointing at Brett, before getting into the taxi, which had just arrived.

"Stop pawning the blame on someone else and take it for once, *Pa!*" James yelled from where he stood. "Let Petra come home, please. This has gone on too long!"

Joel simply gave directions to the driver and headed off back to where his car was parked.

*I don't care if everyone is blinded to that liar's charm; I am not. And I guess it is up to me to expose him for who he truly is.*

Joel was going to do everything in his power to bring Brett down. He wasn't going to wait for the Phoenix Police Department to find Petra. They would only get in the way.

Joel picked up his car, exhausted. It was late, and a lot had transpired that evening. He was still processing everything as he got into the freeway, determined. Intricate plans were already in motion in his head.

Still, he couldn't get over what had happened between him and Petra after the restaurant.

The wait through the next thirty-six hours was nerve-wracking for Kathy, James, and Brett. They hadn't heard from Joel, except for the one time that he called, the day after the incident, to ask if Petra had returned home, followed by another paranoid outburst about Brett being responsible.

Kathy didn't know what to think of him anymore. She could no longer deal with his issues, as she remained on the couch facing the entrance of her house, waiting for her daughter to come walking through the door. She greeted any odd sound from outside her house with great excitement, in hopes that it was Petra.

The sound of a car door shutting sent Kathy running toward the door. She yanked it open so hard it bounced off the wall. Two men stood by the plain car with darkly tinted windows.

Dressed nicely, but not in uniforms, they both donned dark shades, their faces unreadable for Kathy, who scanned them anxiously for a clue of what news they brought.

The taller of them spoke first. "Good morning, ma'am." The other nodded his head.

"Please tell me that you have good news for me about my baby?" Kathy begged, staring at them both as they exchanged a slight but certain glance with one another.

"My name is Agent Scott, and this is my partner, Agent Perez. FBI."

"FBI?" Queried Brett from behind Kathy, dumbstruck.

They moved closer to the house. "We are going to be handling your daughter's disappearance henceforth," said Agent Perez, and they both flashed their badges before gesturing to move the conversation indoors.

"What do you mean? Does this mean that you've officially ruled our daughter to be missing?" Kathy asked as she trailed behind them.

"Yes, we have," Perez replied, removing his sunglasses, revealing deep brown eyes. "We are approaching this as a kidnapping. But there is more to it than that."

As they all sat down on the living room, he continued. "We found some clothes and shoes matching the description James gave of what Petra was wearing, close to Camelback Mountain, along with some other female clothing items. The dress that she was wearing the evening of her disappearance was torn and there was blood found on it."

Kathy was paralyzed with horror.

"And why is the FBI involved in this, and not the PPD?" Brett wondered aloud as he put an arm around Kathy.

"We have reason to believe that Petra's disappearance may not be an isolated incident. There have been several missing person cases involving teenage girls in Maricopa County in the last few months, and the details of the cases match other open cases across state lines," answered Agent Scott.

"Do you guys have any suspects or leads on it?" James asked, joining the conversation from the hallway.

"We have a few leads that we need to run through, and we'd like to get another statement from you all, in hopes that we might catch something missed with the PPD," Agent Perez said as he pulled out his pen and notepad.

"Are you her biological father?" Raymond Perez asked with a glance at Brett, taking out his own pen and notepad as well.

"No, that would be Joel... Joel León," he said.

"Oh, that's right," Perez answered. James looked at him askance, clearly thinking it was a stupid question.

Kathy reviewed her statement, emphasizing Joel as her main suspect, showing them the text messages that he had sent and that he was the last person to see her. James then added Amanda and Mateo's separate confirmations of seeing Petra leave with Joel.

"This is all good. We will look into all of this, and we will be talking to Joel soon to see what he has to say about all of this. He was just detained by PPD." With that, the agents put away their notebooks and headed to their vehicle, leaving Kathy, Brett, and James in stunned silence.

# CHAPTER TWENTY-FIVE | 25

IT WAS EARLY MONDAY MORNING, and Joel was in the worst possible place that he could be—inside a jail cell. He had protested his innocence, but for some reason, he wasn't being taken seriously. He counted each second, too scared to shut his eyes and fall asleep with his current roommates.

Joel knew that the police could only hold him for twenty-four hours before they charged him with a crime. But in order to charge him, they needed evidence. Of course, he had been drilled by the detectives several times, who had labeled him a liar and intimated that they had evidence that he wasn't telling them the entire truth. But he had no desire to let himself slip, remaining silent through the entire interrogation. He knew they weren't telling him everything.

*This is Kathy's handwork, along with that bastard that she's shacking up with!*

Joel needed to do something, and he needed to get it done fast. He got up to signal to the guard. Joel had hoped to fully carry out his own plan, but the incarceration had left him handicapped, confining him behind bars with the lowest people the earth had to offer. Twenty-four hours was a long time wasted, and he couldn't afford the cost. He watched the officer walk over with a cup of freshly made coffee and a doughnut in his hands.

"Morning, Joe," the guard called out, refusing to call Joel by his name, even though Joel had corrected him twice already. "You had a pleasant couple of hours, I'd presume," he added with a soft chuckle that nauseated the León patriarch.

"What are you holding me here for without charging me with anything?" he queried, seeing it to be the perfect time to vent his frustrations. "Do you guys have any evidence to keep me here?"

Joel hoped they didn't, or he'd be screwed.

"What do you want, *Ho-El*? We told you we found new evidence against you regarding your kidnapped daughter," he replied, taking a bite from his half-gone doughnut. "You'll hear soon about all that. You just enjoy your five-star stay for the time being."

Joel sighed in defeat. "I just need to talk to my lawyer," he said in a proud and confident tone. "I am ready."

The officer looked at him with a smirk and nodded before ambling back to his desk.

*That bitch must have done this! I am going to make them all pay.*

Finally given access to a phone, Joel dialed the number he had memorized years ago, relieved to hear the familiar sound of his lawyer's voice. He explained his situation at length but was careful, knowing the conversation was public.

"Okay, sounds good. I'll see you soon, Paul," Joel finally ended his call and anticipated his lawyer's arrival shortly.

It had taken just two hours, as the wall clock read a few minutes past ten, when Paul LeMont, his lawyer, walked in with his briefcase and cool superiority. He made inquiries with the officers in charge, getting more information on why he was being held, seeing that there were no charges filed.

Joel paced around the holding room, staring at the clock.

"Hey, Joel. How are you holding on?" LeMont greeted his client.

"Not too bad, Paul. But not great either, as you can see. I just need to get out of here, and soon," Joel replied, hoping some agreement had been made. "I can't spend another minute in this crap of a place."

"I am sorry, Joel, but I have some bad news. I also have good news, though. The good news is that I should be able to get you out of here soon, assuming they provide you with bail," his lawyer responded.

"Bail? So they are charging me, then? I guess I know what the bad news is, then..." Joel said, already thinking up the possible worst scenarios in his head.

"Well, first of all, they are charging you with kidnapping. Your own daughter, Joel. They don't seem to have much yet, and I think we will be fine. But there are multiple witnesses who claim they saw you leaving with her, being with her at a different location, and they are also saying that you got into an argument with her and assaulted someone at a restaurant," he said. "What were you thinking, Joel? Lying to the police? That's asking for trouble."

"Oh, come on! I didn't lie to anybody. I never denied that I picked her up and that I took her to eat and chat. And I told them that I took her back. I didn't lie. And about the whole altercation thing... well, let's just say that I didn't see it as necessary to share everything at the moment. I simply didn't say anything about it then, but I never lied!" Joel protested. "I didn't kidnap my own daughter. That is absurd! Even worse is the time they're wasting on me that could be better spent finding my daughter."

"Well, that's a new problem for you now. But the fact that you chose to omit certain things is only going to make you look even guiltier."

"I would never hurt or bring harm to any of my kids, Paul! You know that. Or even anyone else in my family... not that my ex-wife doesn't deserve to be punished for all of this. But I just can't. I could never. You know this!" Joel exclaimed.

"Just hang tight, okay? I will get you bail and post it. But you must keep your nose clean and avoid any funny business throughout this investigation."

"My daughter is missing, Paul, and I am going to do whatever I need to do. Remaining behind bars won't help me get that done," Joel snapped, watching his lawyer turn around to go and work his magic.

LeMont was a great lawyer. One of the best in the state of Arizona. He had been his faithful attorney since he had started his company years back. His firm had grown just as Joel's business prospered. And while LeMont was not a criminal lawyer, Joel had full faith in him and his team. If not him directly, someone in his firm would take care of him.

Joel just couldn't wait to get out; he had a lot of things to do. His plan was all in place. First, he needed to ditch his car. He knew it would further incriminate him, since his daughter had ridden along with him in it that night. Then there was her blood.

Joel waited and watched the time tick by slowly, remaining confident and somewhat cocky that he was smarter than any of the officers involved in the case.

He cast his mind over to Kathy. He could recall a time she had found him charming, way before things spurn out of control. He reminisced painfully about how things had further soured upon Brett's arrival.

*You aren't going to fool me like you've fooled everyone else, you bastard.*

Joel finally got bail and headed straight home, with the notable presence of two PPD officers tailing his cab from a distance. He simply smiled, seeing they had nothing better to do than make him their prime suspect. He believed that they had taken him to the station just to rattle his nerves, trying to shake him and make him fall; but he had kept his cool and his focus in perfect shape. He wouldn't break. He knew who he was and what he had to do.

Upon arriving to his home, Joel headed straight into his detached car garage to deal with the most important thing of all. He powered down the electronically controlled garage door to make sure no one could see inside, then began the needed cleaning to his car interior.

With soap, bleach, and a brush that he already had in the garage, he washed the interior clean and free from any stain of Petra's blood. He wasn't willing to provide the police with anything to connect him to Petra's disappearance, making certain he scrubbed through every inch of the chair she sat in, as well as the dashboard, which still held some visible traces of her blood on it. He could picture the horrible moment in his head, knowing he would be done for if any information about it got out.

After making sure his car was spotless, he went back to his condo. He was glad that they hadn't come with a warrant to search his house when they came to take him to the station. If they found his poster board, pictures, and all his notes, it would be taken as evidence. Evidence that would most likely put him away for a very long time. He knew that they just wouldn't understand, and no explanation given would suffice or be believable.

He moved his investigation items to the attic and closed it. It was best if no one saw any of this. Ever. Joel then sat in the living room, taking one cold bottle of water before preparing for the next step in his elaborate plan.

Kathy had waited for the past few hours to watch Joel come back to his home. She had looked around his condo and through his front window to know that he wasn't in when she arrived earlier, even though his white SUV was still parked in his garage. She wasn't sure if he was still in jail or if he had been released. Either way, she could swear he knew something about her missing daughter, and she was more than ready to keep watch on him, if it meant getting her baby girl back. There had to be something around here that could help her.

She decided to go to one of the adjacent buildings that was under construction. A lot of new condominiums were being built in the area, and Joel's was brand new. Being that there were no workers in sight and that it was closed off, she figured this would be a perfect stakeout place.

As she stalked his place through the mostly empty, half-renovated building opposite of his, the sudden touch of a hand covering her mouth muffled her attempt to scream. She twisted and turned as the firm grip around her mouth remained there, a large, hard body preventing her from pulling away.

*This isn't Joel!* Kathy thought wildly, feeling the shorter, wider, and bulkier frame squeezing her.

She was terrified out of her skin, wondering if she was about to meet a terrible fate then quickly panicking that Petra had gone the same way. She stopped struggling, feeling the person's grip loosen gently.

"I'll let you go only if you promise not to scream," the man behind her said. She recognized the voice and sagged in relief.

Kathy nodded in compliance, turning around slowly just as the hand slid off from her mouth and set her free as promised.

It was Agent Raymond Perez. He slowly reached for his pocket while putting a finger to his lips to keep her quiet.

*What's the FBI doing here?* she thought to herself, finding the words actually air past her lips.

"We believe that your husband might be a part of something bigger than just your child's kidnapping," he informed her. "We saw you come into this building while keeping an eye on your husband. I just wanted to make sure everything was kosher here. You should go back home, let us do our job, and trust us to get your daughter back."

"Wait... what do you mean that Joel is involved in something bigger than our daughter's kidnapping?" Kathy asked, ignoring his last statement.

"We have cause to believe that your husband might have something to do with the related kidnappings we mentioned earlier," the agent said.

Kathy gasped in horror and absolute disbelief. She was convinced that Joel had something to do with her daughter's disappearance, if not to be with her then to hurt Kathy, but not as a part of a kidnapping organization. The thought would have never crossed her mind.

"His car fits the description for a car that several eyewitnesses have claimed to see picking up the missing girls. It could be a coincidence, but we think not."

Kathy found it hard to swallow. She couldn't see Joel getting involved with a kidnapping ring. She knew him to be driven toward making money to maintain his expensive tastes, but not at *all* costs.

"Were you aware that your ex-husband is in some financial turmoil at present?" he asked, almost as though he had read her thoughts. "He came under our radar on the list of suspects involved in recent kidnappings after you daughter's mysterious disappearance and the valuable information that we gathered about him. Especially his financial problems, which I'm certain he's keeping from you."

Kathy's jaw dropped in disbelief, wondering what exactly was going on. First of all, what financial problems? He was never late paying the alimony and child support, or the kids' tuition. And their school was expensive. He had also just bought James's brand-new sports car.

And it hadn't been cheap either! How did he pull that off? What else had he been hiding?

Kathy was speechless for the moment, mind whirling.

"We've tried our best to connect the dots in these cases, with several failures, until your daughter's case, which fits the description of the past occurrences." Raymond Perez leaned against the wall, speaking in the same calm but structured tone that he had begun with. "We need your help getting these people, and helping your kid get back home safe and sound, as well as the other victims. What do you say?"

Kathy was still dumbstruck, breathing fast and hard, as well as running the possible scenarios in her mind. She had been married to this man for years before their split, and nothing had ever given her the impression that he was so deeply flawed. She couldn't picture him being *that* evil.

She stared across the street toward his condo, as did Agent Perez, who pulled out a lollipop from his jacket, slipped off the wrapper, and tucked it in his mouth. He looked around the unfinished condo, scratching his temple gently, awaiting some response from Kathy.

"Look, I can tell that you are dumbfounded by what you just heard—"

"I'll do it," Kathy interrupted, without peeling her gaze off from Joel's condo building across the street.

"You'll do *what*, exactly?" Agent Perez asked, clearly wanting some kind of verbal confirmation as to what she was signing on for.

"I'll help you bring him down, if that will help you guys get my baby back safely." She was holding back the tears as much as she could at this point.

"I think that'd be wise. We need to show you what even you don't know about your dear husband, so that you can have a proper insight into what you are up against," Agent Perez said, leading Kathy out the back door toward a stationed van, in which two other agents patiently waited.

"Ex-husband," she corrected as she followed him.

"Right. Ex-husband. Come with us, Mrs. León," he said, ushering her on board the cable company vehicle which was used undercover for scouting Joel. "You need to see the bigger picture past Joel."

"Ms. Potter."

"What did you say?" Agent Perez asked.

"You need to get it right. Joel is my *ex*-husband. And it is *Ms. Potter* now. I changed my name back to Potter after the divorce," she said again, this time clearer than she had done before.

"Pardon me, Ms. Potter. I made a mistake," Raymond Perez apologized immediately, distracting himself with a conversation with the guy next to him.

The vehicle was crowded with all sorts of listening devices and gadgets that she had never seen in her life. She could tell by the coffee cups in the bin that they worked around the clock, having little time to rest or sleep.

She wondered what her kids would come to think of their father, if these suspicions were proved true. She thought about Brett and how strong and loving he had been all through the entire situation. The thought of him finding out sent a frisson of fear through her; would he leave her? She was determined not to let him know about this.

As they neared the FBI building in North Phoenix, surrounded mostly by deserted land, Kathy prepared herself for the moment of truth. She had reconciled within her heart that she knew nothing about her ex-husband.

What she did know was that she wanted her daughter back. And if that meant bringing Joel down in the process, she was up for it. She felt partly betrayed, as well, wondering if he truly was the man that she had fallen in love with, and with whom she raised two beautiful kids.

Entering the building, Agent Perez elaborated on his plan. "Here is the thing, Ms. Potter. We need to get close to Joel, and that's where you come in. Even though you two are divorced, we believe that he still feels something for you, which could be useful to us."

One of the other officers added, "We've been chasing the kidnapping ring for a while with no success, so this means that we need to tread carefully and not spook him."

"I understand. Let's do this. Fill me in and let me know how I can help."

Kathy Potter was about to learn a whole lot about her ex-husband, and it wasn't going to be sweet news to her ears, eyes, or heart.

# CHAPTER TWENTY-SIX | 26

KATHY POTTER WAS IN ABSOLUTE DENIAL with the facts that she had just been presented with. They were all there, both digitally and in hard copy, placed in her hands by the cocky Agent Perez, who had an air of overconfidence she found incredibly annoying. Kathy knew that Perez wasn't letting her in on the entire thing, but he was more than willing to let her know that her ex-husband wasn't the man she had thought him to be. He seemed to almost relish breaking her rose-colored glasses.

"Joel isn't this kind of man. What you're telling me about him can't be real. I know you people fabricate all sorts of things just to get people tied down to something," she snarled.

"Do you think that we'd go as far as to fabricate so much falsified data about your husband's past, when he isn't even the big fish that we intend to catch?" Perez countered. "Why are you even defending him now? You were ready to crucify him not long ago."

Kathy grew pale. She had come with the intent to find out something which could help her daughter, but had gotten something else instead, and it was anything but helpful to her mental health. Evidently, her ex-husband had been a stranger.

"Look, Ms. Potter... this is bigger than you, me, Joel, *and* your missing daughter. Even though you most likely think that I'm a jerk for saying that," Agent Perez spoke in his usual calm tone, right hand in pocket. "Within the past six months, we've had dozens of young girls missing, just about the same age as your daughter, running through underground channels that we've been unable to trace," he explained.

"I know that Joel has something to do with my baby missing, but I doubt that he would get himself in such dirty nonsense. He loves his kids. All I need is for you to threaten him some to get my baby back," she pressed, hoping her emotions would rub off on the unruffled agent. She paced the room, sighing nervously. Then she came back for more. "Joel has my baby, and I know that he has her hidden somewhere. But I am sure that it's not with a kidnapping ring or group, as you are saying!" She vented her anger toward the entire crew in the room as they stared on at her, basking in her level of ignorance.

Agent Perez simply walked away from her, staring at the file that they had presented to her, before moving to the large monitor in the room to punch in some keys, revealing a video of the incident between Joel and her daughter. He folded his arms, nodding toward the screen for her to watch what had transpired between her husband and her daughter at the restaurant.

Kathy recognized the restaurant right way. Watching, she clamped her hand over her mouth. Seeing her daughter storm out of the restaurant in anger, while an equally enraged Joel chased after her, broke her heart.

"Why are you just showing me this? When was this?" Kathy demanded.

"You need to watch the next video," Perez said, with a new scene coming into play almost immediately after he clicked a saved link.

This time, the video was recorded by a traffic camera, which showed Petra wiping some blood off from her face while Joel screamed furiously as his daughter tried desperately to rebuff his hand from touching her. It was an even more damning scene, and she shut her eyes, wishing to see no more of her daughter's anguish.

"A traffic camera picked up that up. But we lost him in some Scottsdale neighborhood."

"I... I just don't understand. How could he? His own daughter!"

"Look, we don't know exactly what is going on. We can only make assumptions and try to connect the dots at this point. But your husband is the only major lead that we have right now. Not just to this case, but to those others who hide in the shadows, running these kidnapping rings all around the Southwest for the past few months. If we are correct, this could be huge. And we also found evidence indicating that he might not have been working alone," he added, watching Kathy rise her head up.

"What do you mean?"

Agent Perez took his time, allowing the suspense to linger on in an annoying manner before spilling out what he meant. "We found out that he had reached out to a boy, one of your daughter's friends, whom sources said had a thing for each other. He goes by Mateo? Mateo García."

Kathy was startled, unsure that she had heard him correctly. She knew Mateo well, and was certain that he couldn't do anything to hurt Petra. He was a good friend of both kids; they had practically grown up together. She knew the Garcías from church. They were good people. This was a scenario that she just could not come to terms with.

"Mateo cannot have *anything* to have to do with this!" she rebuffed immediately.

"Did you know that Joel had reached out to Mateo before he picked up your daughter? I bet you weren't aware of this. Were you?" he asked.

"Mateo likes Petra, and he would never do this. He is... obsessed with her, maybe. But he is a good kid. Trust me, you need to keep your focus on Joel if you want to bring my baby back."

"We are bringing Mateo in as we speak." He turned his attention away from her, waving his colleague to go and prepare the interrogation room.

Kathy had her heart in her mouth as she moved to watch the proceedings from the other side of the viewing glass. She watched them ease him into the seat, the poor boy clearly terrified.

Agent Perez conducted it himself, starting out as calm and despicably annoying as he naturally was. Kathy couldn't stand him, but she understood that he knew and did his job well.

"I swear to you, I had nothing to do with her disappearance," Mateo insisted.

"Why did you fail to mention that you saw Joel León before he picked his daughter up on the night of her disappearance, then?"

"I only met Mr. León after he asked if I knew where Petra was when he was searching for her. It was very quick, and I didn't think much of it. We exchanged numbers after he told me about his concerns with Mr. Brett, and then moved on," Mateo explained, clearly nervous. "I never had any other discussion with the man. And the other time that he called, the following day, was only to ask if I knew where Petra was or if I had heard anything from her. Which I told him no. I let him know that we had had a fight prior to the time that I saw him, and I also told him that she wasn't talking to me anymore. Which was true, by the way."

Mateo's eyes were flooded with tears.

Kathy could tell that he was innocent. She had no doubt about it, turning around to leave the viewing room. She felt time was being wasted there. She needed to confront the man that she suspected the most; she needed to confront Joel León, her demon of ex-husband. *He* had been the last person to see her daughter. And he had hurt her. She had seen it with her own eyes.

She walked back into the briefing room where a few of the agents were. The minor in question had brought his mother and younger sister, who were also in this briefing room. Mateo's mother was talking about wanting a lawyer, her voice strident. Mrs. García was not happy that they were interviewing a minor without a parent or a lawyer present and was threatening to sue. She knew her rights.

Kathy scanned the entire room before plunging Joel's file into her handbag and making her way out of the room without an ounce of guilt running through her. She was surprised by how well she could keep her body from trembling, considering that she was stealing evidence from the FBI.

She knew that she had been recorded on video, seeing the entire building was monitored by cameras, but she couldn't care less. She needed to confront Joel herself and threaten him with exposure in order to get her baby girl back.

Joel León had unknowingly taken the last shower he was going to have for the next couple of days when his doorbell began ringing continuously.

With his bathrobe around his bare skin and his interest piqued, he made his way to the door. He opened the door to the sight of his fuming ex-wife.

They exchanged a tense stare for the next few seconds, neither of the two choosing to speak. The air between them roiled with unsaid accusations.

"What the hell do *you* want?" Joel demanded, disdain clear on his face.

"I know, Joel," Kathy simply said. "I know everything, you sly, sneaky, lying son of a bitch!" She slammed a thick file into his chest.

Stunned, Joel watched Kathy stomp into his home. He looked at the file, which had the marking from the Federal Bureau of Investigation printed in bold words across it. He felt a chill go through him as he parted the file to the sight of pages filled with notes.

He closed the door and walked inside again, emptying the file's contents onto the kitchen bar.

"You lied to me all along. All along, you lived with me and lied to my face, while I slept with the devil!" she accused him.

"What are you talking about?" Joel asked, having trouble tearing himself away from the pages in front of him.

"Really? That's the card that you're gonna play with me?" she asked. "You want to pretend ignorance and tell lies to my face again, you bastard?"

"I don't know what it is that you think you know, but I am asking you nicely to please leave my house right now. I have important things to do. You might not remember this, but our daughter is missing. You know, the one that *you* accused me of kidnapping, while you and your blind police friends keep chasing after the wrong person."

"Why don't you tell me about Petra bleeding in your car, Joel? Did you her, like you were by your grandfather?" she asked, and his face molded itself into a frown. "Yes, Joel. I know all about your messed-up upbringing, which you conveniently chose to keep a secret."

"Where did you hear this?" he asked, surfing through the documents in his hand to see the parts which held interesting details about his upbringing in it.

It was detailed from the time of his birth, including the fact that he never knew his biological father and had to live with his grandfather, who was a piece of work after a few bottles and would make his and his sister's bodies into his personal punching bag, beating the pulp out of them both. It had been a period of his childhood in San Carlos which he had never wanted to remember or share with anyone.

"Where is my daughter, Joel?" Kathy asked, voice shaking with rage. "If this is some sick family shit you're continuing, I need it to end this instant, or you will regret it." She was threatening him now. She then barged into the hallway and began opening doors, looking intently for any trace of her sweet Petra.

Joel had his mind and focus occupied by other things at the moment. He flipped through the pages, finding out more information that even he hadn't known. It was all there.

"Hey, you can't just go through my home like that! Get out of here, you witch." Joel caught up with her on the first room.

"Oh, you've gotten to the interesting page, I see," Kathy interrupted after putting a mattress back down into its place and now staring at the page that Joel was reading. "You failed to mention that your stepfather was arrested on multiple occasions for trying to kill your mother."

"I never knew he did such things. I promise. All I ever knew was that they always fought, and I told you that. Besides, this is an aspect of my life that I never wanted to relive. Why would I ever bring that up?" he demanded. "You must believe me! I am not like *that* guy. And that was my hell to live."

Joel desperately hoped that she would believe him. But Kathy fumed in anger and didn't seem interested in anything he had to say. She continued to the closet to see if she could find anything.

Joel had just read the part about his sister's suicide, just before he immigrated to the United States with his mother, feeling the memory too hurtful to recall.

Kathy was awfully quiet now, but determined in her search. Joel's face grew into one of pain as he flipped through every page, until his eyes widened and his lips tightened as he got to the last page. It had a little piece of information about him that was a total surprise, written in red in the lower corner of the page.

*Currently under round-the-clock surveillance.*

He ran to his window to have a brief look around, feeling unsafe about the fact that he was being watched. He understood what he needed to do next, running back to his bedroom to get dressed.

Kathy evidently noticed the haste in his actions, following him deeper inside the condominium, yelling after him. "What are you hiding, Joel?"

Joel paid little attention to her, shoving as many clothes and items that he would need into his duffle bag. He pulled his drawer open, pulling out two neatly stacked rolls of cash, tucking them into his jacket, as he finished getting ready in a hurry to leave.

"Where the hell do you think you're going, Joel?" Kathy protested, seeing he meant to travel by the looks of things. "What are you planning? Tell me!"

"I am sorry that I have to do this, Kathy, but I am not the enemy," he said apologetically.

Taking one step closer to her, he hit her hard on the head with the base of the table lamp that he had picked up from a small table next to his bed. She crumpled to the floor, head bleeding. He felt bad. He had never hurt her physically, at least, not intentionally. He felt her pulse still beating in steady pace so he laid a wash cloth over her wound and proceeded with his new plan.

Joel removed the screen, threw down his bag, and climbed out a room window that faced the back alley, hoping the FBI wasn't watching the back of the condominium building. He used the trash bin to help him jump the back wall, and kept his head down and hooded as he walked. He peeked around the corner and noticed the back of the white van that he had observed in the neighborhood the last two days. He felt before that he was being watched; and all thanks to Kathy, this was now confirmed. He went the opposite way, hidden from their view.

He boarded the first bus that passed by. Going anywhere, but out of here first. The plan was in motion.

# BROKEN

# CHAPTER TWENTY-SEVEN | 27

JOEL GOT OFF THE BUS, keeping his head low and his eyes sweeping around to be certain that he hadn't been followed.

*I need somewhere safe and less conspicuous for now.*

He spotted an old motel off the road to his left, perfect to use as hideout, as nobody would consider looking for him in such place. After a twenty-five-minute bus ride, he was now in Phoenix, a few miles south of downtown, close to South Mountain.

Joel needed a place without cameras, someplace that would provide adequate cover for him throughout his stay, until he could make his own move. He wasn't ready to be caught by the cops, much less the FBI, and he certainly didn't need to be disturbed by his crazy ex-wife, who seemed to have chosen to make his life a living hell ever since their daughter's disappearance.

He walked in through the dusty front door and tapped on the bell on the empty desk slightly.

*This will do just fine.*

He waited a couple of minutes before tapping on the bell again, this time in continuous manner, until a lanky-looking man with a wrinkled face and mostly bald head came to his call. He had just an open vest on, revealing a hairy chest, and a pair of glasses resting on his crooked nose. He provided enough stench without speaking to assume that he had been occupied with drinking before he came to heed the bell's call.

"Good afternoon. How may I help you in our fine establishment?" the man said in a tone that made it clear what he thought of Joel's impatience.

"Are there any rooms for rent?" Joel asked, feeling rather nauseous from the odor emanating from the man. "I need a room for a few days."

"Yes, sir, we do. We have some rooms, indeed!" the bald man replied, rubbing his sweaty eyes below his spectacles.

"I need something with running water, stable power, and Wi-Fi," Joel informed him, wondering if the crappy-looking place would provide for his needs.

"We have all of that too, sir," he replied with a wink. "Will you be needing anything else?"

Joel remained without a reply for the next few seconds, not sure how seriously to take this guy or what he meant. The thought of the FBI found its way into his head once again, triggered by a picture of a police officer hanging on the wall. "Are you a cop?" Joel asked immediately, ignoring the question that he had been asked. "Are you the owner of this establishment?" he added.

Joel couldn't risk being stupid enough to rent a room in a motel belonging to a police officer, or even an ex-cop. He might as well just go to the precinct and ask them to give him a cell to sleep in. He was too smart to act stupid at this point in time.

"Oh, you mean the jolly old days before the bastards forced me to quit the force?" the old geezer said with a frown. "I was a darn good cop for fifteen years, until they accused me of stealing drugs from the evidence room and also of getting high while on duty. They never proved it, but they still let me go. Now, I confess. Yes, I did take some of the coke, because it wasting away in the evidence room without being discarded, and the hearings involved with these stashes were done by then. It was a shitload of it—hundreds of thousands worth, maybe more, and I only took some of it. But I never used any of it, and I certainly didn't get high while working! I got me some cash through some connections, I bought this old lady of motel, and I have been in the lap of luxury ever since."

*Now, that's perfect.* Joel knew had come to the right place, where he couldn't be meddled with; his plans could fall right into place. He still hadn't paid for the room, while he listened to the old man speak on and on, without ever giving the impression of wanting to stop. He wondered how this man got away with it, being that he was confessing to a person he had just met. He also wondered how much of it was true.

"It took me years to get this old lady up and running. But I kept my wits strong and my desire going with some booze, and my gun always by my side," he said, bringing up a shotgun to Joel's view.

Everything about the bedraggled-looking structure eased his worry. It wasn't what he hoped to remain in for a long period of time, but it was one that he could work with, before his contact came calling. He had been waiting for Ricky's call before Kathy came bearing news of his surveillance. Her news had disrupted his plans slightly, but no bother; he had it all covered still. At least he wasn't under their constant eye anymore.

"By the way, I don't accept credit cards or such," the man said, giving Joel a weird look as he dipped his hand into his pocket to slowly reveal the cash he had intended to pay with.

"I wasn't going to use a card," Joel replied. "How much will the rent cost for say... one week?"

"$350 for the week will do fine."

"I'll pay cash, and I'll even double it, if I can remain here without a record of my stay," Joel replied. "Oh, and... I am gonna need a few things. If you could help me with them, that would be great. I'll pay you nicely for your troubles too, sir," Joel stated without looking up at the man.

Joel counted $700 into the man's hand, who chose to count it again, after initially counting with Joel before he was handed the cash.

"The name is Bob, by the way. It's nice doing business with you," the man finally said, revealing stained, uneven teeth with his grin.

"I can see we are going to get along just fine, you and I. Come on with me now; I'll show you around."

The man waved Joel to come with him, walking east past a door which led to a stretch of rooms on both sides with a narrow hallway between.

"Hope there are no bugs," Joel said as he followed behind. He could recall migrating to the United States from Mexico with his mother, when they had no choice but to stay in similar establishments. The next day's move was accompanied with constant scratching and skin dotted with red spots.

"I do some real nice cleaning in here often," Bob assured Joel. "You have no worries about nuttin', ok?" he assured, jamming a key into the old keyhole and struggling momentarily with the lock before opening the door to a surprisingly spacious room.

*This will do.*

"You've got yourself one fine place here, Mister—" Bob asked with a raised brow.

Joel gave a short shake of his head. "No names, no records. Remember?"

"I just want to know what I can call you, that's all."

"Call me Sam..." Joel said, understanding the number two rule while trying to hide from the cops when they were up your tail—never using your real name during hideouts. This came after the number one rule: never using anything but cash.

"Okay, Sam. I'll leave you be with your room to get settled in now," Bob said, dropping the key on a battered wooden table that stood in the far corner of the large room.

Joel waited for him to leave before walking to the bed, which was just perfect for his height. He lifted the mattress to check for bugs. There weren't any. He walked around the room, looking outside through the large window, which gave him a good view of the dirt road not far from the motel and the road that went up South Mountain. This was the perfect vantage point for him.

He set down his bag, shuffling through for the burner phones that he had gotten the day before his ex-wife's visit. He had gotten just about enough to remain without being tracked by his pursuers, just until he got to his destination. Taking out a sheet of paper with a number inked on it, he began dialing on one of the cheap phones.

He didn't even hear a ring before a deep voice barked out, "Hello?"

"It's me," Joel replied, "Sorry I didn't call earlier; I had some setbacks," he said as he sat on the edge of his bed and kicked his shoes off.

"I got what you asked for. But you could get me in trouble with this, you know?" Ricky sounded worried on the phone. "By the way, I saw that you left your house already. The place was crawling with cops. But I don't think they searched it yet."

"Kathy..." Joel murmured to himself.

"Huh?"

"Nothing. So, you said you got what I needed, right? When can I pick it up?" he asked again, anxious.

"I can't be moving around with this stuff, Joel. You could land me behind bars if you caught with them. Get yourself a P.O. box where I can mail it to you. But be smart," Ricky advised.

"I'll do just that and send you the details soon."

"One more thing, Joel—"

"What?" Joel sighed as he sunk himself into the bed, giving up his bed bug concerns.

"After this, I owe you nothing more, and I'm done with you," said the investigator.

Joel remained silent, knowing exactly what Ricky meant. He had helped Ricky financially on another occasion, knowing well that he'd never be able to repay. But these favors he was doing for him now were more than enough.

"And get rid of my number," Ricky said. The demand was followed by the short beeps that indicated a disconnection.

"That's two different things, dummy," Joel muttered as he charged his phone on the wall.

After a few pensive minutes, Joel got up from the bed and put his shoes back on to go and meet the one person who could provide him with immediate help. He walked the stretch of hallway, checking to see if he could hear anything from the rooms, but nothing came past any of the doors, which he had now counted to be eight in total, four on each side. He walked back to the reception area, where Bob was back to the hard work of pickling his liver and smoking a joint.

"Hey, Bob, is there a post office around here, by any chance?" he asked.

Bob stared at him with a smile across his wrinkled face. He put down his booze on the counter before choosing to reply. "Watchu need the post office for?"

*Man, this guy is nosy!*

"You ask a lot of questions for a cash business. I just need one. You know, to mail stuff."

Bob chuckled then coughed raggedly. "There is one a few miles from here," he replied before burping loudly. "I could help you drop off or pick up any package when I go get my stuff."

Joel weighed the pros and cons his mind. He would be wise to let the geezer get it, but he couldn't risk him getting a whiff of things.

"Okay, I'll pay you to use your box and get a package for me, on one condition," Joel said.

Bob picked up his bottle, downing a long pull before providing Joel his attention again.

"You don't mess with my package, or even peek into it! It'll be under your name, with attention to Sam."

"You got something to hide, Sam?" Bob asked, staring at Joel weirdly.

"Don't we all, Bob?" Joel asked.

"Ha! Honestly, I don't care, my friend. You got a pen and paper with you?" Bob asked.

"Don't *you*? What kind of place is this?"

No response.

Joel took one good look at him before sighing and returning to his room to get paper and a pen.

# BROKEN

# CHAPTER TWENTY-EIGHT | 28

KATHY HAD BEEN DRAGGED BACK to the FBI offices by Agent Perez after a quick trip to the ER to check her head injury. She was simply furious.

Perez was equally livid. With her. Kathy knew that he was upset that she had taken evidence from the FBI office and gone to confront Joel on her own. "What have you done?" he asked her, glaring.

"I needed to confront him. I can't just wait around and pass the time with a cup of coffee and a doughnut," she snapped, earning disapproving stares from other agents in the room.

"You'd do best to watch your mouth now, Mrs. *León*," Agent Perez warned before turning around to run his hand through his hair. "I am frustrated because we lost the one lead to a criminal organization running a kidnapping ring!"

"*Ms. Potter!*" she corrected him.

"Another girl has been reported missing, fitting the profile," Agent Scott came informing Agent Perez with a file in his hand.

Raymond Perez scanned through the file before showing it to Kathy. "I am not trying to be a jerk or unprofessional, Ms. Potter. But, as you can see, there are other parents also living your hell. And we need your help, not your hindrance."

Kathy could barely suppress a sob at the girl's picture, who bore a striking resemblance to her own daughter. She closed the file gently, still in Perez's hands. She was regretful of her actions. She could tell that he felt some level of emotional attachment to the cases and truly cared about them, but her motherly desire to get her own daughter back had threatened to derail the investigation.

"I need you to trust us to get your daughter back to you alive and safe," Agent Perez said. "We will hunt your ex-husband down, if it's the last thing I do, since he has given considerable doubt about himself not being involved in your daughter's disappearance."

Kathy nodded gently.

"A bus camera just picked up Joel riding it a few hours ago," an agent called out from where he worked on his computer. "He seems to be trying hard to avoid cameras," he pointed out, just as Joel ducked his head while walking past a camera by the bus exit.

"He's on the run, people!" Agent Perez announced loudly. "Get an APB out on that son of a bitch. If he sneezes, coughs, pees, or buys gum, I want him traced and found." He walked over to Kathy, "If you really want to help us, now is the right time."

Kathy nodded in acknowledgment and understanding of what he had said. "What do you need from me?"

"Is there anywhere your ex-husband might go if he needs to lay low? It could be a vacation place that you've shared in the woods sometime before your breakup, or a particular hotel that he fancies. A trusted friend's house. Anything at this point."

Kathy couldn't think of anything that would help, as she truly didn't have any idea where he could be. She could tell by the look on the agent's face that he was disappointed.

"If there is anything at all that you can think of, please feel free to share," he encouraged her. "Now, please, excuse me; I have someone to grill," he said grimly as he walked toward the door.

"Is there another suspect?" Kathy asked, looking surprised.

"I got pointed in the direction of a kid who people say stalked your daughter," he replied to her by the door.

"You mean Tobias?"

"Yes, his name sounds something like that. Come to the interrogation room. We'll see what he has to say," the agent said before excusing himself from her presence.

Kathy made her way to the viewing room with a heavy heart. She had been there before. She wasn't sure of where things headed, but she would remain with them as much as possible until they got her daughter back. The information that she had heard about other girls broke her heart. She came to a halt right in front of the viewing glass, seeing a pale, nervous Toby in the metal chair. He clenched his hands together underneath the table, the knuckles stark white with his intensity. His mother sat on his left, quietly waiting. On his right was a man in a suit, whom Kathy assumed was a lawyer. Apparently they had learned their lesson with Mateo.

Agent Perez walked in, slamming a huge file on the table, and Toby jumped and nearly fell out of the chair.

"Just tell them everything you know, Toby," his mother encouraged him. "Let's get this over with, the sooner the better."

"I swear, I told the police the truth already. I know I promised to stop spying on her, and I tried, but I just couldn't help myself," Tobias confessed, on the brink of crying. "I am so sorry. I followed her around that night before her father's car came to pick her up, but I know nothing else," he swore, staring at the battered table, too afraid to meet either Agent Perez's or his mother's stare.

The lawyer whispered something that Kathy couldn't hear, not sure who it was intended for. Toby's mom replied in equal volume. Then the lawyer spoke loud enough for Kathy to make out, "My client has cooperated, and he has nothing new to share at this point."

"I just want to get this clear, that's all," Perez replied. "Toby, are you telling me that you didn't see Petra after she left with her father?"

Toby shook, almost as though he had something to hide. "I don't know if I've said too much or too little." He turned to his mom.

"Okay, that's enough. We are leaving," the lawyer added.

"Mrs. Adams, I'll be frank. We have possession of hundreds of candid pictures that Toby has taken of the missing girl, some of them very questionable and clearly not with her consent. I'm talking *hundreds* of them from different occasions. Stalking is a serious offense, and she's also a minor. All I am saying is that this doesn't look good for him. I suggest you cooperate."

Kathy gasped at that information. She had no idea. *My poor baby!*

Toby's mother didn't flinch, as if she was aware of this fact already. A tear did drop, though.

"I am innocent, Mom! I swear. I do not know anything about her disappearance!" Tobias cried out.

"Toby!" His mother cried, signaling him to stop, as did the lawyer. But his fear had overtaken his good judgment.

"I don't want to get in trouble anymore. I'm done with this! Please, I am scared. I just need you to promise me that I am not going to end up involved in this mess, sir. Promise me. I know I took those pictures. I... I can't help it. I need help. I know. But I swear, I don't know anything about her missing. I would never hurt her. I'm in love with her!"

"Toby, please stop now!" His mother was desperate.

"We are leaving, now!" The lawyer stood up.

"I did see two things happen that night, though. I didn't share this with the police. Maybe that can help," Toby confessed further, ignoring his mother's exasperated sigh.

Agent Perez settled back into the chair opposite the trio. "Now you're talking," he said. "Tell me. What *did* you see?"

Kathy knew that Perez was good at this. He was now asking him in a subtler voice, trying to soothe the shaken teenager.

Toby cleared his throat deeply, looking around the room and straight into the window, as if though he could tell that someone was watching behind the mirror. "I saw her father's car come back just about the time that she walked into the church with the pastor."

"*What* pastor?" Agent Perez asked, genuinely curious.

So was Kathy. First, about Joel coming back, and second regarding her going with a pastor. She leaned forward to the glass.

"Pastor John, the youth pastor from our church. They are very close. Like, too close. It's weird. But I was only watching her because I have a crush on her... but you already know that."

Toby's lawyer sat back down, and sighed. His mother took his hand on hers, assuring him.

"You mean to tell me that you saw Petra go into the church later that same night, and this was after her father had dropped her off back in the same parking lot? Please help me out; I'm confused about the timeline." Agent Perez was taking notes.

"I don't know; I'm confused myself. All I remember seeing was Petra going inside the church with the pastor after her father had dropped her off. He looked really upset, by the way. Her dad, I mean. But I remember the car coming back, and parked in a corner across the street," he explained in clearer words, bringing forth a better picture of things that had happened that night.

Raymond Perez looked at his notes, rubbed his temple, and then ran his hand through his nicely trimmed beard, deep in thought.

"Okay. That's very interesting. Thank you, Tobias," Perez said. "Just a few more questions, and then we will be done. I promise. Did you, by any chance, get to see the state in which Petra was when her father dropped her off? I mean, was she looking hurt or in pain in any way when she got out from the car? Also, around what time was that? And did you go inside the church after she went in with Pastor John?"

"I don't know, I swear to you. I just told you all I saw. And no, I didn't go inside. I saw all of this from a distance. I stayed late at the festival because I was waiting for my mom to pick me up. But I was tired, to be honest." Toby sighed. He took a pause, and then continued. "I saw that Mr. León stayed outside in his car for a while. I just figured he was waiting for Petra to come out, so I didn't think much of it. And that's when my mom came to pick me up. So that's all I know; I swear! Can we go home now, please?"

His mother asked the same question.

"You've been of immense help, Toby. Mrs. Adams, if we need Toby again, we will let you know. Please remain where we can easily reach you, as we still need to deal with the other situation."

Toby sagged in the chair and sighed in relief before popping to his feet. He couldn't walk out the door fast enough, trailed by his lawyer and mother.

"Looks like we need to have a talk with Pastor John, Ms. Potter," said Agent Perez to the empty room, staring at Kathy through the glass.

"Looks like it," she echoed.

An agent opened the door and called Perez out. He whispered something in his ear. Agent Perez turned around and excused himself. They both hustled out the door without saying more, determined.

Katy left without any words, exiting the building with the weight of the world on her shoulders.

Was Pastor John involved? Were all men pigs?

Her phone rang just as she got inside the black car that they had provided for her ride back home. It was Brett. He had been with James, keeping him safe, just in case.

"I am on my way back home," Kathy said, unable to hold back a sob.

"I'm getting involved in this, Kathy. I am going to do my part to help. I have contacts from my military days who can search under rocks the FBI would not dare to look," he said. "I'll bring our Petra home; I promise."

Kathy felt a seed of hope plant itself in her aching chest.

"Okay, honey. I'll be there soon," she replied, returning the phone into her handbag.

It had been three days since Joel made his escape from the prying eyes of the FBI.

Joel had contacted Ricky with specific instructions to send the package to Robert Creel. He was to put his package inside another sealed box, just in case Bob got curious and tried to open the box.

He alone knew how important those things were, for without them, he couldn't make a clean escape, nor move around. More importantly, he needed things within the package for Petra.

He waited impatiently for Bob to return, wondering if Bob could be nosy enough to take a peek into his package. The sound of someone stomping their foot through the hallway brought him out of his whirling thoughts. The heavy man walked like a soldier on his way to war.

Joel was already moving toward the door when a fist banged against it several times, but then he paused and waited for Bob's voice. He couldn't be too careful right now.

"Hey, Sam? I got your package right here, bro," Bob called, a trifle uncertain.

Joel opened the door and was greeted with Bob's wide, snaggle-toothed smile. Joel looked around the hallway before looking at Bob, who now had a cynical look on his face.

"Watchu looking for?" Bob asked, noting his demeanor. "You expecting company?"

*Man, this guy is so nosy! Seriously.*

Bob got nothing but a frown in return.

"Even if I told you, you wouldn't believe me," Joel answered, stretching out his hand to receive the package, a medium-sized box.

"Here you go. Knock yourself out," Bob said, handing it over. He stood rooted to the spot, clearly aching with desire to find out more about his mysterious new tenant. He scratched his almost-bald head as Joel glared at him in disapproval.

"You may leave now, Bob. There is nothing more here for you to do. Don't worry; if there is anything else that comes up, I'll be sure to contact you at the front desk." He began to close the door. "Thank you, once again, by the way."

Bob turned around slowly, obviously not satisfied by the arrangement. He grunted and shuffled away.

Joel slammed his door shut, laying the locks in place, and found himself a comfortable spot on the creaking bed. He tore the package open, retrieved the inner box, also opening it. It exposed a brown cased pack underneath the wrap. He couldn't tear past the encasing as fast as he wished to, revealing all he needed to continue his journey.

"Michael Arteaga..." he called out, reading the name on the new driver's license, which had his Photoshopped photo on it, his black hair a silver white and glasses perched on his nose. "Looks like I'm going silver fox for a while."

He smiled to himself, placing the new identity card on the bed before bringing out another one, but with a different name and a completely different look in it. The alterations of his photograph were superb.

The package contained hair dye materials, a copy of his FBI file, information about the kidnapping ring, the identification cards, a pair of glasses that matched those of the ID picture, and other items. Joel knew that each of these items were important, as he needed to stay up to date with things, rather than run the risk of getting caught before getting his plans enacted.

With the burning desire to exit the shithole that he had been staying in for days, he read thoroughly through the files and pulled out a pink slink of paper containing an address and further helpful information of Joel's next destination on it. It was the most important piece of information yet, and he was certain that he'd be heading out again soon enough.

Ricky was good. He had risked his life for this information, and indeed, his debt would be now forgiven.

"First, I need to look the part," he whispered to himself while picking up the glasses.

He walked to the bathroom with a pair of scissors and the silver dye. He would cut his hair to size first before coloring it. No one would go around looking for a white-haired Joel, and he knew it. It would get him just far enough until he could get things done.

*I always did want to go silver...*

He had just dumped the items on the counter when his current burner phone rang out from the bed. He hurried back to answer the call, but did not speak. He could hear his caller's breath.

"Hello? Joel, I sent you the package," the voice on the other end said in the all too welcomed voice of the one and only person that Joel assumed he could trust now. "You know what to do now. Right?"

"I got it just now. Are you sure about San Bernardino?" Joel asked Ricky, seeking some clarification about his destination.

"You'll just have to find out for yourself now, won't you? Need I remind you that I never gave you anything, and that this is the last favor I owe you?"

"Yeah, no. I know. Don't worry. You told me that already," Joel replied, getting tired of his constant reminders about not being involved should anything go bad.

"Be smart and do not get caught. The heat is up on you right now. Lay low. Stay off the radar as much as possible. You are becoming more popular than the president as of now, Joel. Well, at least in Arizona," Ricky joked before bringing the call to an end abruptly.

Joel did not enjoy his little joke, but took it in good faith. He wished that things had gone differently and he didn't have to be on the run. But it was unavoidable at the moment. He had to become Michael Arteaga now.

He took a few more minutes staring at the crooked mirror on the bathroom wall, with thoughts of James on his mind and what he might be thinking of his father. He knew too well that Kathy and her lover Brett would have worked their magic on him, making certain he was hated. He knew he couldn't do anything to change their thoughts about him now, given Petra's current situation.

The picture of his daughter's beautiful face came to mind. He could still recall their last fight, with his paranoia about Brett getting the best of him. He could still much recall the tears running down her face after their meal, making his heart ache.

*Stay strong, Joel!* He encouraged himself before handling the scissors. *Be strong until the end.* He took the first cut from his hair with a smile.

Joel... No. *Michael* understood what he needed to do next. He was prepared now. He was ready. He visualized where he needed to go.

San Bernardino, California.

# BROKEN

# CHAPTER TWENTY-NINE | 29

I WAS HANDED OFF TO A COUPLE OF MEN I don't recognize. It wasn't *him* who drove me. It was someone else. I am in a new place, who knows where, and I don't like it. I was given a white robe to wear. It's more like a long, white shirt. The men told me that if I want to be treated well I have to be a good girl and obey at all times. Eventually, they said, I will be taken to the group.

I wonder what they mean.

In the meantime, I am forced into a dog kennel. A dog kennel! Of course I refuse. I fight. Of course, they win.

Humiliated, I cry myself to sleep in this small box as they film me and laugh.

# BROKEN

# CHAPTER THIRTY | 30

JAMES SAT IN PETRA'S ROOM, imagining her presence. He knew that she would most definitely freak out about him being in her room, especially sitting on her bed. She always fancied her privacy, as he did his. Boys were just not allowed in her room, ever, since she was a little princess.

"Get out of my room, Jimmy!" she would yell.

It was something that he missed very much right now, as he let the tears rolls in constant streams. He couldn't come to terms with the fact that she was missing, and possibly gone, never to be seen again. He had thought being in her room, with her things, would make him feel better, but nothing was the same without her.

He walked around her room, looking at some old stuffed animals that she had stacked away and hardly ever touched anymore, at least not since she felt herself to be grown up and not a kid anymore. She had grown up too fast, and he couldn't come to grips with it.

He found it difficult to swallow when he found guys hitting on her, and even more when she gave them her flirty attention. But he didn't care about that now; he just wanted her back.

*I miss you, Petra.*

James fell back into her bed, letting himself get flooded by memories of their childhood together. He wasn't a very spiritual person, but he still prayed and hoped for a miracle like never before. He would give anything within his power to make it happen—to return to their life before the festival.

*Lord, please keep her safe! Wherever she is, keep her safe. And… bring her back to us. Please!* He took a moment to think about it before praying it. *Take me instead. I don't care.*

Chaos had ensued at home. There was no order or cleanliness anymore, and everything felt like it was going to hell. Nobody cared to pick up anything around the house. Brett had kept to himself more often than usual, spending a lot of time on his phone, talking quietly and texting, while his mother had become but a shadow of herself.

James got up from his sister's bed and went to the bathroom to wash his face. After slapping himself a few times, he went downstairs, just as Brett received a phone call, a worrisome look crossing his face. He knew that Brett was also worried sick about Petra, and he had just learned that Brett had military contacts who could help them find his dad *and* his sister.

Brett walked out the back door to take his phone call, away from listening ears. James walked the opposite direction, restless. He had no desire to go out to see friends or go to church since the incident, unwilling to leave his mother.

James walked to the living room where his mother sat. She had recently returned home after several hours away, and she had a bandage on her head. He sat opposite her, trembling. He was a nervous wreck. He hadn't had any good sleep in days, with the occasional downing of coffee to keep him awake because he was afraid to close his eyes and miss something important.

"How could Dad do this?" he whispered, fully convinced that his father was responsible for his little sister's disappearance, especially after hearing what he did to his mother. "I mean, what kind of father is that?" he asked again, hoping for some logical explanation to the madness, even though he knew that he wasn't going to get any.

His mother only replied with sobs. She swiped at the tears off from her eyes and was about to speak, but Brett swept into the room with a grim look on his face.

"What is it, honey?" she asked. "What's wrong?"

"I just talked with some buddies of mine on the phone, and they are pretty sure that Joel is involved in much more than kidnapping. James, please, would you excuse your mother and me?" he asked kindly, clearly hoping not to further tarnish his father's image right in front of him.

"No. I want him to hear everything," his mother snapped. "I want him to know how much of a monster his father really is, Brett. He stays."

James remained quiet and seated, desperate to listen to what Brett had to say. He needed to know the truth, even if it hurt.

"If you think so, honey," Brett said with a sigh, taking a seat next to her.

"So? What did you find out about my dad?"

Brett took a breath, not knowing how to start. "It seems that your dad had been stalking this house for months," Brett informed him. "I think he has been planning the kidnapping for a long time," he continued, giving them something to consider. "While we were out, I asked some of my friends to come search this house for anything they could find as clue—which I'm sorry I didn't tell you before, by the way. But I was hoping I was wrong."

"Did they find anything?" James asked.

"It seems that your dad has been watching us the entire time with some hidden cameras he had installed. I don't know how or when he placed them, but they were here. My friends took them down and dumped them in the back bin, which is why I headed out that way upon receiving the call earlier," he explained.

His mother was red, her lips curled into a hateful snarl. "I feel violated. This is disgusting!"

James felt something between hate and disdain, fuming in anger. He walked away toward the back door to get the cameras that Brett had spoken about, returning with the load of them in his hand and dumping them on the table.

Immediately, his mother reached forward to examine them, before holding her head in her hands in disbelief. "We need to get this to the FBI, immediately!" she urged. "They need to find that bastard and bring him to justice."

"I agree with you. But we also need to check out his house for any clues that we can find," Brett suggested. "I don't trust him, at all."

"Wait," James said, "When did you friends come to take them out? I don't understand. And who let them in?"

"Jimmy!" his mother snapped. "That's not important right now. The point is that we found them!"

James gave it some thought, choosing to go along with the plan that seemed more likely to get them to Petra. He wondered if indeed they could find something in his father's house, since the police hadn't exactly raided the place for clues already, according to his mom. Besides, he wanted to see things for himself, since his mom didn't exactly have the chance to search the place all that well. And with Brett's help and experience, he could provide a fresh pair of eyes.

"Okay, but I want to go too," James agreed, finally speaking. "I want to be there when you go through his home."

His mom looked at Brett, who remained silent, and then she spoke, "I was there earlier today, but I was so disoriented when I woke up, all I could think about was getting out of there. Besides, the agents came right away. Like I said, I don't think the police went through it yet, because they didn't have a warrant or something like that, but I am not sure. Will we find something that can help?"

"Yeah, I don't know," said Brett, "But at this point even something small is more than we have now."

"It's worth the try," James added. "It's possible that he cleaned it all out before he took a hike, but who knows. From what you've said, Mom, it seems like he was rushed, and you probably weren't out for too long anyway. So it might be worth snooping around."

Silence ensued. The room was filled with one thought alone — doing whatever necessary through whatever means necessary to bring Petra home. James had recently learned through Brett that any evidence they found would be inadmissible in court, first because there was no search warrant, second, because they were not cops, and lastly, because that was essentially breaking and entering. This would also mean that they would break the law. But if Brett thought it was a good idea, then James was down for it too.

And so they went.

Brett manned the wheels at a nauseating speed, good enough to fool anyone into believing he drove fast cars for a living. He paid attention to traffic lights and speed limits at moments, doing everything within his ability to make certain that he wasn't pulled over; they couldn't afford to get involved with the police right now. But he was still trying to get there as soon as possible. Luckily, the 101 Loop was mostly empty of traffic at this time, and they reached his dad's home quickly.

The drive to Mesa, Arizona, where Joel lived, wasn't as far as Kathy had remembered it to be. She knew the FBI would still be monitoring his place, but she had a plan. She would create a distraction. It didn't need to be long—just long enough for them to get inside unnoticed and close the door behind them.

Kathy had seen their operation and knew that, as of now, they were only monitoring to see who came in and out, as well as tapping his phone and computer. All they needed was just a few minutes. She hoped her plan would work. It was worth the risk.

They parked outside the condominium complex and walked in from the back side, adjacent to the detached car garages. Kathy then called the non-emergency Mesa police number to report the suspicious van to the cops. She told them that she was a neighbor and had seen the van parked there numerous times. She used the words "meth cooking" and elaborated on how she saw suspicious-looking fellows going in and out all the time. She figured no one had called because there weren't that many people living in this brand new neighborhood anyway. This plan could work.

It was only a matter of minutes before several patrol cars came and surrounded the van, guns out, demanding the occupants of the van show themselves. The agents exited, hands up, and were not happy. At that very moment, the trio made their move.

Kathy felt butterflies swarm her belly as they approached the front door. Her guts threatened to fail her, as Brett took to the door lock and picked it in a matter of seconds.

She stared at Brett in shock. He had always seemed like a by-the-book person. The sight of him picking a door lock with ease sent a rush of confusion through her, but there was no time to process, as Brett urged them into Joel's home, and they closed the door back, hoping they had managed to miss the agents. They weren't sure.

"I am scared, babe," Kathy whispered after he locked the door behind them.

Brett had read her thoughts well enough, knowing what scared her exactly. He walked over to her with a warm embrace.

"Everything will be all right, I promise," Brett said as he handed each of them gloves to put on.

Kathy could barely take courage from the words, every worst possible scenario playing in her head.

"Make sure you guys stay away from the windows, and don't make too much noise. Remember, they can't know we are in here," Brett told them.

"How are we going to get out?" Kathy asked, realizing they hadn't thought that far in advance.

"Crap!" James added.

"We will worry about that when we get there," Brett responded. "For now, let's find something to nail this son—" Brett stopped as he looked at James, obviously trying to respect the fact that Joel's son was present and deserved respect.

"You can say it," James said and walked away.

As quietly as possible, James begun going through his father's stuff in the living room, searching fervently for anything that he could lay his hands on, just to help. He began searching through a pile of papers that he couldn't make anything off.

"You should check the bedroom while I go through the living room with Jimbo here," Brett whispered to Kathy, as if hoping not to intrude entirely on her ex-husband's privacy without her having gone through the major parts first.

Kathy needed no more instruction, heading off to Joel's bedroom in search of whatever she could find. It was a relatively new two-bedroom condominium, and his master bedroom was at the end of the hallway. This bedroom had its own bathroom and seemed to function as a home office, with a small desk and some file cabinets and a mattress on the floor.

She had been here before, looking quickly through the closet and under the mattress. She hadn't found anything then, but she'd search better this time.

Her heart weighed heavy, and her body shook at the thought of what could have befallen her baby girl. She began with Joel's wardrobe, searching through his pile of clothing, before heading off to the bathroom, pulling apart anything that her hands could lay on, in hopes that something, anything, would provide her some needed information about her missing girl or Joel's nefarious activities. She hoped James and Brett had better luck.

"These apartments have an attic, right?" Kathy heard James asking. "I mean, this place ought to have a small area upstairs for storage or conduit at least. They seem a lot taller from the outside than what it shows in the inside."

"Yes, you're right. They definitely do," Brett replied, sounding like he had wished he had thought of it sooner. "You should go and search around while I get your mother," he asked of James.

Kathy was already making her way back toward the pair before when he reached her. "There is nothing here, Brett," she said, distraught. "There is nothing about my baby here. The cabinets are full of work stuff, and the rest is just normal everyday items."

"I am sorry, babe. I really am," Brett apologized in a tender tone while embracing her, proving himself to be a gentleman to the core. "Maybe the other room—"

A gasping noise from James froze them both in place.

"That's James!" Kathy hissed. "He could be hurt."

Brett needed no further explanations, making a run with Kathy trailing him behind through the short hallway. They found him in the other room, where Joel slept, an attic door hanging down from the ceiling inside the walking closet, a chair right beneath it.

The most unsettling sight was James. He looked pale, with his hands trembling, as he pointed up to the attic, quietly crying.

Brett grabbed the chair and stood on top of it, jumping into the attic while pulling himself up using his arms.

"Holy shit," Brett murmured.

"What is it?" Kathy asked from below, as she tenderly hugged her firstborn to console him.

"You need to see this, Kathy. But I am warning you; you are not going to like it," came the response from above.

"Help me up, Jimmy," Kathy commanded her son.

The two men helped her get to the attic, one from above and one from below. It was a small storage area. There were some boxes and papers around. There were some old tools and a lot of old blueprints rolled up inside boxes. Joel's normal job stuff.

But then she saw it. The final nail in Joel's coffin. Plastered across the right wall was a poster board, with pictures of different young girls, seven in count. Petra was one of them.

"What have you done, Joel?" Kathy asked. "What kind of evil has overcome you?" This was a man that she did not know—a total stranger.

"We need to call the police," James suggested from below. "Those could all be missing girls."

"Technically, this proves nothing. Yet," said Kathy. "But we all know that this is most likely what it appears to be. Joel has–"

Brett interrupted, "We can't just pick up the phone and call the cops. We broke the law, Kathy. If they get a search warrant, it would be different. In that case, they will find all of this and nail the bastard. But as of now, we would have to admit to breaking and entering in order to get the cops here. And Joel could easily argue that we planted it. Think about it."

"Well, what then? We can't wait around for these fools to decide to get a warrant and hope they find this. We know my dad did it, and this is proof!" James said furiously from behind them, having joining them in the attic space.

"Well, we must do something!" Kathy was determined. "I don't know what, exactly, but something. Anything! And soon." A tear left her cheek. It was a tear of anger rather than sadness.

Brett got emotional for the first time, angry tears welling. "That bastard will pay for all that he has done!" he assured them both, taking out his phone to take some pictures before going down and placing a call to someone Kathy assumed to be one of his military colleagues.

Kathy went down with the help of James. "Hand me your phone, James. Mine is in the car," she ordered once down. She had brought down the poster board from the attic.

"Mom, I don't think it was a good idea to move it. It's true what Brett said; we could be accused of planting it here, trying to frame Dad."

"At this point, I don't care anymore, Jimmy. I just want my daughter back."

Kathy took a good look at the pictures of the girls on the board, followed by some dates scribbled underneath them and addresses of where they lived. It looked organized and pre-planned, with some other information of their possible destinations on a daily basis scribbled underneath each girl's picture. She turned around to make the call to Agent Perez, unable to bear looking at it any longer. She could feel herself tensed up within, worried that she might never see her daughter again.

The emotions translated into her words, as Agent Perez picked up with his usual commanding tone. "It was Joel, Perez. He did it. He—" She found the words hard to conjure in one sentence.

"Calm down, Ms. Potter. Please. What are you saying?" Agent Perez asked, hearing her stammer.

"Joel kidnapped all those girls! Or at least about seven of them," she replied, this time sounding firmer.

"How are you certain of this?" Agent Perez asked, sounding baffled. "As of now, we strongly believe he is involved, of course. But you sound confident."

"I am calling you from inside his place. It was all in the small attic. You should get here fast; I know you're outside," she replied before bringing the phone down to end the call.

"Attic? Did you break in? The PPD is—" Agent Perez was saying as she ended the call.

Kathy knew she had rattled his cage, and it was only a matter of a few minutes before agents would come bursting through the door. And that was exactly what she had intended. At this point, if they got in trouble for breaking and entering, it was worth it.

# BROKEN

# CHAPTER THIRTY-ONE | 31

THEY THINK THEY CAN BREAK ME. *Pfff!* They say my name is no longer Petra. Apparently, I am Eve now. They say I am their pet now. Ironic, isn't it? *Eve*, as in the first woman, created directly by God's own hand, after His own image. A pet.

I curse at them. Of course, they don't like that. They keep trying to break me in different ways, but I won't let them.

I am a rock. I am a lion. I am a warrior.

My name is Petra; I am unbreakable.

# BROKEN

# CHAPTER THIRTY-TWO | 32

B Y THE TIME THAT RAYMOND PEREZ ARRIVED at Joel's home, a PPD forensic team was already in place. They would be cooperating with the FBI's forensic scientists once they got there. This was not a crime scene, but a judge had issued a search warrant, and that was all they needed to hunt for evidence now. However, the fact still remained—they had broken in. And this would be dealt with.

Perez wasn't at the van when Ms. Potter called; other agents were attending the stakeout. He wasn't even at work; he was at home with his wife. It was his day off. After the call came, he made several calls, got ready, and headed there, leaving an upset wife behind. Of course, this wasn't the first time he'd work on his day off. It wouldn't be his last time, either.

Perez walked up to Kathy with a frown across his hardened face. He couldn't make anything else of her other than a determined mother who would stop at nothing to get her missing daughter back. He admired that zeal in her, even though he didn't have any kids of his own. And he wasn't intending on changing that fact anytime soon.

Staring into Kathy's deep green eyes, he could see past the mirage of calm that she had tried desperately to put up. She granted him a tight-lipped smile before exchanging pleasantries.

"I anticipated we'd be seeing you around more and more during this investigation, until we find your daughter," he said with a small smile.

"You got that right," Kathy replied, heaving a sigh indicating how tired she was from the emotional and mental stress that she had dealt with since her daughter's disappearance. "Why would Joel do this to his own daughter?"

"It beats me," Perez honestly confessed, trying to riddle the mind of this particular psychopath, having dealt with some of them before. "I've seen it all in my line of work, and every time that something like this happens, it simply defies explanation."

Kathy looked at James, who stood silently in a corner, and then turned to Perez. "Do you have kids, Raymond?" Kathy asked.

Perez showed his discomfort by the personal question and by her tenacity to leave all formalities and professionalism aside, scratching the back of his head before looking away momentarily. His eyes caught sight of the pictures taped to the board, in what looked like an organized effort at studying each of them, their daily routines, and activities.

"Agent Perez?" Kathy called out to him, most likely hoping he would stop ignoring her. "Is that an inappropriate question?"

Agent Perez wished himself away from them there and then, casting his mind off to a time when he had thought of having kids, until he met his wife and she decided she never wanted any, and the ultimate sacrifice of having a vasectomy came into plans. This was something he had yet to do, even though he remained committed to her.

"I'm sorry. And no, I don't have any kids," he replied, looking at her in wait for her response.

Kathy's expression remained blank. There were no follow-up questions with regard to why he had chosen not to have children. "I guess we all have our reasons," she simply said, casting her gaze toward Perez's shiny shoes. "Still, I thank you for your diligent work in finding other people's children."

The tension grew. Agent Raymond Perez excused himself for a moment, determined to do something that would yield results instead of discussions about his personal life.

The room had gotten crowded with the forensic team now. They went about lifting prints and any other information that might come handy. Kathy and James had to leave the scene.

They had just walked out of the condo when James asked the one question that Kathy had asked herself time and time again. "Will Petra ever come back home, Mom?" His voice was quiet, and a little shaky, showing just how scared he was.

Kathy felt her hand tense on guardrail of the stairs. She had kept her composure for the past hour, and it was becoming increasingly difficult to keep it together.

She closed her eyes, refusing to make eye contact with her son, fearing she might have to tell a lie she wanted to believe in desperately, when she knew well that the worst possible scenario could have happened to her daughter already.

"Mom?"

*Come on, Kathy, answer your son.*

She needed to instill courage and hope in her son. She was sure that James could see her struggle clearly and groped at how to appear honest but optimistic for him. She opened her eyes and stared at his anguished face. She could feel the pain in his watery eyes.

A voice interrupted their moment. "I am going to need you guys to leave the premises. You cannot be here," Agent Scott said from the entrance as he pointed toward the parking below.

*Perfect timing.*

They made their way down the stairs in silence.

"I'm sorry, Mom," James blurted out once they reached the parking lot. "I am *so* sorry! This was my entire fault. I feel this guilt threatening to rip me apart from within. I am so stupid!"

Kathy understood Jimmy's feeling of guilt. If he hadn't left Petra alone at the festival, he would certainly have been with Petra when Joel came around, and things would have likely ended much differently. Taking two kids would have been more difficult than one for their father. But instead, he had given in to his hormonal instincts and gone to Cindy's house.

Jimmy had confessed it all by now.

Kathy looked straight into her boy's eyes, that harbored the same level of guilt she felt. She did her best to absolve him. "You have nothing to worry about, Jimmy." She put on a false smile. "Your sister is coming home to us," she said in a tone too real to be a lie. "She *will* come home. This is *not* your fault."

She hugged her son, who fell against her heavily, like he did when he was little. Her hopeful heart threatening to collapse.

"I should've been there, *Mami*. I should've been there with her. I am sorry," he said between sobs.

Brett approached the pair, after another lengthy phone call. He seemed to be making more of those for a while now, and Kathy wasted no energy worrying whether or not he was embarking on some unlawful means to bring Petra home. It was too late for that, anyway.

"Ms. Potter!" Agent Perez shouted out from where he stood above. "Can you come over, please?"

Kathy looked at James, who was still crying. Brett gave her a nod and moved in, and she left her son with her lover, walking once again back upstairs to her ex-husband's apartment.

Agent Perez stood over a pile of clothes and papers in the mostly empty room with the attic entrance. She had caught sight of something familiar in the pile the agent was standing over, and it made her heart contract in her chest. It was her daughter's, and she herself had purchased it for Petra the Christmas before.

"That's Petra's!" she exclaimed, pointing at the pair of pants she had gotten her daughter, with her mind awash with maddening thoughts. There was a shirt and underwear that belonged to her, as well.

"We just needed to confirm that. I am sorry about your troubles, Ms. Potter," an understanding red-headed female agent said. "It could be here for thousands of reasons," she added as she walked a sobbing Kathy back outside the condominium. "Do your kids ever spend the night here?"

"He is their dad," she replied. "A few times, here and there, I guess. But it's been a while."

"That helps," the agent responded.

"Do you think... Do you think Joel would put her own daughter through something so vicious?" The thoughts of her daughter getting molested ran through in disturbing menace. The idea of her being forced into prostitution, or getting introduced to drugs, or some worse fate, was something that she had desperately tried to debunk from her school of reasoning; but now, nothing could keep these thoughts away.

"We don't know, Ms. Potter. We are just trying to gather evidence and find out what we can at this point. Excuse me." The agent walked away to chat with a partner.

Brett came over, meeting Kathy at the bottom of the stairs and held her in his embrace, warming her heart as best as possible with his body. He whispered words of encouragement into her ears, as if hoping they would calm her nerves. "I love you, honey. I am so sorry. But know that I am here for you. Anything you need, just tell me."

"I need you to find my baby, Brett," she pleaded with teary eyes and broken words. "I need you to do *whatever* it takes to find that bastard and make him pay for everything that he has done." She was ready for him to get nasty if needed. They had crossed that line; there was no turning back anymore.

Brett listened, as he always did, his heart heavy at her hunched shoulders and obvious despair. He squeezed her body tighter, his heartbeat in such a pace that it felt like a herd of wild horses marching across a field for battle—just like hers.

Agent Perez was headed toward his vehicle when he stopped to talk to the distraught family. "I am going to the office to take care of some things. I need to start on some paperwork essential for all this. I need more resources for a full-on man hunt for your husband. Even though this is not standard, once we catch a whiff of wherever he is hiding, I will let you know. I promise you," he assured her, walking away with his hands tucked inside his pockets.

Kathy closed her eyes in search for calm. She could feel the darkness within her, urging her to do horrible things to Joel once he was caught. She wanted him to suffer just as much or more than he was making her suffer at present. She wanted Brett to make him pay in blood for the agony that he had brought upon them all. She wanted more than justice. She wanted *revenge.*

She could picture Petra in a dark, lonely cell, being forced to do wicked things. Years of watching true crime television shows came back to haunt her, the stories and images being replaced with her circumstances and her sweet daughter's face.

For the first time in her life, she felt angry enough that she wished a man could die. She wished Joel would be caught, leading them to where her daughter was, and killed in the process. She would accept whatever punishment God deemed necessary to know beyond a shadow of a doubt that Joel would never hurt her or her children again.

His father's condominium came with a detached, yet enclosed, two-car garage on the parking lot side. James knew this. And the minivan was parked next to his father's garage on a parking spot marked with a *visitor* tagline. The back of the garage had a window, through which Kathy had seen Joel's Range Rover inside the day before.

Out of curiosity, James went to check it out. He managed to open the window from the outside, and popped the screen out. He didn't care anymore. James had locked himself out but still gotten inside his own house at least twice through a window in the back. This wasn't any different.

Once inside Joel's garage, James sat in the hood of his father's luxury SUV, deep in thought. *How did we get to this point?*

He didn't have any idea on what to do. He questioned everyone. There were too many sketchy people around Petra. And then there was his father. The idea of having his same blood made his skin itch and crawl. He hated the man.

James ran the entire night of the festival through his mind once more, before the thought of seeing the one person who had hidden the fact that he had seen Joel from him came forward. He wanted to see Mateo—the unfaithful friend who had betrayed his trust by carrying on with his sister and then spying on her. They would have words. He was sure he knew more than he was letting on. No one was innocent here.

By his father's work bench, James caught sight of a strange-looking patch on the drywall. The paint was brighter, and the texture different from the surrounding wall. His curiosity piqued, helping him temporarily bury the thoughts of Mateo's disloyalty, he decided to investigate.

James looked around, ensuring that he was indeed alone, before crouching to have a feel of the rough patch on the wall, which was just behind the work tools. He scratched at the freshly laid paint, feeling it erode under his fingers, just before the wall came caving through, the fresh drywall patch not dry enough to withstand the pressure of his fingers. What he saw sent him scrambling back in alarm.

Inside the wall was more cash than he had ever seen in his life. It was like something in a movie. He opened the garage door from the inside and yelled to anyone who would listen.

"Mom! Hey, everyone! You need to see this!" he screamed, hoping to alert as many people as possible.

Brett made it there first, asking if James was hurt. He froze in his step upon seeing the rolls of money hanging out of the caved-in wall. He exchanged a with James, nodding at the wall, and James simply raised his hands in the air, indicating he did not have the slightest idea on what was going on either.

Two agents led the way back, looking equally as shocked by the sight of the money tumbling out of the wall. A few other agents stormed in, ready for action, gun extended.

"What the—?" Agent Scott asked aloud looking at his fellow agents.

James knew that the pictures in the attic, the pieces of Petra's clothing, and the newly discovered cash in the garage wall did nothing to help his father's case. There seemed to be a tremendous amount of incriminating evidence left behind.

Scott radioed Perez to come back, as he had already left the premises. He hadn't gone far, though, and was back there in a few minutes.

Once there, Perez motioned for the wall to be brought down completely, with the forensic team doing their part to gather further evidence, which would help them ascertain any possible lead on Joel's whereabouts, or Petra's. Maybe this money had something to do with the girls' disappearance. Maybe not. But for now, it was also evidence.

James felt a tad useful, seeing he had found out about the money hole.

Some neighbors had been coming to see what the commotion was all about. The red-headed female agent was questioning them to see if they could help with any details as to where Joel had gone or if they had seen him come in with any young girl.

The demolition was fast, with the pieces of drywall peeled away from the studs within a few minutes. This led to the discovery of more cash stacked away deeper into it.

"That's a lot of cash. I thought you guys said he was broke?" James asked Agent Perez, who was watching the forensics team with interest.

"From what our sources gathered, he is in heavy debt, or was. But this brings an entirely new insight and perspective into things," he responded, as they both watched the rolls of cash get bagged and taken away as evidence.

"How much do you think could be in there, total?" Brett asked.

"I'd bet at least a couple hundred grand, by the looks of it," Agent Perez said. "We won't know until it's all counted. But it sure is a lot of cash. Which only increases the questions," he added, taking a lollipop from his pocket, unwrapping it gently and tucking it into his mouth. "Sugar helps me calm down when my nerves are getting rattled, believe it or not."

Brett nodded slightly, before leading James and his mother away from the garage. "Let's go home, guys. Our work here is done. Let's let the professionals work," Brett said.

James cleared the sweat off his forehead with his arm and headed toward the van. He couldn't wait to get home. He had someone to see, and it wasn't going to be a fun visit. He was ready to go out and punish a betrayal.

The drive north toward home wasn't as law-defying as it had been when they headed over to his father's place earlier in the day. Brett seemed to have gathered some sense of responsibility once again, driving like a proper citizen, while his mom occupied herself with her phone, dialing his dad's number over and over and again to no response.

"Kathy, he's not just going to pick up his phone," Brett said gently. "He is way too smart for that. It's probably abandoned, broken, or somewhere far from where he actually is now."

She turned to him with swollen eyes that were all cried out, but gently slipped her phone back in her bag. They were all a dry well now. James stared out toward the freeway.

A few minutes later, they pulled into their driveway, with James shooting out of the car before the minivan was even turned off.

"Where are you off to?" Brett asked from inside the car.

James got in his silver Audi and yelled, "I'll be back" from his open window as he backed down the driveway.

"Jimmy!" his mother cried out.

He ignored them both and drove off fast.

Kathy watched her son's car fade into the distance. "Be careful, Jimmy," she whispered.

"Let him be, Kathy. He is obviously upset. He needs to process this in his own way. I mean, he did just find out that his dad is not the person he thought he was, after all. I just hope he stays safe. I don't think we can take another tragedy in this household right now," Brett said with a sigh, turning off the van and making his way to the house.

Kathy opened the door and entered the house, holding a lot of regrets and an immeasurable amount of pain in her soul. She heard the door close behind her as she made her way into the living room, feeling the echo from the door ravage the entire house. Petra's absence was palpable.

*Wherever you are, honey, please hold on… we are coming.*

Kathy sat in the couch, closed her eyes, and thought about praying. She struggled to find her faith underneath all the rage and anguish. It was difficult to believe in a higher power when terrible things happened to the most innocent among them. Finally, she put together some words.

*Please keep my babies safe, God. Bring them safely back to me.*

# BROKEN

# CHAPTER THIRTY-THREE | 33

THE PUNISHMENTS ARE ONLY GETTING WORSE. I am so tired, but they won't let me sleep. I am hungry, but they won't let me eat. The physical beatings keep increasing. I've never craved drinking water, sunlight, a shower, and a bed as much as I do now. I've soiled myself several times, as they won't let me out of this standing closet unless they're abusing me. I have no idea how long I've been here.

One of them comes and tells me I stink. He hoses me down and tells me to wash myself, as he watches. I am his dog, he says. Little Eve, his bitch.

I can't do this anymore. And I'd rather die than live this way.

# BROKEN

# CHAPTER THIRTY-FOUR | 34

MATEO SAT ON HIS FRONT PORCH, missing his parents, who were now out of town as chaperones for his younger sister's eighth-grade trip. He heard thunder, as the impending Arizona weather threatened to rain. Monsoons. They were unpredictable.

He wasn't having the best week, with his fight with Petra, followed by the authorities' inquiries into his involvement. He could still recall the nerve-wracking moments he faced while at the FBI headquarters. He had seen many movies in which agencies like the FBI and CIA framed people or just totally got the wrong guy. He'd never been so terrified in his life.

Mateo flashbacked to the moment when the agent was grilling him, sounding so certain that he had a part to play in Petra's disappearance. The fact that he hadn't done it made him even more terrified of being labeled a kidnapper. Not only was the love of his life missing, they actually thought he had a hand in it.

And Mateo missed her. Petra's absence left a great hole in his heart, as he wondered what she would be doing had she been around and they hadn't had a fight. Most likely he would be at their house, playing videogames with the siblings. Or perhaps, she would have come visit him at his place, now that his parents were gone, and they would have enjoyed some more kissing.

*Man, I really miss her!*

In the past year, they would constantly visit each other's siblings, but they both knew that this was just an excuse to see each other. But then she had changed. So suddenly. And she had replaced him with that pastor.

*I bet that sketchy guy had something to do with her disappearance.*

The days without her had seemed like months, and he wondered if they were ever going to see each other again. He took a sip from the homemade lemonade that his mother had made before she left, feeling the sweet-tart liquid flow down his throat. The fact that her father was the main suspect, and his erratic behavior before she was taken, had given him the conviction that Mr. León indeed had something to do with her going missing.

Staring into the distance, he could see the familiar shape of his friend's silver car coming into focus. He was driving fast.

*Looks like they're back,* Mateo thought, having gone over to James's house just a few blocks away earlier to check up on things. But no one was home.

James shortened the distance to Mateo's house within a few seconds, coming to an audible screeching halt in his driveway. He got out, breathing hard, face red, as if he couldn't wait to vent how he really felt.

"You bastard!" James yelled, storming toward him.

Startled, Mateo dropped the glass of lemonade, surprised by James's tone and choice of words. He jumped to his feet, and opened his mouth to ask what was wrong, but James's fist connected with his jaw before he could get the words out.

"Are you crazy?" Mateo protested, gripping his sore jaw, wondering what had come over his friend. "What the hell is wrong with you?" he demanded, wondering if James had gone insane or was experiencing some kind of mental breakdown due to the current events.

"Did he pay you not to tell?" James asked, making another lunge toward his friend, who had prepared himself this time and easily avoided the swing.

"What the hell are you talking about?"

"Don't act stupid!" James countered, a finger nearly poking him in the nose. Mateo slapped James's hand away with a snarl.

"Get off my face, Jimmy! The first sucker punch, I forgive. The accusations, I can let go, but only because of my love for you and Petra. But you are pushing it, bro."

A nasty brawl started between them, as Mateo refused to let himself be a punching bag for James.

Their tussle lasted for less than three minutes, ending with Mateo holding James in a headlock, trying to keep his closest friend calm. They had both grown tired from the fight and were huffing and puffing with the exertion.

"So are you going to tell me what the heck is going on, Jimmy?" Mateo asked while still restraining James.

James tried to take a few deep breaths, catching his oxygen before replying. "You fool! I heard that you saw my dad's car come back after he had dropped Petra off, and you failed to share that with my family. Not to mention the fact that you kept me in the dark about the fact that he also reached out to *you* after the whole ordeal! What the hell, Mateo? What did he promise you?"

"I am sorry, but I was scared Jimmy," Mateo apologized, finally coming to terms with what he had done. "But you know I had nothing to do with her disappearance! I would never do anything to hurt your sister. You know that!"

"You could have told me the truth!" James spoke in spurts between sucking in air, his neck still in between Mateo's bent arm. "I trusted you. And Petra trusted you too!"

The reminder stung Mateo.

"I am sorry. I should have said something earlier, but I didn't believe your father could be responsible for something like this. Besides, I was so sure that the corny ass youth pastor did it, seeing that she had gone to see him after she saw your dad and all. I just never thought that your dad would be involved in this too."

Mateo finally let go of his grip on James, scrambling backward to sit while James got up, dusted himself free off from dirt, and joined him reluctantly on an adjoining patio chair.

They each took a few moments to lick their wounds, rattled by the physical encounter that they had just had. They had only fought like this once, in elementary school. They had become best friends after that encounter in the second grade.

"I'm sorry, bro. I miss her too," Mateo said. "It's been weird not having her around, to be honest." He spoke in words that James could relate with. "But to be honest with you, I missed her before she even disappeared."

James stretched his arm to have a go at the lemonade. Mateo gave him the glass and James gulped a mouthful, evidently quenching his thirst before speaking. "We found some of her stuff at my dad's place. The bastard took her and ran away."

Mateo's jaw opened. He struggled to contain his shock as he finally came to terms with James's bullish actions.

"That's so messed up of your dad, dude!" he blurted. "She is his own daughter! What the hell, man? I mean, that's just... so wrong... on so many levels."

"I know, bro. Trust me; I know. I'm just tired of all of this crap in my family. I just want to be done with all of this and have Petra back, and live a normal life. You know? And I want the opportunity to tell my dad how I feel about him. It's not good."

"I get you. I am sorry for everything, dude," Mateo apologized once again, reaching out for the glass of half-drunk liquid in James's hand.

They sat there for the next few minutes, silent, but stuck on similar thoughts about Petra, the sister, the friend, the lover. Her absence left a hole within them more than they could have ever imagined.

Mateo had the wild memories of the young girl with whom he shared very private moments, and the shared memories of growing up with both of them. He loved the Leóns. They were family to him. And he was one of them, too.

"You know what sucks, Mateo? The fact that I fought with her so much. It's like every single opportunity we had for fighting, we took it. We argued every day and got on each other's nerves so much, without realizing the amount of time being wasted doing so. Looking back now, we could have chosen to have each other's back. I wish I could go back in time."

Mateo nodded in understanding, not knowing what to say. He took another sip of his drink before continuing the conversation.

"Why do you think your dad took her?" he asked quietly, the question burning within him after a few moments of silence.

James turned around giving him a questionable look. "Huh? Sorry, I didn't hear what you said."

Mateo took a deep breath, shrugging off the urge to ask again. He sat up, staring James in the face. He could see the puffy skin underneath his eyes, indicating he had been crying. His hair was an unruly mess, which was unlike him. He always put up a confident, unflappable face, and never let anything get to him; or at least, he never showed it.

"Why do you think your father did it?" Mateo asked again, this time, sounding clearer than the first time.

James finally broke contact, looking into his open palms before rubbing them together. Mateo knew that James really wondered the same thing as well. It just didn't add up.

Almost whispering, James replied, "Honestly, I don't know. I ask myself the same thing. And it doesn't make sense."

James's father had obviously gone through some sort of psychotic breakdown and wasn't in his right state of mind anymore. The fact that he could or would harm his own daughter, whom he had previously shown immeasurable love for, was baffling and completely disturbing to think of. It just didn't seem as him. And Petra loved their dad too. They had always been close. Well, except lately. Still, it didn't make sense.

"He just lost it all," James finally elaborated, with the few words bearing much more weight and understanding than an entire book describing his father's actions.

"What do you mean by that?" Mateo asked, looking bewildered.

"He, um… he cracked, Matt," James replied. "My mom with Brett. Petra and I allowing Brett into our lives. His company struggling. Which I didn't even know about, by the way. Then there's his childhood trauma contributing to all of this, which doesn't help. I guess he just couldn't handle it anymore."

Mateo finally had an insight into the madness, shaking his head with regards to the troubles of his friend's father. "What if he had nothing to do with it?" Mateo asked objectively, watching James's disapproving stare level at him.

It appeared that James hadn't heard anyone mention his father's innocence, but he wasn't sure he wanted to welcome it either.

Mateo continued, "Look, bro, I'm sorry, but I just think it's possible, you know. Although, thinking about it, it is pretty crazy he did all the things he did. I mean, fighting with Petra, and threatening you guys," Mateo rambled, almost convincing himself he was wrong.

In all honestly, Mateo wanted so bad for John Meyers to be found responsible. He couldn't shake the wary feelings he had about the minister.

"I know he did it, Mateo. No use in defending him or giving him the benefit of the doubt," James replied. "I'm very sure that bastard has my sister somewhere, and he's run away. You don't do that unless you are guilty."

They both felt hurt, in different ways, but connected to the same source. It was immeasurable, and one person alone could help ease their worry.

Unfortunately, she was missing.

Joel couldn't wait any longer. Given the information he had received, he needed to move as fast as he could. His dyed hair had come through flawlessly, with the added glasses and minor facial makeup he had applied equally assisting in a good disguise. He had spent the last few days trapped in the hotel, which had begun to stifle his thoughts and warp his perception of the reality of things.

A sudden racket came from the reception area, where Bob's voice could be heard loudest. He seemed to be arguing with someone, as other voices echoed down the long hall.

The commotion piqued Joel's interest, prompting him to make a slow and cautious walk toward the source of the argument. He could hear three distinct voices as he closed in on the reception area.

"You promised us the cash last week, Bob. Now, don't mess with us," one of them said in a menacing tone.

"I just told you, I have nothing else to give you," Bob shot back in response. "I paid my dues already, and y'all keep coming around to shake me down. This is getting out of hand now."

Joel finally had a good view of the two men, who were dressed in the earth tones of the city's patrol officers. *Cops? Dirty cops?* The last thing he needed right now. *Are they taking a bribe? What is going on?*

Joel had kept himself hidden from them, but Bob caught sight of him. Bob swiftly motioned for him to make no move, but they quickly jerked their heads around to follow his motion.

"Who are you signaling to?" the cop asked, seeming rather interested. "You got someone taping us or something, Bob?" he continued, grimly walking Joel's direction.

It was too late for Joel to make a run for it. He quickly ran multiple scenarios of the worst possible occurrences. He had a rapid flash toward the gun that he had received with his package earlier, which had been neatly hidden away from sight, and how it could come in handy right now. But the thought of shooting cops was only going to make his life and sins graver to bear and harder to run from.

"Evening, officers. I just rented a room here," Joel called out, raising his hands high into the air indicating he had nothing on him. "I just heard commotion, that's all. But I mean no trouble, sir. I'll go back to my room now."

The officer neared, his eyes scanning Joel's person thoroughly for a phone, camera, or weapon. He stood close to Joel, perhaps in an attempt to intimidate him.

Bob, for all his toughness, didn't have much to say in defense of Joel. "Leave the man alone; he's just a guest."

"Can I see your identification, sir?" the officer asked Joel, ignoring the dithering Bob.

Joel wasn't ready to end his journey when it had only just begun. He slowly brought down his hand into his jean pocket, plucking out a thick sheaf of bills and placing it in the cop's hand.

Joel watched his humble donation get accepted with a smile, prompting the cops to smirk their thanks and make their way out the door. They winked at Bob, getting a snarl in response.

"Well, now you've done it, " an enraged Bob snapped.

"I accept your *thank you*, Bob," Joel whispered over his shoulder, as he walked back to his room.

"Thank you? Oh, you mean, thank you for proving those knuckle heads right in their belief I'm a cash cow? Now those hungry bastards won't ever stop coming back here. Soon they will come back to hustle me *and* my tenants, you idiot! Those who pay, those who bribe, are guilty of something. And you just gave them reason to suspect you."

Joel felt a brief pang of sympathy for Bob, having not thought through the consequences of his actions. But he wasn't willing to let himself get too bothered, seeing as he had done it for himself, not for Bob. He knew that Ricky's fake ID was good, but he wasn't willing to risk it before he made it out the door.

Joel just kept walking toward his room.

"Come on, man. I'm talking to you. Sam! Don't walk away from me now," Bob called out, not willing to be ignored. He followed Joel closely, remaining on his tail until they got to his room.

Joel turned around slowly, looking stern in his expression. His lips snarled into a tight curl, his eyes brimming with intent to be taken seriously, before the words came pouring through. "If those guys come back here, you never knew who I was, or where I came from. You never knew my business or anything about me. *Capiche?*"

Bob remained silent. They stared at each other for a few more seconds, before Bob finally replied. "You got a law and order problem?" he asked. "I suspected as much. But you know what, Sam? The truth is that I really do *not* know *anything* about you to begin with. So I wouldn't be lying anyway, would I?"

He grinned at the realization that Bob had just delivered, turned around, and opened his door.

"You can come clean with me, Sam... if that is even your name. I swear by my sweet mother Lucy's grave, I ain't telling nobody shit," Bob promised, obviously hoping for some response.

Joel walked inside and slammed his door shut. He threw his bag on the bed and began gathering and packing his things, when the door behind him eased open, followed by soft footsteps.

*Ugh. Master key. Bastard.*

"You can tell me; I promise not to tell anyone," Bob persisted. "I've seen all kinds of men come here for one reason or another. And trust me, mate, I've seen them all. From the junkies, to the child molesters, to the... Wait, you aren't a child molester, are you?" Bob rammed on without ever giving the impression that he would stop any time soon.

"Get out of my room, Bob," Joel growled. "I have nothing to tell you. So, please, stop wasting my time."

But Bob remained, fixating his eyes on Joel's belongings spread on the bed in an orderly manner. He moved nearer for a better view.

Joel couldn't take any more of Bob's intrusions. Spinning around, he grabbed a handful of Bob's shirt and slammed him hard against the wall.

"You will not mess this up for me. You hear me? You will not ruin my plans, you, nosy midget!" he roared.

Bob put up a token struggle, but he was no match for Joel.

"Okay, okay..." he groaned, and Joel released him.

"Geez! Calm down, Sam. Sorry, man." Bob fixed his shirt and took a deep breath. "I can help you, you know? I know people who don't like the men in blue and can help with things you might need," he offered in a cajoling voice.

"Get out. You just don't know when to stop, huh?"

"Fine. Fine. I'm just saying, I can help. Whatever your deal is, I can help. But whatever. Your loss, Sam. Your loss," he said as he walked outside the room, closing the door shut behind him with a thud.

Joel had bigger fish to fry. He knew all too well that it was just a matter of time before the police would come back asking questions.

He packed as fast as he could, feeling his anxiety heightening and his heart racing. As he packed, he reviewed his options for the most subtle exit from the motel. He felt uneasy about Bob's discontent with being kept in the dark.

*Why is he so nosy?*

His mind then wandered to the officer who had winked at Bob before making his leave; he could come to mean trouble. He zipped his bag and decided to rest for a little while before taking his leave.

After a quick nap, Joel woke up and touched up his new look. Upon checking himself in the mirror from every angle and feeling satisfied with his new persona, he picked up his belongings and headed for the door. The sound of an altercation coming from the reception area once again stopped him in his tracks, with Bob's voice being heard the loudest, of course. He put his bag down in the room and closed the door behind him as quietly as possible. He took a few gentle steps into the hallway to hear better.

"Y'all sons of bitches are back already?" Bob lamented, swearing in loud cries, which told Joel exactly what was going on.

*They're back!*

"*You* didn't pay us, Bob. Your sketchy tenant did," the one whom had collected the roll of cash from Joel spoke. He recognized his voice clearly.

"He be under my roof, meaning he be my responsibility," Bob replied in defiance. "You got paid, now please take your leave, gentlemen. I am asking nicely."

"Haha. Or what, Bob? What are you going to do about it?" It was the same cop speaking. "Are you gonna call the cops?" He laughed.

Joel had assumed the second cop was with him when he heard someone else rush back in, bellowing. "Luke, looks like Bob here is harboring a fugitive," the second cop said, freezing Joel in his tracks.

*Crap!*

He began a quiet retreat back the way he came.

Bob was giving the cops a surprisingly hard time, refusing to reveal the room in which Joel had lodged into.

"I'm not telling either of you corrupt suckers jack!" Bob yelled. "He's already gone, by the way, and you won't find nothing there."

"Let us do our job, Bob, and step out of the way. We are the police, remember? That's what we do—put bad people in jail," Officer Luke warned.

"Not without a warrant. You ain't getting permission from me to search through my establishment," Bob dutifully replied, knowing his rights well enough.

The cops erupted into a short laughter, mocking Bob's words as one dashed ahead while the other prevented Bob from hindering his search.

"You call this shitty, raggedy piece of crap an establishment?"

"It's the same shitty hole you screw your side slut in so that your wife won't find out," Bob shot back.

Joel had made his way back down the hall and slipped into the room directly across from his. He had a couple of day ago that the door didn't latch properly. He closed the door gently, then pressed an eye to the peep hole to watch. He felt stupid for not leaving earlier.

*He couldn't get caught now; he hadn't done what he needed to do yet!*

He blinked intermittently, lying in wait for the man in uniform, who treaded softly as he neared the first room. The officer took a brief halt in his walk, as if he was about to start going through the rooms, but suddenly stopped. He was the one who had recognized Joel while he returned to the car.

Joel could hear them clearly in the hallway, walking slowly. "I knew I had seen that fool before, but I couldn't remember where. I just thought he was a regular Joe, probably fucking a hooker and smoking some shit, like the usual tenants. But he's got the same scar as the guy on our BOLO, plus, he had all that cash," said the cop.

"Get the heck out of here, you bozos! Now!" That was Bob; he was also in the hallway.

"We need a warrant, Gonzo," Luke said.

"Nah, partner. I have valid suspicion. That should be enough."

"You messed it up coming in and screaming about it. You probably spooked the guy. And with Bob causing such a ruckus, he most likely made a run for it already through some other exit." They were whispering now, but they were at the next room's door by now.

"Bob, do you have bars in your windows? I don't remember."

"Wouldn't you want to know?"

"Screw you."

Joel held his breath, as he watched the officers coming closer to where he stood behind the door. One of them walked toward the back door at the end of the hallway. "It's alarmed. Opening it will trigger the fire alarm, and I didn't hear anything. Which means that the only way out quietly is through the front door."

"Or a window," replied his partner.

"True. Either way, I haven't seen anyone leave since we arrived or through the time that we were outside in the car. I'm telling you, the sucker is still in here!"

Joel listened through well enough, understanding the predicament that he had gotten himself in.

"Call it in. Soon, we'll get to search this shithole," Luke informed his colleague. "We can wait out front. We are not going anywhere, and neither is anyone else. We are patient folks."

"This shit hole is worth more than you, asshole," Bob snarled as he stomped back to the reception area.

Luke shot Bob a mocking look, and laughed. They walked back to the lobby area, disappearing from Joel's range of sight or hearing.

The next fifteen minutes passed without any movement from Joel, nor the cops. Joel felt restless and determined not to get himself caught. He wasn't sure if it was all a trick to make him come out of whichever room he was, and they were waiting for him quietly at the corner of the hallway. But fifteen minutes felt eternal, and he was wasting time. He desperately needed to get out now. Joel checked the window of that room and saw the back end of the patrol car parked out front. They were still there. And this would not be a good way out. It would be noisy too.

He opened the door of the room in which he was as quietly as possible. He waited a few seconds before peeking out to see if he could hear or see any of them. It could all have been a trap, after all.

Nothing.

*Where the hell is Bob?*

He quickly and quietly went into his room, grabbing his belongings as quick as possible. Good thing he was fully packed already. He peeked once again in the hallway for any sign of the cops. Again, nothing. His heart threatened to jump out of his chest.

Desperate, but cautious, he knew his time was running out. With the duffle bag on his shoulder and the gun on his hand, he went toward the back door to see if he could open it quietly. The green light on the bar confirmed what the sign said. Indeed, it was alarmed. Good luck was evidently not on his side today.

Joel began examining the door to see if could be opened without triggering the alarm. For a moment, he put his bag on the floor. That's when he heard the steps behind him, quickly closing in. Frightened, Joel turned around, gun extended, ready for anything.

"Geez, Sam! You wanna kill me?" Bob whispered, frozen in fear with the gun Joel had in hand. "Put that shit down."

"I'm sorry, Bob. I thought it was one of the cops. You don't creep up on a man who is in my situation."

"Shh!" Bob signaled for him to be quiet. "If I was meaning to harm you, I could have pointed out you were in room eight," Bob replied whispering, closing his distance to Joel. "I could hear the door creak open when you went into it. I know the sound of every door in this joint."

"I'm sorry I didn't trust you to tell you anything, Bob, but I really can't. And I urgently need to leave here, for your own safety and mine."

"I have the key to the door; I can turn the alarm off." Bob shoved Joel aside, pulling out a small silver key which he inserted into a keyhole on the side of the push-bar, hidden from view.

"What... what about the cops?" Joel inquired, finding it odd that he had gotten away from them without a fuss. Suspicious, at best.

"The dumbass went to take a dump in the lobby bathroom. That guy is like a clock."

"There were two."

"Gonzo went to the patrol car a while back. I better hurry up. I just came to do this really quick and let you know. This is your chance, right now."

Joel couldn't help but smile, watching Bob's mischievous face lighten up with his words.

"They are going to come after you, you know?" Joel felt compelled to mention the fact. "You sure you can handle it?" he asked in concern. He hadn't expected to get any form of help from Bob, but he was glad he did.

Bob chuckled slightly, following it with a grin across his grizzled face. He sniffed a bit and spat out the door with Joel standing by him. "I'd love to see them try their best," Bob said with a snort. "This is the most fun I've had in a while, *Sam*," he said as he gestured Joel to hurry up.

Joel chuckled and walked out before turning around as the cold breeze caressed his body. "Why are you helping me?" he asked, seeking an answer for Bob's actions.

"I hate the police more than you do. And these ones here are the most corrupt bastards, wearing the uniform more for their own gains than others," Bob replied. "Whatever shit you got yourself into, I can tell you wouldn't want yourself getting caught. Besides, I miss action, to be honest. It's been a while."

"There is no going back for me," Joel replied, turning around to journey on. "Thanks again, Bob."

"Wait!" Bob hissed, startling Joel. "Hold on." He went into one of the rooms and came back with an old desert camouflage trench coat. "This will help you blend in out here until you get far enough away."

Joel put it on. "Thank you, Bob."

"Take care, Sam. Good luck." With that, Bob closed the door behind him.

Joel's destination was California, but that meant the airport, which was rife with cameras and face scanners. But unfortunately, driving wasn't an option, and buses were too slow. With his new cut and color, and enough makeup to alter his features, Joel was certain he could pull it off. Of course, that would mean disposing of the gun first. He wasn't too thrilled about that. This thing could come in handy when the time came.

*California.* He closed his eyes briefly and took a big sigh. The journey was on. He picked his way through the rocks, bushes, and cacti behind Bob's place, watching out for the sight of cops or any law enforcement that could get him in trouble, duffle bag tucked under the voluminous coat.

He had found himself doing impossible things the last few days and wasn't sure if he would come out of it alive. But he remained undaunted and determined to see things through until the very end. He finally exited the scrubby desert area and reached the main road, Central Avenue, about half a mile from Bob's, which had little to no traffic. The high-rise buildings towering downtown were close by. It would be easy to get a cab around here. At least he still had enough cash to keep him going.

All Joel León needed to do was to not get caught.

# BROKEN

# CHAPTER THIRTY-FIVE | 35

"BE A GOOD GIRL," he keeps telling me. "We don't want to keep doing these things to you. All you have to do is follow directions, like the other good girls do. If you don't want to be treated like a rabid dog, then stop acting like one!"

With teary eyes, I scan him from his head down to his sporty shoes, taking into full view the sight of a well-built man with a physique screaming consistent workouts. I could never overpower him.

I am hungry. I am thirsty. I am tired. But mostly, I just want to go home.

"Leave me alone. Please!" My begging only causes them to laugh. "Please, just let me go," I cry to him.

"Oh, you are never going home, bitch. This is your house now, and we are your masters."

He towers over me as I lie on the floor. The broomstick in his hand, now more familiar than ever, still has stains of blood. The man calls it Phil. It's his weapon of choice. Yes, the cause of my bruises has a name.

"Remember, though. The stupid girl needs to learn, but we need her in full, or they won't like her," his colleague tells him as he walks in. He doesn't need a tool to beat us. I fear him the most. "This one cost the boss a lot of time and planning. Little Eve is fucking special!"

These are not men. They are demons.

"I know. But she is a feisty little one, isn't she?"

"I like them like that, though. Eve, you are one hot piece of ass. And I'll be the one to break you."

"That's *not* my name," I whisper in between sobs.

The demons laugh.

They want to break my spirit, but not my body. They need that, I am told. But I can't let them have me. I don't want to. I don't want to give them anything.

But I just can't anymore.

And I lose the battle...

# CHAPTER THIRTY-SIX | 36

RAYMOND PEREZ HAD JUST FINISHED his dinner with his wife, at home in the suburban city of Surprise, when a text message came into his phone. He had hoped to brush it off, having received countless calls on matters that were of little importance. He needed a good night's rest before heading off to work early the next morning to grill one of Kathy Potter's neighbors, whose record had some questionable facts. Natasha Olynyk.

She was an attractive, middle-aged lady who had recently moved into the upscale Scottsdale neighborhood, one block away from the León's. Natasha owned a very successful spa and massage parlor in the city of Tempe, and that itself could mean trouble. Rumor had it that Natasha had relocated years ago originally from Ukraine and had been running her home as a brothel.

The allegations had been made by some neighbors, who felt she lured the other pretty young ladies to her house, even though the cops had found no evidence in such accusations and she had been acquitted of every allegation thus far.

The list of suspects in Petra's disappearance only grew. Perez could barely keep up, and it was exhausting. How deep did it go? There was of course Joel León, whom Perez was sure was guilty. There now was Natasha Olynyk, sketchy as could be. The kids, Mateo García and Tobias Adams, who probably weren't sharing everything they knew. And then there was Pastor John Meyers.

Perez's partner, Scott, had interrogated Pastor John Meyers earlier in the day. Meyers had claimed that Petra came to him crying the evening of her disappearance because her father had upset her with his accusations and raging. The youth pastor said that he hadn't been of much help to her. However, he cleared himself, claiming Petra left after his wife, Sandra, talked to her. They hadn't seen her after that. Sandra Meyers acted as an alibi to clear Pastor John. But maybe she was in on it too. Who knew?

This was too complicated now. While trying to narrow it down, the list of possible suspects involved only grew. What they needed to do was find Joel. And soon. He was the one link missing in all of this. The search for Petra had intensified, and the stress of it with it. It was taking a toll on the agent's personal life.

Another text message brought Raymond's phone to life and his state of mind to the present one again. He grudgingly walked over to where he had dropped it with his car keys upon returning home from work. The message was exactly what he had been hoping to get over the past few days. He read it over and over, and then again, just to be certain that he had gone through it correctly. It stated the fact that Joel had been seen boarding a flight to Ontario, California. Unfortunately, they had picked up his picture after the plane had arrived at its destination.

But it was a good start. At least they knew where he was now.

Excusing himself from his wife, Agent Perez dialed through his phone to call his partner. He waited to hear the phone get picked on the second ring. "Prepare yourself, Scott, and get every agent available to travel within the next hours," he stated urgently. "Change of plans for tomorrow. We head to California in the morning. We are going for the bigger fish."

Perez would have little to no sleep that night. He would be plagued with plans and details and logistics until he got on the plane. He could rest after they had him.

Perez could almost feel Joel's time coming to an end, and he couldn't wait to catch him and hopefully bring all the girls home to their parents, should he be caught with their company. Which he hoped was the case. He hadn't really allowed himself to prepare for a worst-case scenario yet, and he prayed it wouldn't come to that.

Early in the morning, his arrival to the airport was faster than expected. He lived on the northwest side of town, but managed to get to Sky Harbor swiftly, in spite of morning traffic.

He stood in watch, as TSA agents replayed the security camera feed of the previous day. They had found the moments when Joel walked in, cleared inspection in a rather calm manner as though he had done it several times before, sitting peacefully in the lobby, and finally boarding the plane.

Perez studied the man who had become a thorn in his side for the past month, wondering what was going through his head. If there was one thing about Joel León he couldn't fathom, it was what he hoped to achieve.

Was he willing to sell his own daughter for money out of spite and jealousy of his ex-wife getting involved with another man? Did he flip and lose every moral and ethical sense he once used to have, according to testimonies from those who knew him? What had gone wrong in him so suddenly? What did it take to turn a man into a monster? Human trafficking was no joke, but your own flesh and blood? That was pure evil!

*This man is a mystery*, Perez thought.

"He boarded a plane headed to Ontario, California," the security man stated. "All we have is the name of his new identity and the location of his destination."

They were on a manhunt, and it would take nothing short of persistence to catch the cunning Mr. León, who now went by Michael Arteaga and was somewhere around Ontario, California.

"His hair is so different," Agent Perez pointed out. "It's shorter and... is that... silver? White? He actually does look completely different with facial hair, glasses, and a dye job."

The fellow agents looked intently into the monitor, taking a still frame of Joel's face to examine it carefully before making their deduction. It was fascinating to see how a common citizen had suddenly grown evasive techniques and maneuvers over a few weeks.

Joel had walked into the airport, avoiding most of the major cameras from the entrance. He wore a baseball cap, which he only pulled off when he checked himself in. His movement was quick and precise, and designed to not attract attention. He finally sat in the corner of the lobby facing outside the airport windows patiently waiting for his flight. He only had one carry-on bag.

*What is in California, Joel? What business do you have there, that you risked being caught at the airport for? Why the rush? Why not drive over there?*

It was only five or six hours away by car, at most. And a few days had passed since he was last seen. Why now? Again, more questions about the elusive man.

"Pull up the information about his flight, and send everything to me along the way. I need eight agents with me on this trip, the sharpest we got," he ordered, watching the agents scramble around to get his orders done. "Have the crew from California meet us at the airport. Within the hour, I want to be with the crew, on our way through Southern California."

A young, female agent hovered at his elbow, and she pushed her phone into his line of sight. "Sir. You need to see this!"

It was a text. New intel had just come in linking Joel to a motel south of downtown. A couple of PPD officers had confirmed it.

"Ugh! This might be important to check out. Change of plans. Let's see what they've got and *then* we go California."

Joel had taken enough precautions to help him get through the airport safe and sound, but was well aware he might have been made, having caught sight of the cameras over his head as he pulled off his cap.

It was nighttime when Joel finally arrived at Ontario, making his way to the first address on the journal he had gotten from Ricky via a random taxi. Lyft and Uber usage could easily be traced, but a taxi paid with cash was easier to overlook. On this journal were dates, phone numbers, and addresses that he was to visit for some things he needed.

His first destination was in San Bernardino, at a neighborhood well-known for trouble, drugs, and every illicit exchange that you needed when you *needed* it. He had an appointment to book with a Russian guy by the name Alex Zhirkoff.

The twenty-five-minute drive going east on the I-10 freeway felt long, and he struggled to stay awake. All he thought about during his flight was how things would have turned out back home. He didn't want things to be the way they were, but there was nothing he could do after he had found out that the FBI had been tailing him. He needed to make a run for it, or risk getting caught and most likely prosecuted.

The taxi driver eyed him from behind the wheel, taking an occasional damning glare through his mirror. Joel knew he looked rough, but that wasn't the driver's business. "You got business in Bedazzled, huh?"

Joel was indeed headed for the place he had mentioned, but wasn't too sure if he should divulge his true destination just yet. He couldn't trust anyone, and certainly not a cab driver who could and would sell him out should the cops ask him for any information he might have. "Not really. Why do you ask?" Joel replied, making the effort to appear ignorant of the business.

"I ask because the address you gave me is next door to Bedazzled, a famous night club in San Bernardino. I know the place. Most people that I take over there are going for the pleasure that Bedazzled has to offer," the cab driver replied with a smile.

"Oh, yeah? What kind of fun is that?"

"Well, you know. I mean, it's the one place you can get away from your wife to have fun, if you know what I mean," the dark-skinned man said with a wink.

Joel gave no reply to the comment, nodding his head briefly before the car pulled over on a dark street near a gated Victorian house planted some distance away from the Bedazzled Nightclub.

"That'll be $34."

"Thanks," Joel replied, handing over the appropriate cash.

Joel slipped out of the cab and hiked his bag onto his shoulder, walking down the sidewalk at a leisurely pace. The taxi lingered longer than he would have liked before giving up and turning the car around to go back the direction from which they'd come. Once the car was out of sight, Joel turned around, summoning some composure before heading toward the large Victorian house. The vibrations from the heavy bass of the nightclub half-a-block away could be still be felt. As he continued the walk, the bright red lights of the club washed in and out, giving the dark street an eerie atmosphere.

Upon reaching the large, ornate gate, Joel pressed a button. Only a voice was heard— "Come on up"—before the gates opened for him. He turned around briefly to scan the area once more, making sure he hadn't been followed. He trekked up the long driveway, bag in hand, and noticed several armed man scattered throughout the property. Two walking, one standing in place, and a couple of them chatting and laughing while taking a smoke break. They paid no attention to him.

After giving himself a moment to slow his breathing and settle a cool expression on his face, Joel knocked the door, hearing a silken voice greet him in response just before the door opened.

"Hello, good evening," Joel greeted.

"Hi," the young girl responded. "He's been expecting you," she said, urging him into the house with a sweeping arm.

The girl gently closed the door back into place. His pulse skyrocketed, and he steadily clenched and unclenched his fist as he trailed behind the pretty girl, who couldn't have been much older than his daughter.

Joel looked at the watch on his wrist; it was time to get to work.

# CHAPTER THIRTY-SEVEN | 37

I NEVER IMAGINED IT WOULD BE THIS WAY. The pain is excruciating. Not only do the demons have their way with me over and over, while taking turns and filming it, but Phil, the stick, also partakes in the unholy acts. The demons only laugh as they see me writhe and beg to God for help.

All my dreams and expectations of how beautiful my first time would be fade away.

My heart aches. I feel splinters inside my soul.

# BROKEN

# CHAPTER THIRTY-EIGHT | 38

HIS PRESENCE WAS HIGHLY ANTICIPATED. From the stories Joel had recently heard, he was the man in charge of running the operations—at least locally. Even he had a boss. The real boss lurked in the shadows, more of an urban legend than actual flesh. Very few people had ever seen him; most got to deal with the next ones in command. Joel was here for one of these.

From his source, Joel had been told all he needed to know, or at least, he thought he had. He had been warned against complacency, since operations were run with an iron fist, and nothing short of full loyalty was accepted. He needed to bring his A-game and prove his unflinching loyalty before he could be granted any access to the networks.

The how-to was given to him plain and simple: he needed money to begin any form of trade, and he needed a network to run things for himself in an environment free of law enforcement interference. Being in this business demanded certain things, and the Russian was meant to bring Joel up to date.

Joel was uncomfortable, continually shifting in the chair he'd been directed to. He scanned around the sparse, dimly lit room—the neutral-painted walls were undecorated, and the surfaces were clean but barren. It was not what he was expecting to see in such an opulent home.

Joel was seated in the second chair of the two available. The barely-covered girl that had received him said "Wait here," before disappearing through the only other door on the opposite end.

He looked around the room, memorizing everything he could about this place. He held his duffle bag tightly on his lap. He was anxious about the amount of cash he carried there, and only too aware that he had no weapon to protect himself or his property.

Hiding from the authorities and the public eye was exhausting. His back ached from the sagging mattress at Bob's and the lack of sleep since.

A sound of something scurrying sent him shooting to his feet, bag clutched tightly to his chest.

*It's probably just a rat! Get yourself together, man.*

Joel dropped back in his chair, wondering what was taking so long. He knew well that there was no turning back for him, should he partake in what he was about to do. There was nothing on earth that would cleanse him of his sins, and no form of proof to clear his name. He needed to get it done, though. There was no alternative.

He dipped his hand into his pocket, pulling out a piece of gum to try to calm his anxiety. There was something odd about the room. The absence of proper illumination sent streams of worry through him, as well as the fact that he had been waiting for quite a long time and couldn't hear anything.

*I wonder how many rooms this house has. It's huge.*

Joel got up and walked toward the window, looking out over the countless orange trees encircling the odd house, some SUVs, and the armed guards. He could see no other houses around, just more orange trees and the flashing lights of the nightclub in the distance. Beyond that was barren San Bernardino county desert land. Everything had been planned well, and it was most likely the reason they had been able to operate for years without being troubled by the authorities.

A minor storm had begun brewing. The fearsome Santa Ana winds bent the soft-bodied trees in a bullish manner, spinning debris in circles. The threatening storm reminded Joel of the troubles he had been faced with.

*You can do this, Joel.*

He had made just one mistake, and it had cost him dearly. If he had the opportunity to make things right by being presented the choice of revisiting the situation, he would probably make the same choices, though. He had gotten to the point where coming to harbor any form of self-pity or regret was nothing but nonsense at this point, and he couldn't allow himself the luxury. There was no time for that now. This was his reality.

Time trickled by, and no one came. The room was warm. Sweat trickled down his back and forehead. The rain outside began, and he felt like a trapped animal in an ornate cage.

*What's taking so long? What in the world are they trying to prove?*

"Hello! Anybody there?" Joel said as he tried to open the door. Locked. There was no response.

Joel's nerves frayed through like a worn rope. He picked up his bag and dashed toward the door behind him, wondering if, by coming here, he had made the biggest mistake of all. He couldn't trust these people, even if he needed them to trust in him.

The door was locked. He tried it again, but to no avail. He looked around the room one more time before attempting to open it with brute force, but it wouldn't come to budge. He could feel his rage begin to set in. He yanked at it some more, making a ruckus, then froze at the sight of the small, black camera placed just above the frame of the door.

It had been keeping tabs on him since he had walked in, meaning his every move had been observed and most likely recorded. He looked directly into the camera in the dark corner, raised his arms in question and started pacing the floor.

"I can't keep waiting here. Come get me, or else I will break the door down and walk!" Joel threatened, even while knowing it was unlikely to work. "I mean it. Shit, I'll break the window if I have to," he snapped, jabbing his pointed finger to the only window in the dingy room.

The sound of footsteps closing in on Joel from the other side of the other door shocked him. He turned around and went back to the chair, anxious to appear cooperative in spite of his tantrum.

In bustled a scruffy-looking man sporting a bright red Hawaiian shirt, voluminous cargo shorts, and a walking stick. "Hello, *Michael.* We are so sorry for the wait," drawled the man. "We had other matters of urgency to work through while you waited. I hope that's not a problem."

Joel was temporarily stricken by the sight of the man, who reeked of cologne and showed off a full set of grilled teeth as he spoke. The smell was familiar; first, from the slender girl who had opened the door for him, but also deeper back in his memory banks. A coincidence, he assumed, and shoved those thoughts aside to focus on the moment.

Joel closed the distance and stretched out his hand to meet the stranger's, his eyes steadfastly focused on the man's body. "Um, yeah, no problem at all. It's nice to finally meet you," Joel greeted, still flummoxed.

"Call me Mr. Brown, and nothing else from here henceforth. Gregory Brown is my name, but Mr. Brown will suffice," the pale man replied, a heavy Southern accent dripping off his words.

"That sounds good. I'll call you Mr. Brown and nothing else, as you ask."

"Yes. And one more thing, Michael; you need another name different from your real one, should you fully commit to the colony and agree to become one of us," Mr. Brown explained to Joel. "Your lovely gift has been received, and hopefully, when the boss is back from his deeds, I'll let him know all about you. But for now, you and I deal, and with nobody else."

Joel could tell that he was serious. He hadn't thought of choosing yet *another* name if he were to begin working with them as said, not having time to really think extensively about the logistics. It would be hard keeping tabs with all his different identities. At this point he had Joel, Sam, Michael... and now, something else.

"I heard that nobody is ever allowed to meet with the boss. Is that true?" Joel-slash-Michael asked.

Mr. Brown looked at him with an unflinching gaze before walking back to the chair left behind from where Joel had dragged his away. He eased himself into the seat, motioning for Joel to do the same. Joel did as he was told, and Mr. Brown began his reply. "Nobody is allowed to meet with or deal with the boss but *me*," he boasted, tapping his walking stick on the hard floor as he made his point known. "Understood?"

Joel nodded.

"Now, about the name. From here on, I will call you *Lion*," he said with a smirk, staring at Joel as if waiting for some response.

*Lion? What the heck?* Joel could tell that he was messing with him, but he didn't care. He wanted in, and that was all that mattered. *Really? Why Lion? That is my last name, after all, but in English. Is that a coincidence, or does this guy know something?*

"Do you have a problem with that?" Mr. Brown asked him, flashing his grilled teeth once more.

"No, um... not at all," Joel responded, shifting in his seat. "I like Lion."

"Good. Because it was either Lion or Doberman. I kinda like those animals. Lion fits you well."

Joel didn't say anything, his thoughts running wild. *What kind of crazy mental issue does this guy have?*

The man continued. "First of all, however, I must ask why you want in. I mean, reading your profile and all that you were, you don't seem like the type ready to trade in the kind of merchandise we move. One doesn't normally just happen to switch careers into ours, if you know what I mean?"

"I'll be honest, Mr. Brown. The truth is that I have nowhere else to go, and I need the cash," Joel replied, looking as serious as he could ever be. "I need fast money badly. Although, if I can be frank, I also like the thrills that come about working with the girls. If *you* know what I mean?" Joel grinned, then winked at the man.

Mr. Brown took a few seconds, as if processing what Joel had said, before nodding his head slightly in agreement and then responding. "For a moment, we thought you were a cop. So, I felt like I needed to watch you for myself before coming out to greet you. You would have been dead the moment that I found out you were one, by the way. But then I knew you weren't one. For starters, a cop would have noticed the cameras in the room the moment they walked in. But an idiot like yourself only noticed one after an hour and didn't make any attempt to contact for a long, long time."

Mr. Brown was mocking him. But Joel could give no response to his statement. He needed something from him, after all. "I can assure you that I am legit. And no, of course I am not a cop."

"Good, because if I find out that you are lying to me, they'll have to look for your remains in the dog shit out back," Mr. Brown said with another placid smile, standing up from where he sat. "Walk with me, Lion. You need to begin work this instant. I hope you brought enough investment money to begin with," he said as he led the way. "Follow me."

"I believe I have more than enough for my start," Joel replied, holding his bag tightly.

"Good. We'll sort all that soon."

"By the way, Mr. Brown, I thought I was to meet Alex Zhirkoff here."

Mr. Brown gave him a skeptical look. "No, you won't be dealing with him. Only I deal with him. You deal with me."

"I'm not complaining—"

"Now, let's go inside. I'll show you a place where you can stay for now."

Joel... no, Michael... no, *Lion* walked through the mysterious door, wondering what awaited him as a human trafficker. A mover of sex slaves and drug mules across state and international borders. This was to become the new chapter for him, and he hoped to have the intellect and endurance to accomplish whatever was needed.

It was a new life. A fresh start. Or perhaps his final chapter.

Down in south Phoenix, Agent Perez and his team were scrambling to assemble as much data about Joel as they possibly could.

"Turn this shit hole upside down. And I mean *upside down!*" Perez said to his team.

He had gotten to south Phoenix as soon as possible upon getting the news. He was furious that they were constantly one step behind Joel, and especially now that they knew he was in California.

He was further irritated by Bob, who was successfully making life a living hell for them. He had initially denied ever seeing the police officers who had pointed out his establishment as Joel's hiding place, then finally admitted that he had allowed a man to stay there, but insisted that he didn't have any idea that this man went by the name Joel or anything the man was up to. He wasn't lying.

"I'm telling you, I ain't got no Joel in here. Although there was one fool acting weird and all," he explained.

He also didn't let them know that he had helped Joel pick up what had apparently been a very important package from the post office, choosing to not get himself roped into the whole mess.

"Is there anything else that you can tell us about his time here?" Agent Perez asked with a long-suffering sigh.

Bob shook his head vigorously. He bit his nails before giving the same reply that he had given them the entire time they'd been questioning him. "I am not a criminal, but I sure as hell don't snitch either," he replied in a rather annoying manner. "I've told you what I know."

Perez had had it with this strange man. He couldn't comprehend what manner of loyalty he felt he had for Joel, a virtual stranger. Or had they never met before?

"You do understand that you're committing a crime for choosing to obstruct an ongoing investigation by refusing to give us valuable information, which might lead to capturing a federal offender, a wanted man, right?" Perez said with a glare, attempted to scare Bob. But it didn't work.

Bob simply sniffed, bit some more of his fingernails, scratched his ear, and stuck to his story. "I told you, I don't know shit. But even if I did, I'd probably tell you the same thing. I ain't no rat, so I've got nuttin' to tell you, folks. Sorry I can't help you, officers."

Perez walked out of the foul-smelling motel to take a brief walk around. He pulled out a small purple lollipop from his breast pocket and put it in his mouth. He took the time to clear his mind, wondering what exactly Joel's game plan was. He was now a federal fugitive. He had no one on his side to work with, as far as they could tell. And he was on the run.

*What are you doing, Joel?* Perez asked as he stared at the desert mountains behind the building.

He could come to no reasonable explanation why a man of his standing would decide to kidnap his only daughter, keep her hidden, and choose to become a fugitive for the rest of his life. The logic eluded him, and he only wanted the situation to come to a wrap as soon as possible.

It was evident that he didn't take Petra with him to California, so where was she? Where could she be?

Perez walked back inside the motel lobby while raising his phone to his left ear to pass information to his assistant. "Get me any information that you have on Robert "Bob" McGee," he said, thinking they could scare the living hell out of him to make sure he'd told them all he knew.

"We have some news, Perez," one of the other agents assisting with the investigation informed him. "We spotted Joel in the security cameras of Ontario Airport. It seems he took a taxi somewhere. But here's the good news—we were able to get an image of the full license plates of the cab."

Perez halted briefly to listen to the details before passing out some new orders. He hung up and hurried back to the black SUV in the parking lot.

Perez had no intent on relaxing a bit until he nailed the bastard. It wasn't an option to let Joel go and not recover Petra and the other girls he might have been involved with. The situation had turned from a small squall to a hurricane.

*Watch out, Joel; here I come.* The astute agent strapped himself into the backseat of the SUV, and the driver took off back to the Sky Harbor.

Raymond Perez and the assembled team headed off to the FBI offices in downtown Riverside straight from Ontario Airport. The local team had already reviewed all the information gathered in Arizona and were tracking down the taxi that had taken Joel to his next destination.

The sight of the almost-cramped room in this relatively new building, with all the agents present, doing their best to make certain that they brought Joel into custody, warmed his heart. But it also brought with it a level of concern that he had harbored all along.

He would never have believed that a civilian, with no military training whatsoever, could have given them a run for their money like he had. The fact that he had been able to escape every security watch that they had put up was remarkable. He must have been getting help. It was the only explanation that made sense.

Perez ground his teeth together when one of the Arizona agents approached him with a piece of paper. His eyes squinted and his mouth felt dry and bitter upon hearing the latest update.

"Another girl has been taken in Chandler," the agent said in an equally disheartened manner. "She had been missing for a while, but no connection was made to the kidnapping rings due to her history of running away, and her parents assumed this time was like the others. But she didn't. They reported it in Phoenix today. But here is the thing... she was friends with one of the girls whose picture we found in Joel's room," the older man detailed.

Perez felt his heart threatening to tear out his chest. The burning desire to apprehend Joel was taking a toll on his physical and mental health, making him restless with untapped fury. He rubbed his temples before walking the man back to his post, where he had compiled every bit of information he could about the new missing girl.

Perez needed to find some connections between the girls, and what made them the pick of Joel and his kidnapping syndicate; he couldn't be doing it on his own. He must have some level of organized network through which the girls were transported.

"Why and how do you pick them, Joel?" Perez asked quietly to himself as he walked to the wall where the pictures of the young girls, including Petra, Joel's daughter, were taped.

They were all pretty. They were all young. Full of life and promise. But they were of every ethnicity possible—a group as diverse as the country itself.

He gazed at each picture, knowing every kidnapping organization had a modus operandi, and it worked well to their advantage, provided they had a market waiting to buy or rent the girls from them. The past year had seen child kidnapping and trafficking cases rise by more than five percent nationwide, which mainly had to do with young girls and kids like Petra being bartered as a commodity.

A local agent came and stood next to Perez, also looking at the pictures. "Any connections between them?" he asked.

"We are connecting the dots," Perez replied. "What I don't understand yet is why he came here specifically," he added.

"You don't know?" Surprise showed on the younger agent's face. "Well, places like the Inland Empire here in Southern California serve key areas for traffickers, due to their large populations as well as the well-connected routes with other major metro areas in the region. One could easily go north and in just a few hours be in the Bay Area or Las Vegas. I mean, this metro area is literally connected to the greater Los Angeles metropolitan area *and* Orange County on the coast. A little bit south of us is San Diego and the border. And east of us, of course, is Phoenix."

"It's the perfect hub."

"Exactly."

"That's why traffickers prefer connected areas like this zone to operate. They can easily bring fresh *merchandise* from any of these areas around, as well as take and move these kids to any of the other areas with ease."

"Yup."

Perez flicked the picture of Joel with a forefinger. "If we don't find Joel soon, it's going to be much harder to track the organization."

"We will, Perez. We will." The man left Perez to go back to his desk.

Perez grabbed a chair and sat to think it through. He went through some files, trying to learn anything new about these kids that could lead to the abductor or their connection with each other. He figured the kids would either be sold or handled personally through a pimp to perform any task that the organization deemed useful.

He needed to find the connection between Joel and this network. Even his divorced wife, the mother of their daughter, had attested to the fact that Joel didn't have many friends. His life revolved around work and occasionally church. And this begged more questions.

What about his company? Was he leaving everything he had worked so hard for behind? His employees hadn't heard anything from him in a couple of weeks. How was he financing himself now? Perhaps this is why he was having financial problems, although that didn't explain all the cash stashed away in his garage. Then there was the church.

Things didn't add up.

"You won't be going into any church, will you?" Perez mused before fixing his eyes on the photo of Petra. She looked happy, innocent, with eyes mirroring the Caribbean Sea. She was a beautiful girl. She was a smart girl.

*How could a parent ever do this to their own kid?*

Perez wanted so badly to bring Petra and the other missing children back home, safe and sound. He also knew that the longer it took them to bring Joel in, the less likely they were of an even remotely happy outcome.

He closed the folder, not able to stand another pretty face or heartbreaking detail. The sound of his ringing phone brought Perez's focus back to the room. He gently pulled the phone out from his jacket pocket then sighed as he saw the caller.

*Ugh, I wish I hadn't shared my number with her.*

He finally summoned the courage to slide the button to the right, in hopes that her call was not another round of ranting about their incompetence or interrogating him on his personal life.

"Hello, Kathy," he sighed into the receiver.

She had come to be a thorn in his side, probing and jabbing at him with her constant criticism. He usually simply replied with one-word answers, acknowledging that he could hear her, as well as the occasional grunts depicting that he was still on the line with her.

"Hi, Raymond. What is the update?"

"The same as before, Kathy. I need you to trust that we are trying everything in our power. We are getting closer," he quasi-lied, hoping to calm her down a bit. They had no idea where he was. Yet.

"I really hope so," she said before hanging up.

Perez was relieved the call had been brief. He stood up from the comfortable chair and headed out the office. He needed some fresh air to calm his rattled mind. He took a piece of gum—no, two—out of his pocket and jammed them into his mouth as he walked toward the sunlight, wondering if Petra could feel the sun where she was.

# CHAPTER THIRTY-NINE | 39

I'VE MET MOST OF THE KIDS HERE IN THIS ROOM. Well, the ones that talk. The room is full of kids. They keep us all together and bring food once a day. The majority of us here are around the same age, and most of the girls are nice. The few boys that are here don't talk much, as they tend to be younger. I don't think some of them even speak English. The kids only get pulled out of here whenever one of us had a job. I haven't been taken out of the room yet. Supposedly, once outside, they clean us and dress us up, before meeting a client.

At least I got moved into this bigger room with other kids. For that I am thankful. I was starting to believe I was a dog. Being here was my reward for being finally broken, they said. The demons told me that I should start enjoying it, being that this would be my life and purpose now—pleasing evil men like them. They also say I will bring them good money. Of course I won't see any of it. But they assured me that if I am a good girl, I'd be taken care of better than the rest.

The place stinks, and it is dark. There is only one toilet for all of us. The constant crying, especially from those returning from a job, makes it hard to sleep.

I wish I was at home playing my piano. Singing.

The first couple of days here I imagined myself on the piano, moving my hands in the air. I could hear the melodies and harmonies in my mind. It kept me going. I sang for the kids, and it soothed them.

But my heart no longer sings. There is no more music left within me. I might not be a dog anymore, but I am certainly not Petra either.

They finally come to get me. Eve's first job. The first of many, they say...

# CHAPTER FORTY | 40

KATHY STILL HAD THE PHONE IN HER HAND, racking her brain to find ways to help bring her daughter home. She was furious that she wasn't able to assist or provide any helpful tips to catch Joel.

Her fear and rage had escalated, and no one could console her anymore. She hadn't been able to pray either, feeling abandoned by God. Perhaps He simply didn't care enough about her family. About Petra.

*What kind of God would allow such a thing?*

Kathy fell back into the bed, weeping, just as James came into the room. She knew that her son had also changed. She was worried about him. The last two nights, James had gone out and come back late. Last night he smelled like alcohol. She had lost her daughter and was losing her son right before her eyes.

"Come here, Jimmy."

James came and sat next to her, silently, his own tears wetting his face. Kathy embraced him, and together they wept.

After a minute-long silent embrace, Kathy cleared her face and then her son's. "We will get her back, Jimmy. We will get her back."

"But what if she doesn't come back home, Mom?" a calmer James asked. "What if she never comes back home and we don't get to see her again?"

Kathy had no sincere response to her son's questions. He lowered his head into her lap, while Kathy stroked his hair, as she used to when he was younger.

"Please stop taking whatever you're putting in your system, Jimmy. I can tell that you've been up to something not good. I don't want to lose you too."

James simply nodded.

It was a trying time for them all, and one man had been the source of it all. She had cursed the day she married him, with the only joyful thing about their union being the two beautiful kids that she had given birth to. Besides James and Petra's existence, she wished she hadn't met Joel León at all.

She ran her fingers through James's dark, wavy hair, with everything about him reminding her of Petra. The soft texture of his hair was the same with her daughter's, except James's was curly. She could feel his warm breath, with the hot drops of his tears soaking into her pants.

"Everything will be fine, you'll see," she lied, trying to convince them both.

"Why do you think Dad did it?" James asked. "Why do you think he would kidnap Petra? The more I think about it, the less sense it makes."

Kathy took her time to reply. "I'm guessing it's all my fault," she replied as sincerely as she could. "I made him into the beast that he became."

James sat up to see her eye to eye. He looked hurt and unlike himself. "It's not your fault, Mom! Don't say that. Don't blame yourself for any of this! We just need to find her. We need to get her back, no matter what."

"I know. The FBI is working hard at it. And Brett is doing whatever he can with his connections to help too."

The thought of Brett brought a smile to her face. Brett had been gone a lot more, which had begun to really worry Kathy, not knowing what he was up to. Still, she trusted that he would do whatever it took to help. But she couldn't bear the thought of losing him as well, finding comfort in having him there with them while the FBI searched for her deranged ex-husband.

As if on cue, Brett came in through the front door. Kathy and James hurried downstairs to meet him. Brett was unusually disheveled, but still with the usual smile across his face. He looked at Kathy and James, slowly closing the space between them, a sympathetic frown developing. "Babe, you look like a mess," he said, wrapping an arm around her.

Kathy didn't pay any attention to his words, her gaze fixated on a spot on his shirt. She pointed at it, concerned that he was injured. "Brett, are you okay?"

"I'm fine. I should be asking *you* that!" he replied, shooting her a quizzical look. "Why do you ask?"

"That looks like a blood stain on your shirt."

"Oh, this?" he asked, shrugging. "A colleague of mine got injured, and I helped him off to the hospital," he explained without concern.

Kathy was scared that he was going down some dark lane, all just because he wanted to help her out. She wanted him safe, and not going out to do some military crap which might get him hurt.

"You know that I trust you and I appreciate all your help with this mess. But the more I think about it, I think I would prefer it if you stuck around to keep James and I safe here, instead of going out there to hunt Joel or anyone else," she said.

"You don't have to worry about me, love," he said, as his face wore the same sincere smile that she had caught sight of on the first day they had met.

He would say nothing and yet everything when he smiled, and it made her feel safe. He had been with her through the good times, through the worrying ones with Joel, and still remained here, even now, when she was a mess and her daughter was missing.

"But I *do* worry about you! And I can't lose you too." She grabbed his hands, squeezing them.

"I understand," he replied. "Look, I *will* keep you guys safe. I promise. But I am working on something that might yield results. You just have to trust me on this one. And don't worry, we will get Joel, and we *will* find Petra."

Kathy was grateful to have reassurances from someone, leaning over to kiss him without saying any more words. She held his face in her hand, staring into his deep blue eyes.

James finally spoke. "Honestly, Brett, I would love for you and your buddies to go on one of those ex-military missions like the ones on TV, where the main character goes hunting for the bastards who took something belonging to him. Don't you ex-military guys have all kinds of cool guns, hi-tech gadgets, and resourceful means of tracking people down?"

"Oh, Jimbo. If only it was that easy!" Brett chuckled.

"Well, can't you do something like that?" James asked.

"Can't I do *what*, James?" Brett asked, "Be the guy from *Taken*? Pull a James Bond on your dad? Call some friends and become the A-Team?"

"I'm not joking around, Brett!"

Brett sighed. "I know. You are right, Jimbo. And I am sorry. I wasn't trying to mock you. It's just that it doesn't work like in the movies. Believe me, as I told your mother, I am doing something. Don't worry about that."

"Just find that bastard like the military people do and bring my sister back, please. Whatever it takes."

Kathy looked at James, then at Brett. She wanted to say something, but there was nothing meaningful to add.

"I wish it was that easy, Jimbo. But, unfortunately, it isn't," Brett replied softly, breaking the awkward silence.

"Well... how hard can it be?"

"James Cameron León!" Kathy yelled. "Don't take that tone, young man. Brett is only trying to help here, and he is doing his best."

"All I am saying, Mom, is that if Brett reaches out to those he knows, still working in the military, they could help track Dad," James explained stubbornly.

"Listen, Jimbo. I left the military a long time ago, and my buddies there are mostly either retired or dead. Also, like I said, it doesn't happen like you see it in the movies," Brett clarified.

"Please do something; I'm begging you. Do something. *Anything!*" James pleaded.

Brett looked at Kathy, as if not knowing what to say. Kathy knew that Brett had gotten tired of trying to make James understand. In all honesty, she also wanted Brett to do something, even though she had initially asked him not to go on a bender, doing crazy things because of her. She could tell from James's plea that he would have no peace until Petra was found, and hopefully alive.

"We are *all* doing what we can, Jimmy," she said.

Brett stood up and walked to the kitchen to fetch some water. "I would advise that we left this to the proper authorities to handle," he declared, as if hoping it would come to appease them both. "I am trying, but I don't know if it will work."

Kathy stared at him, confused. She still didn't know exactly what he was actually doing, and with that statement, she wasn't sure if he was doing anything at all.

James kicked an innocent dining room table chair not too far from where he was standing. "The FBI is useless. Haven't we seen that already?" James asked them. "I mean, with all the resources that they have, and they still can't find my dad, who isn't even that smart. I am just so tired of everything. I don't care anymore."

"What do you mean, you don't care?" Kathy asked.

"I don't care what happens to Dad anymore. I just want life to be normal again. To be honest, deep down, I've been loyal to him most of this time. I've been giving him the benefit of the doubt. But not anymore. At first, I thought he was simply driven by jealousy and nothing else. But things have become clearer now. So yeah, I don't give a shit about him anymore. I want justice. I want Petra back. I want things to make sense again. *That's* what I mean."

"Baby..." was all that Kathy managed to say. She was lost for words beyond that.

Brett walked over to James, placing his hand on his shoulder in show of support. "I don't know what you must be feeling right now, but

I can imagine." He then gave him a glass with water and pulled a chair for him to sit on, the same one that James had kicked.

Kathy joined them in the dining room. "Brett, James isn't wrong, though."

"What do you mean?" Brett answered, confusion visible in his face.

James also gave her a puzzled stare.

"Well, to be honest, I'm frustrated too. Maybe we do need to do more on our part, like James suggests. Whatever it takes. Right? Just tell us what to do," she pleaded. "Whatever it is, we are going to do it. I have decided that I am done waiting too."

"You too, babe?"

She didn't reply. She stood by James's side and gave him a side hug.

Brett took a deep breath and pulled another chair to sit on. "Look, both of you. Let me explain something. This kind of stuff doesn't come easy or cheap," he finally began.

"What do you mean?" James asked, sounding interested.

Kathy also sat down.

"I'll explain it as best as I can. But first, let me be clear. Getting this kind of information—on Joel's whereabouts and whatnot—would require a lot of money. This stuff doesn't come for free. And they aren't the same people I served with, so I can't call in favors."

Kathy heaved a short sigh, without really looking like she was daunted at all by what he had just mentioned. James didn't have any objections either, instead hanging on Brett's every word.

"I'm not talking about some chicken change, guys; I am talking about thousands of dollars," he warned them. "There is one fact, though, and it is that we could find him with *their* help," he said with a shrug.

Kathy was conflicted. She had some money saved up, but wasn't sure if this was the way she wanted to handle Petra's disappearance.

"How much do you think we will be needing?" she asked, readying herself to play hard ball as needed for her baby girl.

"Well, if we can pay for the needed information, we can find Joel; but it still isn't a guarantee that we would find Petra," he warned them. "I just don't want you to get your hopes up, when there is no certainty."

"I know, Brett. Don't talk to me like a child," Kathy shot back. "I'm sorry, babe. It's just that I am a little bit tense right now," she said as she held his hands. "How much do you think we would be needing?"

"For information of this magnitude, using their equipment and resources? I'd say no less than fifteen thousand dollars," he said flatly.

"I told you that it wouldn't come easy," he warned again. "These guys will be risking their own jobs and reputation. But for the right amount, I am sure that they would be willing to at least try."

Kathy sighed some more, looking at her worried son. She had kept the money as a kind of rainy-day fund. Most of it had come from

Joel anyway. It had been *his* idea to save it for such a situation, after all. But the idea of handing it over to strangers was daunting, even though it couldn't be measured against the value of her daughter's life.

"We'll do it."

James looked at Kathy, surprised.

"You need to be sure, Kathy," Brett emphasized. "I know how badly you want to find your girl, but that kind of money is huge. Don't jump the gun so quickly without thinking it through," he warned again. "Like I said, yes, it could help. But, can you actually even get fifteen grand?"

"You said it yourself, Brett, that it could work. It's worth a try."

"I know, but—" Brett had begun talking when Kathy interrupted him.

"I'm sorry, but she's my daughter, and I want her back. Even if it would mean robbing a bank for it," she said, resolutely. "Stay here. I'll be back." With that, Kathy disappeared into her room while James and Brett remained in the living room, giving each other a silent shrug.

Kathy came back within the minute with several packs of cash in her hand. She tossed them to Brett, who did well to catch them. "That is almost thirteen thousand dollars in cash. Just a couple hundred short," she said. "I'll look for a way to get the rest. But, please Brett, find that son of a bitch and make him pay. Whatever it takes."

Brett nodded, gathering the cash and taking his phone out of his pocket. "Whatever it takes."

He headed straight for his car keys and out the door, and they watched his car fade into the distance.

Kathy felt a sense of calm breeze through her. She could trust Brett was on it, and fully into it. She would wait while he did his best, and hope that it wasn't too late for Petra, even though deep down in her heart she was terrified at the possibilities.

"Brett will find him, and he will lead us to Petra, Jimbo. I just know it," Kathy told James as they both looked outside the window.

A sense of peace finally filled her heart. She gave James a kiss on the cheek and headed upstairs back to her room, closing the door behind her. She kneeled with her hands together and her head bowed, praying fervently for the first time in weeks, even as she felt slighted by God for some unknown reason.

She was desperate.

Divine intervention was her last—and now only—resort.

# BROKEN

# CHAPTER FORTY-ONE | 41

ONE OF THE YOUNGER GIRLS, whose name is Passion, reminds me a lot of Carla García, Mateo's sister. Passion is innocent, sweet, and funny, just like Carla. How someone can remain cheery under these circumstances baffles me. But I like her. She reminds me of home, of friends, of loved ones. She reminds me of family.

I miss Carla. But I really miss Mateo. I was so mean to him, and I wish I could take it all back. He never deserved to be treated in such a way.

*Matty, I am sorry for being so selfish.*

I also miss my brother. As much as we fought, he always took care of me.

*Jimmy, I am so sorry for being so annoying. I love you and I miss you, brother.*

My thoughts get interrupted, as I am called, once again, for another job. I am exhausted, but I must go get ready...

# CHAPTER FORTY-TWO | 42

JOEL'S FIRST NIGHT AT GREGORY BROWN'S place in San Bernardino was more stressful than he anticipated. Brown's men kept asking him questions about his reasons for wanting to become part of the group and getting involved in their operations. Some wondered how he had even heard about them.

Of course Joel would never mention Ricky. In all honesty, he himself wondered how Ricky got all of his information. But Joel knew that mentioning his friend would most likely put him in danger.

Michael, or Lion, needed to be trusted before any major responsibility could be handed over to him. And to prove himself, he had to complete a "pick-up and delivery" the following day, which was to take place at the San Pedro port, with the "merchandise" arriving from overseas, probably Southeast Asia. Joel had reviewed the details of the deal all night in his head.

The merchandise was being sent by the Russian, and Mr. Brown was to handle it upon receiving it.

"Lion," he said, slapping Joel on the back as he spoke. "Tomorrow you will drive the truck back with the goods. It is very important for you to understand that you cannot stop for anyone or anything, not even the police, no matter what. If anything goes wrong, you are on your own."

"I understand."

"No, Lion. I don't think you understand the gravity of all this."

"What do you mean, Mr. Brown?"

"What I mean is that if anything goes wrong, you better pray that the cops find you and kill you before Zhirkoff's men find you. Shoot, before *I* find you!"

Joel had simply nodded, agreeing to do his best. He already knew what the merchandise being spoken about was to be. But he was ready, with his full focus on the task at hand. Still, though, he was anxious, thinking about everything that he had done so far. But then again, everything he had done so far was nothing when compared to what he was about to embark on the following day.

Mr. Brown showed him a room where he could stay until he found a place of his own. It wasn't much, but it would do. And staying here for a few days would be beneficial for his cause. The small room, one of the many in this enormous mansion, had its own bathroom. Very convenient. Joel left the door unlocked to alleviate any lingering suspicion about himself.

Exhausted from his trip, soon Joel was in bed, trying to rest so he would be at his best tomorrow. He turned and shuffled around in bed, unable to get any sleep. He felt guilt. Cursed. He felt terrible because of Petra. But now, he was doing everything that he possibly could. He was too deep in.

Joel was given precise instructions, and the pay for this first job would be $10,000 cash, should he deliver the goods as ordered without damage.

There could be a lot of money made in this business, that was for sure. At this rate, just as it was promised to him, it would not take long before making back his initial investment of $50,000. In a few months he could multiply that amount exponentially.

He had recently closed a deal in what was now his previous life, and it had brought him a lot of money. He cashed the check, and since he didn't trust banks all that much, he had made sure that his money would be safe. As long as the IRS stayed away, he would be fine.

So, this gig, whatever it took, would get him one step closer to earning the needed trust for him to be taken more seriously by the group. He still hadn't met any other important members of the organization, but from what he had learned, the network was extensive. But the bosses were powerful men, protected from scrutiny, hidden in the dark. What was important is that he was in now.

The thought of what James and Kathy would think about him, should they hear about his new life choices, came to mind. He wondered what nonsense Brett would continue to tell them about him. He could still see the self-righteous face grinning and smiling wherever he was, pretending to be an angel. Joel didn't buy it.

A tap on the door to his newly acquired room jolted him upright in the bed.

"Just a minute," he said. He quickly put a shirt on. "The door is unlocked. Come in," he continued.

A female voice on the other side called out to him. "Lion?"

The real reason behind the name still eluded him, though he was hopeful he would learn more as time passed.

"Um, yes, it's me."

Joel watched his visitor walk in, a young woman wearing nothing but a golden G-string, a shiny wristband around her left hand, and a matching waist chain. She was attractive, slender in frame, and a pretty face. In spite of her undress, she seemed rather... innocent.

"Can I help you?" Joel asked nervously.

"I hope so," she said with a wink.

Her facial features reminded Joel of Petra, though her hair was lighter in comparison to his daughter's. A strawberry blonde. She was older than the girl who had welcomed him earlier that evening, but she couldn't have been more than nineteen or twenty at the most.

Joel got goosebumps at the thought of that. She was, without a doubt, one of the girls who had been forcibly taken away from their parents and subjected to the life that she was living now.

Joel bowed his head gently, feeling a sense of remorse take over him. He couldn't bear to look at the girl, for she brought memories of Petra to him. He felt disgust.

*What on earth have I done?* he asked himself, resting his head in between his hands. *What have I become?* Remorse settled in his heart.

He looked up to the teenager, who had drawn closer, who also wore the same scent he'd smelled on Mr. Brown and the young girl he'd met first. He had been provided the same scent in cologne form, and it remained unused in his drawer. He hoped to leave it be for as long as he could.

"I am your gift for the night, Lion," the young woman spoke in a seductive voice. "Think of it as your welcome gift. Do as you please with me, for I am yours tonight," she added as she curved down to where he sat on the bed.

Now that she was closer, he saw marks around her wrists and her elbow joint, indicating that she was one who occasionally used drugs. Also a cutter, based on his observation of linear scars on her inner thigh.

Joel wondered how long she had been involved with the group and where they had gotten her from. Thoughts of Petra doing the same thing came through his mind, and it disturbed him further. But he had no time to think about that for the moment, not least when he had an important day ahead of him... and a naked girl seducing him.

"You mean to tell me that you are my gift, and I can do whatever I want with you?" He feared what the answer would be. But deep down, he wasn't dumb. He knew exactly what this was.

*Is this a test? They are most likely spying on me.*

The girl nodded, taking her seat by his side on the bed, her bare skin against his making him shiver, not with lust, but revulsion. "You can do anything you want with and *to* me."

She grabbed his right thigh and tried to continue her hand up, but he stopped her arm with his. He didn't want this, and he wasn't going to lean into this temptation. Sleeping with someone who was being coerced into the affair was not okay. His moral sense remained, even if he had come to do some other despicable things during the past months. But *not* this. He wasn't even aroused. It was disgusting to even think about it. He was old enough to be her father, and he couldn't even entertain the thought of someone else having this experience with his daughter.

"I am sorry, *mija*, but I really need my head focused for tomorrow."

"But the boss sent me over to you personally. I get paid for the night with you," the young girl explained. "Otherwise it will be bad for me. Very bad."

Was she was sad? No; if anything, she seemed more... afraid. Alarmed.

Joel understood her predicament. She couldn't head out without having done what she was asked to come in to do. Should he ask her to leave? But then she would miss out on getting paid, whatever that meant, and she would most likely be punished. Who knows what would happen to him too? Either way, he couldn't partake in this.

"How about this? You remain here through the night, but we don't do anything. You can even have the bed. I'll sleep on the floor."

She looked at him, puzzled, almost as though she hadn't met his kind before. As if she was not used to be rejected. "Wait. Are you for reals? You mean to tell me that you *don't* want to fuck me?" she asked, to be sure. Her voice wasn't seductive anymore. "You just want me to *chill* here?"

"Yes. I'm not here to have sex with young girls like yourself," he explained to her directly as he stood up from the bed. He smoothed his hair and cleared his throat. "This is all a business move for me. It's about the cash." Joel spoke loud enough to be heard, just in case he was indeed being observed.

She looked disappointed, but he didn't care. More than anything, she was confused, uncertain on what to do. Evidently, she didn't want to get in trouble.

"I tell you what... just help me out instead. I have a few questions that I need to ask you," he began, sitting on the floor.

"I mean, I guess that since you are not going to f–, I mean, since we are *not* going to have sex, it's the least I can do," she replied while grabbing the pillow and putting it on her lap to cover herself, as if suddenly feeling exposed and self-conscious.

"First of all, what is your name? And how old are you? Also, how long have you been here?" he asked, staring at the now-shy girl, whose mostly naked body had become much more of an eyesore to him, prompting him to toss his blanket at her to cover her body with while they talked.

She gently wrapped the blanket around her bare skin before granting him some responses. "I am eighteen, and I've been here for about two years. No, wait, maybe more like three now," she corrected. "My name is Rosette."

Joel nodded, thinking that this couldn't be her real name, since organizations like the ones they were involved in functioned on fake names. But he didn't care. What got his attention was the fact that she had been here for three years.

Before he could say anything, she continued. "Well, that is... was... my real name. I've never used my real name with clients. I don't know why I even told you that. But you can call me Star, like everyone else, if you'd like. In fact, it'd probably be best if you did."

"Where are you from, Rosette?" he asked further, ignoring her last statement.

She smiled.

"I am originally from San Jose. But I don't think that I will ever be going back there again," she replied with a frown.

"Why do you say that?"

"Because of... reasons," she said, looking toward the door as if she was scared that they were being eavesdropped on.

Her paranoia was noted, indicating how well things were kept under supervision around here. He needed to be careful.

"Are we being watched?" he asked her, even though he feared the answer.

"You never can be too sure around here."

"Rosette, tomorrow I am going to pick up some new... *merchandise*, if you know what I mean. Tell me, do you know by any chance how it is during these runs?" he questioned her, feeling some information would do a lot of good. "I mean, do you even know about these things?"

"Well, from what I've heard of the guys talking, it sounds like shipment pickups can be quite difficult, especially if the police are on your ass from the point of pick-up." She sat down on the bed again before continuing. "I guess the cops get a heads-up at times." She shifted on the bed and began to whisper. "Look, my suggestion is that, if you really must do this, do not stop for any anyone or anything! Do your thing, get out, and drop *them* off wherever you are told to do so," she warned. "Just do exactly as you are told. You don't want to make mistakes with these people. Trust me."

Suddenly, Joel considered the fact that Rosette's scars in her inner thighs might not have been self-inflicted.

When she saw him staring at her scares, tears welled, and Joel felt empathetic, choosing to remain silent. No word seemed appropriate.

"Have you been told the place where you are supposed to drop them off?" she asked, wiping a lonely tear from her cheek and meeting Joel's puzzled gaze.

"All I know is that am picking up, but haven't heard anything regarding a drop-off location." He sat up straight, waiting for Rosette's response. "I assumed I'd bring the truck back here."

"You weren't told *any* of this?" she asked, surprised. "Shipments are never brought here! They are taken to *safe* places."

"Safe places? I have no idea of what you are talking about," he confessed, and he wasn't lying.

"When you deliver the... um, girls... I assume that's what you're picking up, right? Well, of course you are."

Joel nodded in acknowledgment. He felt a chill down his spine at the admission.

"Well," she continued, "you keep them safe and away from here or any of the other houses, until the boss or someone else clears you. Because you can never tell who is tailing you, even if you think you aren't being followed. So, you can't just bring them back here directly. You have to go somewhere else first, until given the okay to come to whatever your base is. But don't worry, they have places where you can take them temporarily in case of emergencies. I still remember *that* room." Her body shuddered as she said the last statement.

Joel was shocked. First of all, how did this girl know so much about the business? How involved was she really? And also, he didn't have any idea that he had so many responsibilities lying in wait with this pick-up-slash-drop-off gig. He wondered why they hadn't given him the whole story, though. Maybe they didn't want to provide addresses to him until the moment came. Mostly, however, Joel wondered again how this Rosette girl knew so much of this process, and it made him doubt if he could even trust her.

"I see. And for how long am I to keep the girls before the boss comes to pick them up or until I can bring them here? I mean, how long does that normally take?" he asked, finding her presence insightful and helpful, nonetheless.

"I actually don't know that. I guess it could be a couple of hours, or perhaps a few days."

*What? Days?*

"And once you are there, you must make sure that they're well taken care of with the provisions in the truck that they will give to you. It's normally not a one-man job, so I don't know if they'll pair you up with someone else. Again, I know all of this *only* because I've heard some of the guys talk. Believe me when I say that you get to hear a lot of things when you're essentially invisible."

Joel didn't have the slightest idea on what to do, as he sat still, wondering how he would come to pull it off. He really wanted it, after all, and needed to see it through successfully. He had just one more question he needed answered, though. "How many girls do they bring in normally per shipment?"

"Well, it's not always shipments, really. Many times the girls are simply moved from place to place or from city to city."

"That's true, I guess. But Mr. Brown mentioned that I was picking up a shipment, and it is at the port... so, yeah."

"To be honest, I don't know how big it will be. But when I was..." She got silent, clearly parsing her words. She swallowed hard before continuing. "When I was brought in, when we were first put in some big room... I think it was a storage place or something like, because we were cramped, and it was dark. There were maybe about a dozen or so, maybe. Then someone came, a couple of really mean guys, and they put us in a truck and drove us down here. Only two of us stayed here in this house from that time. We were all American, but I've seen one foreign group before. This one group was brought here last year for a few days until they moved them somewhere else. That one was larger, about thirty or so."

"Thirty?"

"Yes, maybe even more. They took them straight to the basement. But I'm not allowed down there, so I don't even know what's down there."

Joel had just found out that he wasn't going to have any sleep now for sure. He needed to plan this properly. He didn't even know this area all that well! Suddenly, he wasn't so sure if he could even do this anymore. The stakes were too high.

But he had to.

There was no turning back. Not when he was so close.

The next morning came too soon, and with as little sleep as he had expected.

"It's time, Lion," Mr. Brown said, opening the door and ushering himself in without a care in the world for Joel's privacy. "Get ready."

Joel watched Rosette taking a pink envelope from Brown, which presumably contained cash for a job well done. Without saying a word or making eye contact with either of them, she headed out the door, leaving the blanket on the bed and slamming the door behind her, permitting them some privacy to talk.

Mr. Brown bit his lips as he stared at her back as she left. Joel was disgusted. But he could feel the nervousness drench him with cold sweat, as he awaited some needed information from his new boss.

"She is a good lay, isn't she?" Mr. Brown said, rhetorically without expecting an answer as he adjusted his pants. "Lion, you have about four hours to pick the merchandise up from the docks. And you know the drill; keep them safe until I, and only I, tell you to bring the truck," he instructed the listening Joel.

"So I'm bringing them here?"

"You are going to pick them up at port thirty-one. The gate guards know the truck and will let you through with this pass. Once there, some men will be waiting for you; you will give them the truck keys. They'll load the truck for you with the merchandise, while you go talk to Mr. Gary Lopez from customs. You will give him this sealed envelope and a briefcase I'll put in the truck. Make sure you give it to him, and no one else!"

"Got it, Mr. Gary Lopez from customs. No one else."

"The men that load the truck will place a laminated sign in the window once the truck is ready. After that, you are to exit via the same gate, not any other one, or they will inspect the truck before leaving the port. You DO NOT want that! The gate guards will take the sign and let you pass. You shouldn't have any issues, as long as you follow my directions exactly."

Joel paid the best attention he could, unwilling to miss anything and mess up.

Mr. Brown continued, "Once you exit the port, you are going to leave the container locked until you get to a safe place. Do not stop to look into it for any reason. Just because you are out doesn't mean that the coast is clear. Go somewhere safe and stay there until either I come or I tell you it's okay. Do not park in a crowded place, or any noise coming from the container might bring about attention. And again, DO NO fucking open the container."

"I understand, Mr. Brown. Is there a particular place you recommend I go? I mean, is there a specific place I *should* go?"

"I don't give a shit, Lion! That's your problem. Just don't get caught, don't lose the merchandise, and chill until given the okay. It's not that hard."

"Understood."

"And once I am sure that you aren't being chased or pursued, I'll contact you to give you further instructions. Just be somewhere between San Pedro and here." He handed Joel a burner flip phone with which they would communicate during the operation. "Remember, you have just one rule for the job at hand."

Joel didn't need to ask any further question, knowing exactly what was being asked of him.

"You can never get caught, Lion. *Never.* That's why I chose to hire you, along with your recommendation and the gift you brought in. I couldn't ignore your desire to become one of us fully," he elucidated, walking toward the door. "Do well on this one, and you'll have a good future with us."

Mr. Brown was about to exit the room when Joel asked, "If at any point I get caught, what happens then?"

Joel saw Mr. Brown's face fold into a frown after he turned around. He walked back into the room, coming near Joel before bending over toward him, close enough for Joel to choke on the cloying signature scent once again.

"Remember what I said. If that happens, then there are several outcomes to consider, which eventually leads to one end and one end alone..."

Joel swallowed hard, watching Mr. Brown not blink at all.

"You either refuse to tell them anything about what you think you know, which is nothing, and let them take you in and process you, and do your time peacefully... or you speak, still go to prison, but you will then meet your end through our network in any prison that you get sent to." Brown stated his two options vividly while counting with raised fingers.

"Crystal clear, Mr. Brown."

"A third option would be for you to pull out the pocketknife which will be provided underneath your driver's seat, slit your throat, and die peacefully of your own doing and accord." Brown walked out of the room while stating, "Like I said, get ready."

Joel got the picture being drawn for him. Either way, he was screwed, and there was no getting out for him now. Most likely, he wasn't coming out alive, should he get caught.

He knew that he was in way over his head. The cash in this business was good, but his life was at risk from the moment that he had walked through the outside gates the previous night. But he was determined to see it through until the end. The alternative was simply not an option for him. There was too much to lose.

Joel went to the bathroom and saw Miguel Arteaga, the Lion, in the mirror. He let out a heavy sigh and closed his eyes, trying to get a good picture of how things could come to turn out. He could feel his soul drifting away, fully transforming into a different person.

He had his plan set, and he would do anything to make it work out. He opened his eyes, now with thoughts of the people that he cared for.

"I am sorry, Kathy. I am sorry, James. Please forgive me, Petra," he said, as he began buttoning up his shirt.

With that, he started shutting down any stray emotions or reservations.

*Bring it on. Let's do this! There's no backing out anymore, Joel. You are a Lion!*

# BROKEN

# CHAPTER FORTY-THREE | 43

THE DEMONS MAKE US USE OUR NEW NAMES. I don't like it. Most of the girls just play along and don't seem to mind anymore. But I can't get used to being called Eve. I know they're just trying to strip us of our identities.

The demons have taken some girls who had been here for a while, and we haven't seen them again. Every time one of us is taken for a job, we all gather together and hug silently. Some pray.

The rest of us that remain in the room and are not on jobs are still taken at different moments for different purposes. Mostly for the demons' personal gratification. They say we must keep on *practicing*. It'll make us better, they say.

Lately, though, it seems as if I've been selected more often than others. At first I hated it, but as much as I dislike it, I'd rather it be done to me than to any of these other poor girls. It destroys my spirits to see them being used in such vile way.

So, I have made my peace with it. It's okay if they like Eve the most. I'm not Eve, anyway. And they like it that I pretend to enjoy it. I've realized that when I do, they won't hit me as much. Like I said, it's okay with me, as long as they leave the rest of the kids alone. I will be their protective mother if I must.

I will be Eve from now on.

# CHAPTER FORTY-FOUR | 44

BRETT HADN'T GOTTEN RETURNED since Kathy had given him the money. He wasn't answering his phone or replying to text messages. She waited anxiously with James in the living room, vegetating in front of the TV. She got up frequently, pacing around the room.

"Mom, calm down. You're making me *more* nervous."

"I know, baby. I just can't help it," she replied, biting her nails.

"Are you worried about Petra or Brett now?"

Kathy took a long breath before replying, "Both."

"Come, sit with me."

James put his hands around her the way she did when she wanted to show her support. She hugged him back tightly.

"I am sorry that you are having to go through all of this with us, Jimmy. We should have done better to protect you guys, but we failed. I am very sorry, baby."

James listened on to his mother's apologetic words quietly. After a few more endless minutes like this, he retreated to his room.

In silence, Kathy wondered if James had conceded defeat about finding Petra. She wasn't willing to accept that fate yet, though, with Brett promising to bring her back at any cost possible, she had some hope. She trusted Brett; *everybody* trusted Brett to deliver his promises whenever he gave them.

The night unfurled upon them, and the silence was deafening. The house felt bigger and even lonelier than usual. James had asked her to make Petra's favorite meal, blueberry pancakes. She had understood his reason for asking and was happy to oblige.

The making of the blueberry pancakes was catastrophic. The first batch were burned. The second batch were still too dark on the outside and somehow gummy inside. It took three tries before she could produce something tolerable, which now lay on the table, cold and stiff. In her mind, she could hear Petra's excited giggle the entire time that she was making the pancakes, remembering so many years around the table with this meal.

"Pancakes for dinner!" Petra would excitedly exclaim.

*If only she could be here now.*

Kathy was depressed, and she tried desperately to hide it. She was living in a state of denial, although she was doing quite well so far for a woman whose daughter was missing and had been taken by her ex-husband, who was involved in a kidnapping ring. She certainly had reason to feel this way.

"Jimmy, come down! Your meal will get cold if you don't eat it," she called.

But James was silent in his room.

She understood that he had asked for them not because he wanted to eat this, but because he wanted something about his sister around. He wanted to act as if she was just out with friends, and they were holding dinner until she got home.

The fact that nobody knew in certainty what Joel had done to or with Petra only made things even more frustrating. Had her body been found, indicating that she was killed, there would have been some form of closure to look forward to. But nothing new about her had been found, besides the clues found in Joel's house.

It wasn't an easy situation to deal with, and Kathy had still not shaken her feelings of impending doom. She wasn't one for superstitious beliefs, but all that she could sense around herself were vile thoughts of what would or could come to be. She hoped she was wrong.

James swallowed a piece of the now-cold pancakes. He and his mother ate in an awkward silence, trying their best to keep moving through the daily motions of life. A hard knock came on the door, prompting James to jerk in surprise. He exchanged looks with his mother, knowing exactly what was running through her mind as well.

"Can that be Brett?" she asked.

"Why would he knock if he could simply come in?" James got up to tend to whomever was at the door. He opened it gently to the sight of Mateo, trembling, his phone in his outstretched hand .

"I have something I need to show you, Jimmy" he said, shoving past him into the living room. James shoved the door shut and followed.

Mateo was shaking and breathing hard, obviously rattled by whatever he was about to show them.

"I haven't spoken about this to anyone yet."

"What is going on, Mateo?" James asked.

Mateo scrolled through the phone briefly before handing it over to James with a look of regret.

Spread across his phone's screen was a picture of Petra, dressed in a tight, short dress that exposed a lot of skin. She was pale, and had cords around her ankles and wrists. It was evident that she was still alive, but she did not look well.

James staggered back at the sight.

"I got this from an unknown number not very long ago, and I didn't know what to do," Mateo explained frantically. "I got a text message with it too. I didn't tell my parents or anyone else. I just ran straight here. I didn't know what else to do..."

James's mind was swirling, and his mother plucked the phone from his hand before he realized she was there. At the sight of Petra in such condition, she gasped. "How did you get this picture?" she asked. "Tell me, Mateo!"

Mateo trembled with immense fear. "I– I got it with a text message just a few minutes ago. I was just telling James."

"Show me the text message!" James demanded, snatching the phone from his mother to scroll through the phone. He finally came across the message, reading it aloud. "It would take more than a few thousand dollars to get her back. Her price was high and she's a moneymaker."

"What are we supposed to do?" asked his mother. "I wish Brett was here. I bet his sniffing around was yielding results, and that's why we got this."

"What do they want from us, Mom? I don't understand. And why text Mateo?" James asked, hoping his mother would know.

"I don't know anything! I swear," Mateo said.

James took note of his mother's countenance, and it displayed confusion equal to his own. They didn't have any idea why the text message had been sent to Mateo's phone, of all people, just as his father had also contacted Mateo before. It reeked of his father's actions and the thought made his stomach churn in anger. He wished that he could see him and let him know how much he wanted him to rot in hell.

"This is so messed up," Mateo said as he collapsed in the chair behind them.

It was evident that Petra's disappearance had gotten to him too. He was pale, and his usually buoyant face was twisted in anxiety.

"Brett must have found them some way and paid. Otherwise, they wouldn't demand some more money," his mother said, trying to reason though the message.

James still had his suspicion, bringing it to air. "Still, why are *you* the one getting this text, Mateo? It doesn't make sense."

Mateo looked dumbstruck. "I wonder the same thing! I swear to you, James, I have no idea why all this is coming to me," he swore, tears now lining his cheeks. "I told you, I was even scared to show this to my mom! I only shared my contact info with your dad because he had asked me. And I swear to you, I've never contacted him on my own. I am too scared to even reply to this text or call it. Besides, this is not the same number that your dad used before."

"I hope you're telling me the truth!" James warned him.

"What is that supposed to mean? You think I'm involved in this? That's bullshit, man! That's just not fair."

"James, stop," his mother added. "Mateo is right; that's not fair. Besides, he is showing us this."

James didn't know who to trust anymore. First, his father dealt his sister such pain by trading her for money, or whatever, and now he felt he couldn't even trust his own friends. Everyone was sketchy. Except for his mother and Brett. He wished Brett was around to help; he always knew what to do, and he had been the one tasked with doing his best to reach out to his colleagues in hopes of finding Petra.

But Mateo was most likely telling the truth. What reason did he have for running here with this news?

"I am sorry, Mateo. I apologize. This is just... too much."

Mateo nodded, "I know. And I understand."

"Guys, we need to show this to the FBI," his mom was saying, as the sound of the door opening came their way.

At that moment, Brett walked in, looking disheveled. He had sweat running down every visible part of his skin, and he seemed a little shaken.

"Babe, are you okay?" his mother asked.

"What happened?" James asked at the same time. Mateo stood up to join the concerned train of people moving closer to the stricken Brett.

"We might be dealing with some really nasty people," he said as he politely nodded toward Mateo to say hello.

They all had guessed as much, but it was alarming to see the unflappable Brett in this state.

"What do you mean, babe?"

"I was able to pull some contacts of suspected people from the military guy that I paid, but they wouldn't budge for the amount I offered. It's too much of a risk to them, apparently."

He looked like he had gone through hell and back. He was filthy, with a reddish bruise under his eye. He dropped into a chair, seemingly unable to stay standing.

"I think I have a lead, but this is not a small-time operation. These guys mean business."

"What do you mean, *they mean business?*" his mother said, a note of hysteria creeping into her voice.

But before Brett could respond, James felt it right to let him in on what was going on. "They made contact, Brett."

"What—what do you mean, they made contact?" a surprised Brett asked, looking from face to face for answers.

"I think you snooping around made Joel and whoever he is working with reach out to Mateo, the same way that Joel did the night that Petra went missing," his mom elaborated.

Brett's jaw dropped momentarily, before clamping shut again. "What exactly are they asking for?"

She simply handed him the phone, refusing to look at her daughter's picture again.

James and Mateo averted their eyes as Brett looked through the phone, his mouth growing tight and his brow furrowing. It was uncomfortable for anyone to witness Petra in such a state.

"Looks like Joel did this for money," Brett confirmed. "He *sold* her!" he concluded, throwing the phone onto the nearby couch with a fury.

"That bastard sold Petra for money. How could a father do that?" he whispered.

Up to this point, they didn't really know what had happened to Petra. But now, things were becoming clearer, and it was somehow even worse.

"Now that we know they can be dealt with, I suggest that we reach out to them to get Petra back," Brett advised. "Whose number did it come from?"

"We don't know. I don't recognize this number, and I was afraid to reply or call back," Mateo said.

"I understand," Brett said. "If I'm right, then the same people that I reached out to must be the ones with Petra, meaning we're on the right track to get her back. I'll get my contacts to set up some kind of meeting with them again like I did today."

"And then what will you do?" James asked, intrigued by the covert nature of Brett's job.

"It's best that you don't know, Jimbo. But trust me, meeting these kind of people means risking my own neck," he replied gravely. "I have some contacts who know a lot about these kinds of deals, but the guys remained adamant that they knew nothing about what I was asking around for. Unless, of course, I had the right price."

It dawned on James why Brett looked so worn down. He had met with *them*, and it was evident that it wasn't an easy meeting.

"I guess I will have to set up meeting with my contacts to try and locate whoever sent that text message and the picture, and find out what their demands will be," Brett explained some more. "Kathy, I'm sorry that I couldn't get her back."

"What if I don't have the money, Brett? I gave you all that I had, and I'm pretty sure that these people are going to ask for more," she wailed.

"If these are the same people that I met with today, who dragged me into their car blindfolded to an undisclosed site before pushing me out of their car, then I'd suggest we look for ways to pay them and get our baby girl back, whatever it takes. You asked me to go in search of them, and I did. From the looks of it, Joel got some really heavy cash in exchange for her."

"Brett, first of all, that is assault! I don't want to lose you too! Who knows what they will do to you next time. We should go to the police with this. Or straight to the FBI! We shouldn't give in to ransom; this is a hostage situation now. And we have proof. There are people who specialize in getting kidnapped people back, Brett. The money I gave you wasn't for ransom, it was to pay off whoever you needed to from the military to help out. This is getting out of hand, and I don't like it. I am scared that something worse is going to happen, to you and then to Petra."

"We need to tell Agent Perez," James urged. "He could help out with this."

Brett turned around to him slowly, eyes fixated in a rather deep stare. "I don't think that would be a good idea..." he warned.

"Why not?" a confused James was forced to ask. His mother shared the same perplexed look. "They could help catch these bastards and set my sister free at the same time!"

"Guys, I am telling you. Letting the authorities know will only make things worse. This is all about money for them. They don't care about Petra. As long as they get a certain amount, they will let her go.

I've heard about a lot of kidnapping cases gone wrong, and how they many times end up not delivering on their word once they find out that the authorities are involved. And never ends well when this is the case. Trust me."

"I don't know what to do! I'm not supposed to be figuring out how to negotiate with kidnappers," his mom halfway sobbed.

"I'll make some calls to find out what I can. Mateo, I need your phone to track whoever sent that text, and try and reach them for some proper negotiations," Brett stated. "This is risky, I must confess; but I think it is the best way to go about this."

Mateo heaved a heavy sigh. "It's fine. You can keep it. Just give it to me back when you are done, I guess."

James could tell the persistent mindset of a soldier had begun finding its way back into Brett. He looked focused and determined to find Petra. The fact that he had done something as risky as setting up a meeting with a kidnapping group only demonstrated just how far he was willing to go to get his sister back safely.

"I can assure you guys that these people will not go free after they let Petra go. But we will prioritize her release above any other thing, first and foremost," Brett assured them. He got up and headed upstairs. "I'm gonna get cleaned up, if you don't mind."

James, Kathy, and Mateo watched on, admiring the kind of dedicated and fearless man that Brett showed himself to be with every action and word. He was ready to stand and drill through any means necessary to get Petra back, and even in more ways than the FBI had.

"Mom, Brett isn't going to get himself killed, is he?" James asked, sensing that Brett was about to embark on something even more dangerous than the one that had gotten him tossed from a moving car.

With her silence, James knew that his mother couldn't honestly give a response to the question that he had just asked her. She was most likely torn between wanting her daughter back at any cost and making sure Brett came back in one piece as well. It was a conundrum they were all trapped between, and one brought upon the entire family because of his father's actions.

# CHAPTER FORTY-FIVE | 45

THERE WAS A NEW BATCH TODAY. But one in particular, a little Asian boy, broke my heart. He is so young! He wouldn't stop crying, and none of us could console him. His constant crying puts the demons on edge. As sad as it makes us, we all just want him to shut up. If he doesn't, we all get it bad.

"Shut the fuck up, kid!" one of the girls cries out, obviously terrified by the potential consequences of his hysteria.

He doesn't even speak English. I feel so bad for him, I really do. But, it's just that... I am tired too. And I don't want to get beaten anymore. I just want to sleep.

"If someone doesn't shut him up soon, I swear, I don't know what I'll do to him," adds another girl from the other side of the room.

I don't know whether to hug him or slap him.

*Please stop, baby boy. I feel your pain too.*

# BROKEN

# CHAPTER FORTY-SIX | 46

JOEL STILL HAD HIS HAND UP IN THE AIR when the five men approached the vehicle. They looked unlike any cops that he had seen before. He thought about making a run for it, but there were too many variables involved that would spell disaster.

"Don't be stupid!" one of men yelled, pointing his gun directly at him, striking further fear into Joel's heart. Joel simply raised his arms to show he wouldn't try anything.

"What do you have in the truck?" one of the others asked.

Mr. Brown's words of warning rang in his head. He wouldn't to let out any word, no matter what he had to go through. Still, he couldn't believe that he was so unlucky to fall prey to a hijack on his first day.

*What is this? Why are these guys dressed as civilians? Are they cops or are they robbers?*

They hadn't identified themselves yet, simply rammed him to the side of the road and overwhelmed him.

"I don't have anything in the truck," Joel lied, trying not to stutter. "I am just going to my storage unit to move some furniture."

"This son of a bitch is lying," snarled a stout-looking man, who spoke with a lisp. "We know you got Brown's merchandise. We need the key now. Otherwise, you are going to start losing digits from your body one after the other," he threatened.

"I don't know what you're talking about or what you mean by 'brown merchandise,' but I am telling you that I've got nothing but an empty container back there. The furniture I'm picking up isn't even brown."

The men looked less than impressed, with the closest one ramming his gun hard into Joel's head, sending him to his knees with a lightning bolt of jetting through his body. Joel screamed in agony, doing his best to avert any more incoming hits, to no avail, as a left jab connected with his ribcage from the stout man who had deemed him a liar earlier.

"You are going to show us what you have, spic," the man growled. "Or we can just kill you and take the whole truck."

"I'm telling you the absolute truth! I have no idea what you're asking," he protested as he cowered, watching the men grow less patient with him, his thoughts on the burner phone that Mr. Brown had handed him earlier, but he could see no way to use it.

He was trapped, and Joel, the Lion, was out of options. More like a scared cub, now.

"Damn, boy! You are one loyal beaner; I'll give you that. But you must know that your death wouldn't even give pause to a man like Brown, and you would only be replaced by another money-seeking cockroach like yourself," another coaxed.

His words did nothing to soften or melt away Joel's resolve. He steeled himself, taking the single small padlock key securing the container with the girls in it, which he had in his hand, and shoving it down his throat to prevent it from been taken forcefully, should that be the case. He would rather put them through hell than allow easy access to the girls. He choked on it, but managed to swallow it, as the men looked on, confused.

*Of course, they could easily simply shoot the lock off. Shit, was this all for nothing?*

The men were furious, pouncing on him in unison, beating him so furiously he could not distinguish one hit from another.

"That's enough!" a familiar voice called from behind them. "Let him be; you are going to kill him!"

Joel recognized the voice coming from one of the SUV trucks behind; he had heard enough of the man's twang in the last 48 hours. With his sight blurry, and his head aching badly, he desperately tried to confirm who had spoken. Gregory Brown's figure finally came into view just before his vision was clouded by dizziness.

With his eyes closed shut and his hearing equally fading away, Joel heard the words. "He is not bad, huh? Fucking Lion sure has balls on him. I am impressed."

Joel could feel nothing but relief as he lost his grip on consciousness and slipped away.

Perez wasn't having much luck in his pursuit. The last frame of Joel that they had gotten was his time at the Ontario Airport, trying hard to maneuver his way around the cameras and through the security guards in there. Perez hadn't had much sleep since the incident, either.

Perez needed answers, and so far, he hadn't been getting what he wanted. He sat in the comfort of his temporary desk chair, staring at Joel's face on the large screen. He wanted to know a lot of things; he needed to know what drove his actions and what made him just so hard to figure out.

He wasn't ready to slack off, though, turning around to the sight of the team working hard around the clock to find Joel as soon as possible. The taxi driver hadn't paid off. Apparently, these guys had some kind of honor. Or maybe he really didn't remember, as he had claimed.

The kidnappings had further increased by two percent, meaning more children were being kidnapped within the space of two months. The American Southwest had become a hunting ground for those who sought pretty teenage girls for their illicit affairs. If he could at least have this break and catch Joel and this ring, it would make him feel like he was doing something about it.

"Perez, we might have something here," a local young agent, by the name of Boulder, called out.

Agent Perez walked toward where the local agent had been stationed and working. He stared into the screen, watching the images of some men, through which the facial recognition software had begun compiling their names and every valuable information from the database.

"Tell me what we have," he requested, without peeling his fixated gaze away from the computer monitor.

"I ran Joel's face through our various facial recognition programs, with the same picture we had gotten of him from the Phoenix airport in disguise and makeup, and it came back with a hit just now," he explained.

Perez wanted to jump for joy, but managed to remain professional. He took a closer look at the large screen, which had no less than seven people splattered across it, with their personal information getting compiled as well.

"A traffic camera in a low trafficked area of Rancho Cucamonga picked up some shady looking men with guns accosting each other during the early hours of the morning. Joel was one of them, as well as someone else that you wouldn't believe," Agent Boulder explained, playing the video feed again for Perez to look through.

Perez was more interested now, sitting down and drawing himself closer to the monitor. He took the next few seconds to watch the video, ascertaining that it was indeed Joel and a group of armed men in the video of the heist, or whatever this was.

"What is Joel's connection with these men, and why were they hitting him? And what is he doing driving a truck?" Agent Perez needed answers. "Let's get those plates and find out who owns it. Also, what do you mean that I wouldn't believe who he is with?" he asked.

The overachiever Agent Boulder excitedly shared, "The man who came into the scene after he was being beaten, sir, is none other than Gregory Brown."

"Greg Brown!"

"Yes, sir. He is wanted for serial counts of murder, drug trafficking, money laundering, and a rap sheet of kidnappings longer than any man alive."

"Among other things. I know who Brown is."

"We know that he is connected to the Russians. The thing is, though, that he is a ghost. I am surprised that he was this careless."

"Wait a minute. Is Joel is now working with Brown?" Perez pressed his temples in disbelief. "What the hell is he doing with these guys? Is this the ring he is involved with? This is worse than I thought."

"Well, it looks like Joel has become part of something much bigger. Right now I am trying to chase after them by following their different vehicles with traffic cameras and hoping to get a location on them soon. The problem is that they all ended up splitting at some point, so I am going to need help. That's when I called you."

"Let's get you some techs to help."

The overwhelmed agent felt his anxiety begin to get the better of him. He needed to find Joel, and fast, before things grew even worse.

"But stay on Brown *and* Joel. We'll assign others on the other truck."

"Already on it."

Perez turned to the office group. "Let's pull up everything we have on Gregory Brown from the database," he asked no one in particular.

Just a few minutes later, Perez looked at Brown's rap sheet on the computer monitor. It was a sight to behold. His various wrongdoings included masterminding the kidnapping and trafficking of hundreds, if not thousands, of teenage boys and girls through various means in the entire country for the decades, as well as various identity thefts and blackmails of high and mighty people around the country. Originally from Columbia, South Carolina, he was also a wanted man in Russia, Ukraine, Belarus, Cambodia, Thailand, Mexico, South Africa, France, and the UK.

Perez had read enough about Brown's organization, and the fact that he knew how to cover his tracks well too. Brown was the face and representative of Alexander Zhirkoff. Zhirkoff was the bigger fish. But taking Brown down would be a big blow in the organization. Unfortunately, he had always been one step ahead of the authorities, and he had good contacts in high places, thereby making him a difficult catch. Joel's association with him had brought things into a new perspective as well.

Smaller fish always brought about bigger fish. All he needed to do now was hunt Joel, and he would catch Brown red-handed. Zhirkoff would be next.

"How is the chase with the traffic cameras going?" Perez asked impatiently.

"We are still on it, but the low light of early morning and lack of street cameras in many places isn't helping. We lost the main truck that León was originally driving around an abandoned winery in Ontario. As you saw from the video, one of the other goons drove it after the encounter. There are no traffic cameras in that area, so we don't know where exactly they went. Brown and León followed them," Agent Boulder explained, watching the last camera come to a null view afterward. "The other two SUVs reconvened in a remote area of San Bernardino, close to the 210 freeway. It's mostly orange groves and old Victorian homes."

"Ontario, you say?" Agent Perez asked again to be sure. "How soon can we dispatch a team there to find out about the surroundings? We will probably need a chopper too."

"No less than an hour," another agent in the room replied. "There is not much around that area but old abandoned industrial buildings, though."

"That would be a perfect hideout for whatever this is that they're doing. I need you to assemble a team as soon as you can and send them over there. Play the video from the roadside once more for me; I need to watch it again. If we need to contact NSA to access satellite support, so be it."

One of the assigned agents did as she was told, watching Perez scrutinize the video, almost as though he could read their lips as they spoke, even though the video quality wasn't the best. He watched the video over again and again, watching Joel get hit and shoved to the ground before Brown's intervention.

"What on earth have you gotten yourself into, Joel?" he asked in a rather concerned whisper while shaking his head in disbelief. "It looks like he swallowed something. What is going on here?" he murmured.

There were too many questions that needed answering. Agent Perez thought it best to inform Kathy about their findings, both to keep her apprised of things and to assure her that Petra had not been forgotten. She answered on the second ring.

"Hello, Raymond," she said, sounding rather weak and very much unlike herself.

"Hello, Kathy. I am sorry that I haven't reached out to you in a while. I need to run some information by you, though."

"You have something important to tell me?" she asked, going straight to the point.

"Yes. Yes, I do. We just found Joel with a bunch of... *kidnappers*, I guess." He wasn't really sure what or who they were, but he could only assume. "But we have yet to establish their base to apprehend them. Really quick, I just need to ask if you ever saw him with anyone by the name of Gregory Brown or heard him speak about anyone of such name?"

"I've never heard that name before, that I can remember. It doesn't even ring a bell. What has this got to do with Joel?"

"We believe that your ex-husband is working with Brown, who is a very, very bad guy. He is wanted in multiple countries for human trafficking and drugs, among other things. I just wanted to know if you ever heard anything, that's all."

"Oh. Yeah, no. Sorry." There was a short pause. "Um, Raymond?"

"Yes?"

"No, never mind. It's nothing." Her voice was unsteady.

"Okay...? Are you sure?" Perez felt that something was wrong.

"Yeah. Sorry. Forget it."

"Alrighty, then..." After hearing no response from her, he kept going. "Well, I'll keep you informed about our findings. Talk to you later."

"Perez," she managed to say before he actually hung up.

"Yes?" He brought the phone back up to his ear.

She took a big sigh. "I just wanted to apologize to you. I am aware that I haven't been easy to work with. I know I can be a bit... much, at times. And I am sorry. It's just that I feel my whole life is in crumbles, that's all. I know that you are doing your best, and I appreciate it. So, yeah. I just wanted to let you know that."

"Um, thank you, Kathy. I appreciate your words. Don't worry, I understand. You've lost a piece of you, and we will all continue to work together until we find her." He thought for a moment. "I promise you, we will bring Petra back."

"Yes, we will. I'll let you go then. Talk to you later."

"Bye, Kathy."

Perez felt unsettled after the call with Kathy. It was as if his sixth sense picked up on something wrong. Of course, it's not as if anything was going right in her life. He decided to put his feelings aside and return to Gregory Brown's bio and other data on the screen, especially the known aliases and the allies.

Alexander Zhirkoff, Carlos Wong, Jacob Doyle, Mitch Petersen, and other known associates. But no Joel León. So, they would start with those names. These were the men to be found, and perhaps the major link to finding Joel and the missing girls.

Perez found some more information about Brown popping up on the screen, which included his travel information in the past months, one of which was taking a flight with under the name of Jonas Kidd along with Jacob Doyle from LAX to Phoenix, Arizona, the same city where Petra and a few other girls had been kidnapped from. Phoenix – his city. Jacob Doyle needed to be found.

Perez had no time to waste, watching the selected pick of agents gearing up to head to Ontario. Another team in Arizona was on the hunt for Jacob Doyle. The real chase was on, and it was only a matter of time before Joel's actions would catch up with him.

Perez took out a lollipop from his pocket, this one pink, and placed it in his mouth.

*Here we come, ready or not.*

# CHAPTER FORTY-SEVEN | 47

I ALWAYS THOUGHT OF MYSELF AS RESILIENT, but I am destroyed. I thought the whole point of being a solid foundation was that it was unbreakable. But this rock is broken. More like fine sand now, impossible to glue together. There is no more resolute warrior left in me.

Petra León is nothing, but a memory. A shadow of a past life.

Petra is no more. My name is Eve.

I am Eve, and I will do as I'm told. I promise to be a good girl now.

# BROKEN

# CHAPTER FORTY-EIGHT | 48

THE DISTINCTIVE SCENT OF MR. BROWN greeted Joel's nose before his eyelids opened. Cracking a lid, he saw a freshly made doughnut as well the steam from an equally freshly brewed cup of coffee on the bedside table.

Joel couldn't recall how he had gotten into bed, let alone when Mr. Brown had walked into the room and sat in the chair opposite of where he was. He had an uncanny smile across his face, as Joel struggled to sit up, his head still aching. His body was bruised. Everything hurt. Everything.

"Take it easy, Lion," Brown warned, sounding concerned about his wellbeing.

"What happened?" Joel blurted, his voice still thick with sleep. "Those guys came out of nowhere, asking for your merchandise, and they kicked my ass," he recalled groggily. "I don't think they were cops."

"I know. I know, Lion. But it is all good now, and you need to have a good rest before we continue our journey," Brown replied, handing him the cup of steaming hot coffee and a doughnut.

Joel pushed up to sitting and accepted the offering, stuffing the tasty chocolate doughnut into his mouth first, feeling the explosive taste in his mouth, before washing it down with a sip of his hot coffee. He tried desperately to recollect everything that he had seen and heard before passing out, and it slowly, but surely, came back to him.

His eyes widened as he recalled the last bits before he got totally knocked out, with the voices he had heard and the words almost precisely as they did. Brown could tell that he had caught up, and the smile dropped off from his face immediately.

Joel took down the half-eaten doughnut from between his lips in slow and dramatic fashion.

"Tell me you had nothing to do with what happened to me on that street!" Joel demanded, hoping for some sincere response.

Gregory Brown chuckled, manically, getting up from his seat and moving to the window. He stared into the distance, surveying the surrounding trees that danced in the wind.

"What the hell did you put me through? Was that really necessary?" Joel asked in rage. "Everything went as planned for the pick-up at the port. I was nervous, but there were no complications. And then, I was driving around, when–"

"You still don't get it, do you, Lion?" Mr. Brown interrupted. "You don't understand that it needed to be done," he added without looking back at him.

"*What* needed to be done, exactly?" Joel asked furiously.

"All you need to know right now is that you're one of us now. The manner in which you held your own, refused to cave in, and gave no information about the entire operation showed your genuine loyalty to the organization and our cause," Brown explained as he turned around to face him. "The test was needed to ascertain that we could truly bring you into the fold fully. It's standard procedure, Lion. Don't take it personally."

Joel figured that this was what he was going to say. He could still feel the ache all around his body, while his sight had only begun getting better after a blow had struck him right across his head. He hadn't imagined such treatment, but he was willing to take it in good faith, choosing to make no fuss about what had happened now that he understood. All that mattered was the fact that he was in now. This was all he desperately wanted.

"But man, Lion. When you tried to swallow the key! I never expected that."

"Um, I'm pretty sure I did swallow it."

"Shit!" Mr. Brown snickered. "You're one crazy bastard."

Joel took another sip of the coffee, wondering how he'd get that key out of him. He understood this was a normal practice needed to gain better ground in the group. He was glad that he hadn't flunked, though, by telling his assaulters anything that might have given Mr. Brown up or losing the merchandise. He wondered what would've happened to him if he had. But he dismissed the thought quickly, knowing exactly what would have happened to him and not wanting to dwell on it.

"What happens next from here?" Joel asked. "I mean, now that you can clearly see that I will be loyal, can you come clean with me?"

Mr. Brown made his walk back across the room to where Joel sat with his cooling cup of coffee and his half-eaten doughnut.

He sat down next to Joel. "I need you to run a sensitive part of our operations from here, while we try our best to expand. Things are looking good for us, and we need more men like you to enlarge our operations. You know, I am starting to think that I chose the right name for you, *Lion*."

Joel heard the encouraging words. He had waited long enough, and it finally came after some bruises and injuries inflicted on his body in form of a loyalty ritual.

"You can count on me," Joel replied.

Mr. Brown got up and brushed imaginary lint off his pants. "Evidently. However, before we continue, I still need to ask you an important question," he insisted, sighing deeply, almost like a man overwhelmed by something at heart.

*What would that be?*

"Why do you *really* want in? Why do you want this... this life?" he asked looking him straight in the eyes. "I mean, everyone has a reason for wanting to go dark, and you've yet to tell me yours. And I mean, the *real* reason. Some of us found our way into this because we had no choice. But you... well, enlighten me."

Joel took his time to give a response. He laid down the piece of junk food in his hands, and sat straight on the edge of the large bed. "Is the cash not good enough reason?" Joel responded awkwardly.

Mr. Brown listened to him, slightly nodding his head. "The money isn't always the only reason we do this. The cash is good, of course. But like I said, everyone has a reason for wanting to become part of something as big as this. It takes serious commitment and an end to your previous life, when you want to dine with the devil the way in which we do here. What's your story?"

"Honestly, Mr. Brown, I just like money. And I like girls."

"What about power? Being in charge of other human beings?"

"Yeah, that too." Joel mind was really somewhere else. But this would suffice for now.

"Okay, then. You begin work tomorrow with the girls," the older man noted, bringing Joel to the present. "This time for reals, though. The shipment you brought in contains some of the new recruits, and I need you to handpick them into the various categories tomorrow."

*So, the truck did have girls, after all! But I didn't hear anything. I wasn't even sure, but I was scared to look. What if I was being watched? And, of course, I was.*

Joel's face wore a confused expression across it. He couldn't believe that he had actually helped traffic minors. He hadn't dared open the door, trying to follow instructions as best as possible. He also didn't have any idea of what he meant by categorizing the girls.

"What do you mean *categorizing?*"

"You said you wanted in, didn't you? Well, this is how we get things done," Mr. Brown shot back. "The transports won't keep you busy. But this will. So, you'll begin the process of learning to pick the right ones to move drugs around without drawing attention from the pigs, while those well suited to other endeavors will be sent to the clubhouse or the massage parlors to be trained. The remaining ones we sell on the streets. That's how we run things. It's simple. Three groups. Three different purposes. *Capiche?*"

He nodded in acknowledgment, even though not everything was clear.

*Wait. So not all of them are prostituted? I don't understand.*

"Good. Now get some rest, Lion," Mr. Brown said, "so that I can come pick you up this evening for more work. I know you didn't sleep much last night, and you'll need to be rested. There is a full bathroom behind that door. Your bag is in the closet with all your shit. You'll find a gallon of water under the bed too. Just stay here until I send someone to get you," Brown added, before heading out the door.

*What time is it? How long has it been? Where the heck am I?*

"Sounds good. Thanks." Joel knew he could use the rest.

The man left, and Joel was once again reminded that he had smelled the cologne on someone in his past life—if only he could remember who.

He shrugged it off and resumed munching on his doughnut and sipping from his now tepid cup of coffee, with the satisfying feeling that he had been accepted. He could tell that he would be taken more seriously and would be handed more responsibilities now. Of course, he wouldn't be able to sleep now that he had drunk the coffee.

Joel hadn't really taken note of his room, previously occupying his thoughts with the conversation he had with Mr. Brown. This room was entirely different from his first one, with a flat-screen television on the wall. This bed was much better. He looked out the window and noticed that he was back in the same house in San Bernardino. He recognized the shady club in the distance beyond the orange groves from his view. It was evening. He then saw the brown parcel to his left, placed on the table only a stretch away from him with the words *Lion, You Deserve It*, inked on it with a black marker. The was also a bag of fast food left for him.

He reached for the parcel, unwrapping a neatly stacked pile of Benjamins. He grinned from ear to ear, seeing his efforts begin to bear fruit. Everything had begun falling neatly in place, and all he needed was to continue in hopes of meeting with the real boss, the Russian, Mr. Brown's superior, should his efforts really get acknowledged.

His plans were working well enough, even though his heart yearned for his entire family, especially Petra. But he put the thoughts aside. He had done too many shameful things. He had wronged God, as well, having barely sought Him out since he began this soul-tainting journey.

For the first time in a long while, Joel closed his eyes to pray; with embarrassment, he asked for nothing but forgiveness for all that he had done and for what he was about to do. He wondered if God was even listening to him. Somehow, deep inside, though, he hoped that God heard him and understood.

As the night came, he had got himself dressed. He had his favorite pair of blue jeans on, topped by a black jacket, and a black, round neck shirt underneath, revealing his trim, muscular body. He wanted to look the part.

A knock sounded at the door. He turned the TV off and raced to the door, yanking it open without asking who was on the other side. There was the familiar face of Rosette, who had fed him so much false information about what was needed of him, which he assumed had been an instruction from Mr. Brown himself.

"Star," Joel nodded, choosing to use her captive name. He was one of the group now, after all.

"Mr. Brown is asking for you," she said, turning around and leading him away.

*At least she is clothed now.*

Joel trailed behind her slowly as they entered a room filled with several young girls. He wondered if these were the ones he had brought from the docks in San Pedro. They looked frightened and disoriented, clearly drugged. Several of them were dressed in ways leaving little to the imagination and sporting heavy makeup. Asians, Latinas, Europeans. It was a mix. There were both, girls and boys. All young. Too young. Maybe these weren't the ones he drove—if he even had anyone in that truck.

Mr. Brown sighted Joel first, calling out to him with an outstretched arm. "Here is our newest member," he said, embracing Joel in a hug. "Lion will personally be taking care of things on my behalf hence."

*In charge? What the…?*

Joel briefly swept his eyes around the room, taking into account the sight of eight armed men.

"You should have fun even while we work tonight," Brown encouraged, slapping Joel slightly on his back. "Come on, let me show you how we pick them into the right category so that you know what to do tomorrow with the other group."

*Other group?*

Joel was still confused, and his chest tightened as he looked over the group of children. If these were the ones that he drove, he hadn't seen them at all while picking them from the docks at San Pedro. He wasn't there as the truck was loaded, as he was instructed. He was told to simply drive that truck as it was without opening the back, and he was glad that had been the case.

"What are you going to do with the boys?" Joel forced to ask. "I mean, they are a little too young to indulge in any of all this, don't you think?"

Mr. Brown snorted then drew back as he realized Joel was legitimately asking. "Oh, you are you serious! Well, some of the boys will fetch a handsome price from their parents, if they want them back. Otherwise, they will serve the same purpose as the girls. You'd be surprised how high the demand is for them," Brown said with a smirk. "We profiled their parents before we took them, same as most of the girls, whom we know for certainty are from wealthy homes, and will bring us large sums if they want them back. Although most of the time they never make it back home anyway, to be honest. There is quick money in ransoms, but there is much more to be made if we keep them and break them."

Joel forced a neutral expression on his face. Brown excused himself to receive a phone call, and Joel tried to move closer without trigger the notice of the armed guards.

"I believe they got it," Brown said. "I told you it would work, provided it came from the same Mateo kid he sent it through."

Joel had heard the name and froze. It couldn't be a coincidence. He strained to hear more, but a group of men entered to room and stood between him and Mr. Brown, and their conversation made it impossible to eavesdrop.

Joel took some steps back, keeping an eye on Mr. Brown. His mind was swirling with what Mateo—if it was indeed his kids' friend—

had to do with anything. He was worried that something else was going on, and he needed to find out soon.

Brown finished his conversation and strode over with a file, thick as a book, which he handed to Joel with a flourish.

Joel needed no introduction or permission to surf through the files. He brushed through the pages to read the perfectly detailed profile about each one of the kids – medical information, demographics, financial state of their parents, pictures, as well as other valuable information about their education, age, talents, and every valuable thing they could dig up about the kids.

"It's quite impressive, isn't it?" Mr. Brown asked, clearly proud of the thorough and organized nature of his organization.

"This is very well detailed and specific," Joel replied, surprised by their level of sophistication.

"We like to take our time and do thigs right. There is power in details. It takes time, but they payoff is always better."

"That makes sense."

"You see, Lion, when you run things the way that we do, it becomes paramount that you do it well, or you risk being caught. Or at the very least, exposed. And that can be a problem because we have a certain clientele that wouldn't want to be discovered, if you know what I mean," Brown explained. "So, we take our time with each of these kids. Yeah, sure, we get a runaway from the streets here and there. But most of the times, these are quality kids. We hunt them. We study them. Sometimes, we infiltrate their lives, if we think they're worthy.

And they always are. And in return, we guarantee that they are all beautiful, smart, and talented. The cream of the crop. The cherries on top. *Gifted*, if you will."

Joel nodded in acknowledgment. He understood exactly what Brown meant. "I can see that they are all special."

"Indeed. And now, I'll leave that to you so that you can go through it all and determine who goes where. Read their stories. Look at the pictures. Come back out with a good categorized distribution that makes sense. I know you could be tempted to take the easy route and think that they could each do it all. And perhaps you're right. But remember, Lion, some are better than others at certain things. That's why you must choose wisely."

"I will take my time and do my best. I promise."

"I know you will. I'll be back later. I have several phone calls to make."

Joel nodded in acceptance of his role. He was still very much engulfed in the details that the file held, mesmerized by the specificity of the psychological and physical profiles. Information ranged from the height of each kid, to their weight, clothes and shoe size, allergies, birth order, languages spoken, hobbies, school grades, extra-curricular activities, as well as other attributes. They were ranked in different categories with a specific rubric rating from A to F. Most of them were ranked As or Bs. These kids were all *gifted*, indeed.

Joel noted something, which prompted him to depart the group and return to his new room to continue going through the list of kids and their respective files. What got his attention was the fact that the files also contained a few profiles of other kids not in the present group. Some dated back in years and a few were recent, with the list of new kids tagged by date on the top right corner of each file.

"Where are you?" he asked himself, sifting through the pages.

The lack of information irritated him, and he tossed the binder across the room in frustration. He needed to know who Brown was speaking with, and he had to find a way to get his hand on his phone.

*Come on Joel, you can do this. You've come this far.* He dashed out the door to visit Mr. Brown one more time. *You are a lion! Go hunting. It's not too late.*

# BROKEN

# CHAPTER FORTY-NINE | 49

ONE OF THE DEMONS told me that the boss is coming tomorrow. I hope he likes me. Apparently, several of us are ready to be moved to another location and be given our new purpose. I wasn't even aware that there were different purposes for each of us.

I wonder what I will be. I wonder how *he* will be. All I know is that I don't want to be in this crowded room anymore. And the other place they take us to meet the clients is not much better either. They said that once we are moved, we will have to share a room with only a couple of other girls. The demons also said that the houses we will go to meet clients are very nice. They'll even give us new clothing. I can't wait to get out of this stupid white thing that barely covers anything.

But honestly, I don't even care anymore. Take me wherever. Make me whatever. It doesn't matter. The truth is that anything is better than being in this shithole.

Shoot, I'll suck and fuck whomever. Like I said. I don't care anymore. All the demons seem to like me, after all.

My name is Eve. And Eve has found a new purpose.

My name is Eve. And Eve is ready for her new life.

My name is Eve. Bring it on.

I just... I can't with life like this. There is no more fight left in me.

# CHAPTER FIFTY | 50

BRETT HAD BEEN ON A CALL for the last hour, leaving Kathy to twist in the wind while he talked. He made no eye contact with her, and instead walked outside the house to the backyard, waving to her once and averting his eyes.

"Do you think he can reach out to them?" James asked, putting his hand on her arm.

Kathy jumped visibly at his touch and whipped around with wide eyes.

"I'm sorry; I didn't mean to startle you," James apologized.

"It's all right, Jimmy. You didn't do anything wrong. I just think I'm a little shaky these days."

"Do you think Brett can locate them again and strike a bargain with them to bring Petra home?"

"I believe in him," Kathy said. "I know that he can get it done." Kathy wasn't sure if her words were reassurance for James or herself.

"The more I think about it, the more I worry about not saying anything about this to Agent Perez, though," James murmured. "He has a team, and resources. They do this for a living, Mom."

Kathy provided no response to her son's words, as Brett had started back toward the house. He didn't look too pleased.

"They are demanding a really large sum of money," Brett said, shaking his head. "It's crazy, them thinking a normal family can put their hands on this kind of cash."

"Just tell me; how much are they asking?" Kathy urged him as she followed him into the living room, where Mateo was still waiting, having begged to stay on the off chance he could help.

"They want thirty thousand dollars in cash," Brett replied, his lips taut with anger.

Kathy could see that the entire thing had begun getting to him. It was obvious that Brett was emotionally drained. She stepped closer, holding his warm hands in hers, and staring him in the eyes.

"I know this is hard for you, honey, but you've been the bright spark for us in these dark times," she said in a loving, tender tone. "If that's what they ask, I believe I can get it, and we can then get my baby back."

Brett's expression was priceless. He was both shocked and moved by her determination to find her daughter. "Kathy, I am so sorry that you've had to go through so much pain and worry." He squeezed her hand, letting her know that he was with her throughout all of this.

"Mom, we don't have that kind of money. Do we?" James butted in. "We need to get Agent Perez involved. I'm telling you!" he warned. He then turned to his friend, who had been silent this whole time. "Mateo, come with me."

James walked away briskly, obviously discontent with their plan, Mateo following right behind him.

"I need to explain things to him," Kathy told Brett, slipping her hands out of his.

He pulled her back in restriction.

"Don't worry; I'll take care of it. I know how to tell him how wrong he is," Brett assured her, planting a kiss on her lips before heading off toward James's room.

James was panicking, realizing how awful their decision could turn out, including costing Petra her life. He wasn't willing to sacrifice his sister's life or waste so much money, when they couldn't even be trusted to deliver her to begin with.

"Why are they so adamant about keeping the FBI on the dark, Mateo?"

"Beats me."

"James, can I come in?" Brett said as he tapped on James's door softly.

"I don't want to talk," James rudely replied, knowing all too well that Brett had been sent to reason with him on the issue.

"We need to talk, James. At least listen to what I have to say," Brett said from the other side of the door.

James looked at Mateo for reassurance, who simply shrugged.

"Brett, what you both want to do is suicide for Petra, if it goes wrong. Why can't you see that?" James asked from inside his room.

Mateo was clearly uncomfortable being in the middle of a family dispute. "I think I'm gonna go, Jimmy."

"No, stay. Please."

Mateo nodded. "Okay, fine. But I think you should listen to anything that he has to say first," he advised, walking over to the door to open it for Brett, who walked in right away.

Brett remained silent while taking his seat in the only chair in the room, adjacent to James's bed, where he now lay.

"We need to talk, James. I need you to listen very carefully to me," he urged.

James simply stared back at him in silence, clearly upset. Mateo closed the door and sat on the floor, using the wall as a back support.

"I've seen things like this happen before, and I've participated in it during my time in the military. Most times, these kinds of negotiations break down when the authorities show up, making things more complicated than they have to be."

"Are you trying to convince me that getting the authorities involved in a kidnapping case is much riskier?" James asked back, seeking a direct answer. He sat up while still in his bed.

"No, that is not what I am trying to say or do. Besides, the authorities are *already* involved. They can still do their part, and this would be additional. It's a different angle; it can't hurt to try. All I ask is that you trust me to get this done and do it well," Brett replied. "I need you to trust that I know what I'm doing."

James had heard him out, but was not entirely convinced. He nodded his head briefly, with Mateo listening on, seeming to soak in everything that Brett had said like a sponge.

Brett stood up and simply added, "Please, just trust me on this one. Okay?" With that he left the room.

Mateo remained quiet until Brett went downstairs. "I know you, Jimmy. And I think you're going to tell the FBI anyway. Aren't you?" Mateo spoke with so much certainty.

"You are damn right!" James replied, taking out his phone to dial Perez's number. He had saved it from before.

"Brett is going to be mad at you, you know? Your mother isn't going to take it lightly either. Better get your plan straight," Mateo continued, without really telling where his loyalty lied.

James wasn't interested in anyone trying to dissuade him, determined to do what his heart told him to. He couldn't bear the risk of Petra getting hurt in some shady deal with people none of them knew. He trusted Mateo to keep quiet and say nothing.

"Can I trust you, Mateo?"

"I'm with you, Jimmy... whatever you want or need. That's a given," Mateo reassured him, standing by the room door and locking it, as James began to speak to Agent Perez.

Joel knew his curiosity would most likely get him in trouble. But it was worth the risk. He lurked around the entrance where Gregory Brown was, seeing him drop his phone into his jacket and stepping into the bathroom. He knew by now that Mr. Brown liked his privacy, so he made certain that there were no guards around before sneaking in through the main door. He also knew now that there were no cameras in this area, so he'd be safe.

Joel hadn't been in Brown's room before, and hardly anyone was allowed inside. The room was considerably larger than the others he had seen in the mansion, and better furnished, too, with a massive screen pinned to the wall on Joel's right side, opposite the bed, its own fireplace, and a lavish desk. Joel knew that this wasn't where Brown lived, but it was his home away from home. This house was also mostly where guards and movers slept whenever on duty and also where some of the *merchandise* was kept, at least temporarily. But still, this room served as Brown's headquarters whenever he was in this house, and it sure was nice.

Joel briefly searched through the room once more, ascertaining that he was alone, before sneaking toward the jacket with the phone in it to see if he could unlock it to scroll through toward the last dialed calls. He could hear Brown's humming coming from the shower.

The phone was locked, and there was no way to figure out his access code. But at that moment, a phone call was coming through. Joel nervously put the phone back in the jacket and quickly hid under the desk.

Brown simply continued with the shower.

Joel got up and went to the phone again. The same number called again. And then again. Three missed calls, all from the same number. It must have been important. The number had no name on it, but the actual number was visible. Joel quickly saved the number into his own phone before returning the boss's phone into the jacket. As he slid the phone into the jacket, his hand felt something else inside the pocket.

*What do we have here?*

Joel looked around, as the sound of the shower and the whistling continued. He could tell that Brown wasn't done with his shower yet, providing him enough time to take out the object. He pulled out his arm with the object in hand; it was a key ring with one key on it and a blue flash drive.

Joel's eyes swept around constantly, cautious of where he was and the risk of getting caught. There would be no way out for him should he get caught doing what he was doing. He weighed the idea of taking them, but it was too much of a risk.

There was no computer or laptop in the room. The desk drawers were locked, but this key didn't open any of this. Where could he see the contents of this flash drive?

Joel thought it through long and hard, clenching the ring in his hand tightly, before tucking it all away deep inside his socks, in the shoes, and bringing his pants down to provide enough covering to it, should he get caught and searched.

He headed out of the room, with the next vital mission in mind, which was obtaining a computer with which he could view whatever was on the USB drive. He also wondered what this small key opened, as there seemed to be no apparent safe or box in the room. Of course he didn't have time to search, so maybe he had missed it.

Joel was onto something; he could feel it. He headed off to the designated room of one of the guards, whom he had noted had been among those who had assaulted him while during his "test."

The Lion had a plan, and it was one to save his own backside, should it work. Rosette had just walked out of another room, adjacent the one belonging to the guard, when she saw him.

"Hey, Lion! It looks like you're getting a hang of things around here, aren't you?" She was high. Higher than he had ever witnessed her to be.

"What can I say? I'm living life, Star!" Joel replied with a bogus smile. "Hey, by the way... I need your help with something," he asked of her, knowing she alone could assist him with the information that he sought, even while he couldn't and wouldn't trust her in any way.

"Oh, is that right?" she said with a wink. "And what exactly would that be? Because if it's some hits, I don't really share. And if it's something... *else*, it's going to cost you. Only the first one is free, and you already wasted it." She came close to him and put her finger on his chest, running it down.

"No, no. I am not talking about drugs *or* sex." Joel replied, taking her hand off of him. "It's nothing like that. I was just wondering... is there anywhere around here where I can get any access to a computer?"

Rosette eyed him briefly, almost in a suspicious manner.

"What do you even need a computer for?" she eventually asked, speech slurring. "Don't you have like a smart phone or something?"

"I need information about a lottery ticket that I played before coming over here. And my phone isn't really working anymore, for some reason. Besides, its Wi-Fi is damaged, so it wouldn't help me anyway. I'm shit out of luck, I guess." He let out a fake chuckle.

Rosette stared at him like she didn't believe him, but finally pointed east, toward the door. "There's a computer in that room, rarely used by the girls, except for watching porn and funny stuff whenever Mr. Brown lets us, and only under supervision," she said, walking away, giggling at nothing. "The guards use it all the time. I'm sure you can use it too, if one of them is not on it. But good luck with that, 'cuz apparently you don't have good luck."

He could barely make out her words, between the trailing off and slurring she was doing. But there was no time to worry about Rosette. He disappeared cautiously into the guard's room, getting his business done there. He would leave behind a clue to send suspicions away from him. He then quickly headed off to the computer room. Luckily, it was empty. There was a desk, with an older desktop computer and a printer, in a corner in the living room that he had walked into on his first night.

He needed no permission to wake up the computer from its slumber—no password required, which was great. It ran on a rather slow and very much outdated OS, but it was still good enough to view the contents of the flash drive. He pulled the ring from his sock and slid the drive into the computer. He watched it load the files, taking some time to complete its task.

*Come on, stupid thing!*

It was a frustrating wait for Joel, who could barely afford another minute before the muscled men were sure to be back.

The files finally loaded, coming to display in full on the monitor. He scanned through it in disbelief. It had been all he needed. There were multiple folders, nicely organized. One had kids' profiles, others contained folders within folders, with intrinsic plans, as well as various cells of the organization in different places all around the country. Their mode of operation, as well as the communication channels, methods, and merchandise—drugs, children, weapons—transport details, and channels all around the country were in full view on the monitor. Finances. Names.

Joel had in hand enough evidence and required information to bring Gregory Brown and the entire organization down. Or to blackmail them. But still, he could find the one piece of information that he needed. The sound of approaching footsteps had him ejecting the drive and stuffing it back into his sock.

*Ugh, I need more time!*

He needed a plan, but first, he had to be smart enough to fool Mr. Brown, who would most certainly come looking for his flash drive. The moment of truth was upon him. He waited in patience for the storm coming; he would ride it as best as he could.

*Crap! What am I going to say…?*

# BROKEN

# CHAPTER FIFTY-ONE | 51

WHEN I WAS YOUNGER, I used to love piñatas. I liked how they looked and what they represented – a new year of life. Mostly, however, I enjoyed them because they were full of sweetness. I remember one of the times my dad took us to Mexico, and we got to see how they made them. They were pieces of art. No two were the same. The artisans took their time to make each one of them, pasting the strips of paper carefully over the form, winding the colorful tissue around the hardened shell.

It dawned on me then, that all that time and hard work put into each of them was taken for granted. Kids would hit them with a stick at birthday parties. We only cared for what they carried inside – the small toys and sugary treats. And once the piñatas were broken and ravaged, they were worthless. Their purpose had been fulfilled.

I feel like a piñata.

I am broken. But I don't want to feel unloved. I am broken. But I don't want to feel like trash.

I feel like a piñata.

I am broken. I've been broken by a stick, with a line of men waiting their turn. I am broken. And there is no more sweetness within me.

I feel like a piñata. And I am broken, indeed.

# CHAPTER FIFTY-TWO | 52

"THEY CAN'T BE THAT STUPID!" Raymond Perez snapped. He dropped the call, feeling outraged and frustrated at Kathy Potter's foolhardy behavior. But he couldn't head back to Phoenix at this moment; that would mean leaving Joel and the ring to roam free somewhere in this area, when he was almost at their fingertips to be nabbed.

*You gotta be shitting me!*

He took the next few minutes to process his thoughts and emotions, clenching his fists in anger, and blinking intermittently. The reality was that he needed to get the kids back safe, in any way that he could.

He called out to one of his most trusted agents that had come with him from Arizona. "Hey, Frank!"

The brown-haired man hurried over with an anxious look across his face.

"What is it, boss?" he asked, with his glasses resting perfectly on his nose.

"I need you to get some guys back in Phoenix to prevent the Leóns from doing something stupid."

"What exactly are they trying to do?"

"They intend to make a proposed exchange with the kidnappers—if they even really are the ones who have Petra, that is—for a large sum of money."

Frank looked perplexed. "What the hell? How is that even possible? I mean, Joel and the kidnapping ring is here. And most likely the daughter too!"

"My thoughts exactly. And they could be falling into the hands of some phonies, or possible kidnappers all over again. James, the boy, was the one who alerted me of his mother and her fiancé's plans. Get to Scottsdale, quick. Find out everything that you can about this situation, and make certain that you prevent it from happening, no matter what. Make whatever call you need to make. I'm about to call the office back home too to give them a heads-up."

Frank nodded in acknowledgment, heading off to prep for the next flight back, while also agreed that this was a completely idiotic idea.

Agent Boulder had just walked in the room and witnessed Frank's rushed departure. "What's going on?" the local agent asked, looking at Perez's dark. "Everything okay?"

"Joel's ex-wife back home and her new man are about to do something utterly stupid, and I asked Frank to get a hold on things over there in our absence. I trust him better than anyone else back home," he replied, looking around for a chair to fall back in. "Any news on Joel, Brown, this Jacob guy, or any of the other names we got?" he asked, feeling a headache begin to settle in.

"We are running everything we got through the system, and hopefully we will get some feedback soon enough," Boulder said. "I have a few thoughts that I'd like to share with you, though."

"Go on… spill it," came the reply.

"Well, from what we know from Zhirkoff's men, they seem to be the kind of guys who betray those that they deal business with," Boulder explained.

Perez didn't understand with certainty what the agent was talking about. He needed more clarification, "What do you mean?"

"Well, just by looking into Brown's history, Joel might be getting into something way over his head."

Perez now understood the complication. This meant bad news for Joel, whichever way he wanted to play or look at it.

Boulder continued voicing his concerns with further elaboration, "So, if Joel dies, we might never find the underlying cause of all of this. This means that we definitely need to get him soon, whichever way we can, before the inevitable happens."

"That makes sense. And I can feel it coming," Perez sighed, feeling exhausted by everything going on. "I feel like something is coming for them all, and it won't be with mercy."

Agent Boulder looked at a message on his phone and excused himself.

Perez was losing his patience, wanting desperately to call Kathy to warn her about her planned actions, but concerned that he would only spook them and force them underground. He could imagine the desperation growing within them, but committing suicide by a foolhardy plan wasn't going to help the situation.

He fondled his phone in his hand, feeling the temptation to place the call through and warn her, but he dropped it on the desk. Almost instantly, a text came through. He picked it back up, his eyes widening as he read the notification.

"What the—?" he exclaimed. "This has to be him!"

Perez shot out of his chair in search of Agent Boulder. He found him battling through some data at his workstation.

"Boulder, I need you to run through this text that I just got with your tech guys, and try and trace the source," he instructed, laying the phone on the table before him.

Agent Boulder picked up the phone, running through the text, an expression of wonder crossing his face. "*He* sent this, didn't he? This *must have* come from him."

"I don't know what to think yet, but I assume it truly is from him."

"If what he is saying is true, then he is on a suicide mission," Agent Boulder said, returning his attention to his computer. After entering the texted phone number into the system, he began running codes on it to trace the specific point that it had been sent from.

Perez all but danced by his side, eager to find out more. "That's if we can trust that lying, conniving bastard to begin with," he replied, determined to find out one way or another.

And their only means of finding out was to find him, and fast, from the hint of caution the text message read.

The clock was ticking, and time was running out.

# BROKEN

# CHAPTER FIFTY-THREE | 53

JOEL WATCHED BROWN shake down his entire team of guards, turning their rooms upside down to find his missing ring with the key and flash drive. He was enraged, determined to find his device. He personally went through the guards' rooms, yelling upon finding the ring with the key hidden within the belongings of one of his guards. But it didn't have the flash drive.

"You bastards!" he raged. "Nobody leaves this house until that drive is found!"

Everyone was afraid, but no one as much as Joel. He needed to escape quickly. He needed not only to get himself to safety, but also to get some needed information out to the authorities. He still hadn't found out everything he wanted about the enterprise, such as the true boss, the Arizona connections, and other essential information that he had come specifically for, but that would come to follow soon enough.

Hopefully.

If he survived this.

Joel was pretending to look for the drive as well, trying his best to blend in with the rest. Quickly, he sent a text message and found some of the vehicle keys from outside before Mr. Brown saw him. He had gotten to the back door, wishing to sneak out unnoticed, when the boss called his name, angrily. *Accusingly.*

"Lion! Where do you *think* you're going?"

Joel turned around slowly, feeling that he was being suspected, but he needed to play it cool, at least until he got an opening to make an escape.

"I need to check something out back," Joel replied. "Just in case it fell outside or something..."

"But I just told you: nobody is allowed out of here."

Joel felt trapped. "Oh, yeah. I wasn't actually going anywhere, though. Like I said, I just wanted to—"

"You actually think I don't know who you are?" Mr. Brown asked, a mean glint in his eye. Then he started laughing out loud.

Joel walked back slowly, watching the intimidating man move closer.

"You of all people should know we would find out," Brown continued. "*Ho-El Lay-on*, father of *Pay-Tra Lay-on*, and ex-husband to one cute Kathy Potter—a fine piece of ass, if I do say so myself, by the way. Like mother, like daughter. Maybe we should've gone for her too."

Joel could feel his heart threatening to come out of his chest. But in his anxiety, he remained unable to move.

Brown continued, "That's right. I know it all. You are the *lion* who came all the way from Arizona to find his daughter, by becoming someone else, all in a bid to penetrate our organization. Ha! Look at this lion... looking more like a cub to me, just like the other time."

The guards all laughed.

Joel was genuinely surprised. He didn't have any idea that he had been made out. He thought he still had some time to get things right and rolling.

*How long has he known?*

"And you know what?" Brown added, "I wouldn't even have found out, had a little birdie not clued me in," he explained. "I was glad to have you along. But ever since then, I've been marinating my plan to deal with you. And now you've made me rush, by being so stupid to steal from me. You little idiot! Give me back the flash drive, *Ho-El*, or you die as slowly and as painfully as I can make it!"

*How did he find out? Who told him? What do I do?*

Though Joel was full of questions, he knew beyond a shadow of a doubt that the warning was not simply a threat to scare him. He also knew, however, that they would most likely kill him no matter what kind of deal he made. *No!* He couldn't lose now. He was so close. He had more than enough to implicate Gregory Brown and his entire organization, at least locally, and hopefully the location of his missing daughter.

"I'll give it to you, on one condition alone," Joel offered, not really knowing what else to say and trying to buy precious minutes to think.

"Trust me, you don't want to mess with us, little lion. Or should I just stick to calling you *Joel* now, since we're putting our cards on the table?"

Joel didn't answer. During Mr. Brown's little speech, Joel had made good contact with the door, gently opening it.

"*Ho-El Lay-on!* Give me back my fucking device, *now!*"

"Give me my daughter, and I will return your flash drive to you," he said. "I hid it, and I will tell you where it is. I don't care about your organization or even the money. You can keep it all. I just want my baby girl back."

But Gregory Brown wasn't having any of it, motioning for his guards to apprehend Joel, who made an immediate run out the back door. He headed straight for the car parked outside the building. He had been fortunate enough to see that they kept the keys for this particular vehicle in a living room coffee table, and he had snagged them before trying to escape and being discovered by Brown. All those years of a steady workout and running regimen finally paid off, because he had just enough time to throw himself in the car and start the engine before Brown's men reached him. He locked the doors just as one jerked the handle and banged menacingly on the glass.

Joel put the car in gear and stamped on the accelerator. One unfortunate foot soldier was in front of the car, and the solid thump of his body under the wheels made Joel slightly sick, though no less intent on his goal. Another group of men had clearly gone for their vehicles instead of giving him chase on foot, and they right on his tail, guns pointed out the window of the huge SUV.

Joel had one destination in mind, and it was the one place that Gregory Brown had his *merchandise* locked and secured away in for most of the time, up until they were distributed and structured to begin work. Now he knew where it was.

He dialed 911 on his phone, multitasking as he maneuvered his way past some trees and through the gate. Brown's men were chasing closely behind, and he knew they weren't afraid to use lethal force.

"Come, on, answer!"

"Yes, 911, what's your emergency?"

Joel reached the freeway, as the men continued to tail. Mr. Brown had also joined in a car behind. "Yes, I have something important to tell you," he screamed into the phone as he focused on his drive.
*I hope you got my text,* he thought, thinking of Agent Raymond Perez. *Please don't fail me.*

# BROKEN

# CHAPTER FIFTY-FOUR | 54

MY GREATEST WISH to perform my own compositions in front of thousands of people. I would give anything to do that. My biggest fear, on the other hand, has always been that people wouldn't like my songs. That they wouldn't like me. That they would make fun of me.

Right now, however, I don't care if I never touch a piano key ever again. I don't care if I go mute and can never sing again. All I want is to be with my family. I sit in the corner of the room, grab my knees, and weep. God is silent. Perhaps this is my destiny, after all.

The boss is coming today. Even the demons are nervous. I am petrified.

I know I said before I was excited to get out of this place and go into my new life and a new place. I know I said I was willing to do whatever. I know I said I was okay being Eve.

But I am not.

I need to get out of here! Please, please... someone please listen. Don't forget me.

Somehow, I manage to pray. *Please, Lord, I can't bear it anymore. Save me! Take me home.*

Gunfire, shouting, and commotion is heard outside our captivity room. The kids scatter to the corners and under furniture, wailing and clutching each other. We hear the demons yelling, scared.

Is that the boss?

# CHAPTER FIFTY-FIVE | 55

AGENT PEREZ AND HIS ENTIRE SQUAD arrived at the location Joel had texted to be. A SWAT team from LAPD had just settled in place upon their arrival. It wasn't a pretty place, but at the same time, the metal-sided warehouse gray building didn't look like a den of iniquity either. It was a normal commercial edifice, like many other ones in the area.

"Can we trust this guy?" Agent Boulder asked his partner, wondering why they should even believe Joel's text asking Agent Perez to send over an FBI squad and an arsenal of cops to an unmarked building with a large parking lot.

No sooner had they gotten there and settled, a car came careening into the parking area, screeching to a halt just feet away.

Guns were pointed at the vehicle, fingers were one the trigger.

"Wait, don't shoot!" Perez screamed as he saw who was driving.

The sight of Joel stumbling out of the car with his hands up high, his body shaking with fear as more cars tore into the lot from behind him, was a sight to behold. The ghost had appeared, and had brought the trouble to them.

Deadly trouble.

"I'm unarmed, and I believe you'll find the missing kids in there!" he screamed as he pointed to the building while hunkering down on the pavement. "I can tell you everything about their operation. This is why I went missing and became a fugitive. It is all on this flash drive," he explained, holding the flash drive up as he kneeled down and then laid fully on the ground.

"But they're coming! And they're armed!" He was holding the USB device up, just as a bullet whizzed past him. One of the uniformed officers crawled out and grabbed Joel, dragging him to the relative safety of the squad car barricade.

Agent Perez, the rest of his team, and the remaining officers turned their attention to the incoming firestorm. The SWAT team did their part to unbalance the terms, making this fight heavily one-sided , though several of Brown's guards poured out of the warehouse's front entrance, making for a two-front battle. The agents and Joel were in the middle of the line of fire; it was a full-on war.

But it was no fair match for the outnumbered and outgunned criminals. The battle didn't last long. Several were apprehended, most were killed on site.

In the middle of the fire exchange, Joel ran toward the side of the building to evade the bullets, as if on a mission, with three members of the SWAT team following him closely. He led them to the rear side of the building, where a large door stood. They could hear the muffled sounds of screaming and crying from the other side.

"I think they're in there," Joel informed the SWAT agents, who went about their business to get the door opened, while the fight continued on the other side of the building.

The officers brought the door down, revealing a large warehouse. Inside were smaller compartments set up as housing units. Two men came running out of the building with guns, but were shot down right away by the SWAT members.

Joel ran inside, screaming for Petra. One of the agents grabbed for him, trying to keep him safe until the building was secured. Joel shook him off and continued to run, looking for the one person he had gone through hell to find. Nothing would stop him now. He knew she was here, somewhere. The agents were soon distracted by apprehending the remaining guards inside the compound.

"All cleared!" one of them yelled.

"Clear," echoed another from the other side.

As the agents cleared the area and one of them caught up with Joel, he was already opening a large metal door to an inner room. With guns pointed inside, the agent saw them.

Children. Dozens, boys and girls. They were petrified. They were from a broad range of ethnic backgrounds, ranging in age from eight to nearly grown, malnourished, and cowering.

Joel looked around, in search of the one person that he had gone through hell for. "Petra! Baby, are you here? *Papi* is here."

Petra's frightened, squeaky voice replied from behind the group of kids. "*Papi? Papi.* I am over here!"

Joel made his way in between the children and grabbed her in a fierce hug. He sobbed. So did she.

"I am sorry, *Papi!*" she wailed as she dug her face in his chest. "I am so sorry that I was so mean to you the last time that I saw you and told you that I hated you and that I never wanted to see you again. Please, forgive me, *Papi!* I am so sorry! I wish I could take it all back. *Perdóname!*"

The almost-naked teenager was crying and trembling hysterically in her father's arms. She didn't dare to look up and see the look in his eyes. She was embarrassed and ashamed. "I had given up," she added in between sobs.

"*Mi amor!* You are my everything. And I would *never* give up on you. I forgave you the moment you said such things. I love you, and I would give my life for you, *bebé.* It's okay; I am here now. *Papi* is here. I came for *you,* my love."

Joel felt Petra's embrace stronger than ever. She held him tighter, as her tears continued to flow.

"I prayed, *Papi*. I prayed to be rescued just before you came."

"Let's move them out," one of the SWAT members ordered before Joel could say anything. "Come with us, sir."

The armed officers led the group of children, including Joel and Petra, who were last, out the front doors of the building. Outside, Agent Perez and his team were dealing with the kidnapping ring's guards, cuffing the ones left alive, and compiling the list of dead bodies sustained during the shootout. From what Joel could see, no agent had been lost, only a few wounded.

The kids were given water and blankets to cover themselves. Police officers were now taking information from their behalf. Many parents would soon know the joy that Joel was experiencing, that their child was alive and rescued, and that the culprits had either been arrested or killed.

Petra, now wrapped in her father's shirt, was still at her father's side, refusing to let go of the man who had risked it all to rescue her. She had just heard the story. He was her hero, and his bravery had helped expose a criminal ring, and most importantly, discovered where all the kidnapped children were.

Reporters from local news and newspapers were showing up to report on the happenings, as a helicopter had followed along when multiple 911 calls came from other drivers in the I-10 freeway as Joel had sped down the road. Now, there were multiple helicopters flying in circles above them.

A female reporter from the *L.A. Chronicle*, Genesis Gill, had been doing her own sleuth work trying to expose criminal organizations that trafficked children for the purposes of sex slavery and child pornography in Southern California. Her partner was snapping pictures of the father and daughter as Gill was finishing an interview with the duo, when Agent Perez came to talk to them.

"Joel León, you are one difficult man to understand," he said, shaking hands with Joel.

"I am sorry that I put you all into so much trouble, but I needed to find my daughter. I am sure you understand. I couldn't be detained, knowing that the longer time passed, the more difficult it would be to ever find my baby. You have no idea the kinds of favors I had to ask to pull this off."

"I do understand, Mr. León. And while I don't have kids myself, trust me, I would also do anything for my loved ones. However, we still have a lot of questions that need answering, as I am sure you'll understand."

"I'm sure you do. I'd be glad to do whatever I can."

Together, they walked toward one of the FBI vans, where Agent Boulder was going through the files on the flash drive that Joel had given to them on a laptop.

Upon arriving, Petra began to speak. "It was Brett. Brett did it..." Petra noted in a weak tone.

"What?" Agent Perez asked, confused, as if wanting to make sure he had heard right.

"Brett Miller, my mother's fiancé, and his friend—they abducted me," she said, this time firmer and looking at the agent straight in the eyes. "I mean, it wasn't him, exactly, but his colleagues. He had them do it," she said angrily, as a tear dropped to her cheeks.

"How do you know it was his doing, if he actually didn't do it?" Agent Perez asked.

"I knew there was something with that bastard," Joel roared, throwing his hands in the air.

"It was this couple, good friends of Brett. But I heard them talking to him when they took me. I heard him clearly, and they talked to him several times." Petra said, followed by a sip of water from a bottle that they had given her.

"I believe she might be right," Boulder said. "Brett isn't even his real name. And it seems that he actually is the mastermind behind this entire operation. I think *he* is Jacob Doyle. Everything is in here. Look." Boulder showed Perez the laptop. Joel could also see it clearly.

It showed information on Jacob Doyle, alias Brett Miller; Alexander Zhirkoff, most likely the boss; Gregory Brown, and some guy named Carlos Wong, as well as detailed information on their victims and their clients.

Apparently, this was an international alliance, working in different countries around the world, trafficking minors from one place to another. They would identify a potential recruit, and then study their schedule and life patterns. Sometimes, if the prize was worth it, they would even infiltrate their social group, whether at school, church, or even the family, in order to gain their trust. They would then take them away at the given right opportunity.

"Oh, my God!" Perez exclaimed, taking out his phone to place a call to Frank, whom he had tasked with handling Kathy and Brett's decision. "The bastard tricked Kathy into believing he had contacted the kidnappers to get cash from her."

Frank took his time to answer, but finally did.

"Whatever you do, detain Brett Miller!" Perez ordered into the phone on speaker mode. "He *is* the kidnapper. *He* is Jacob Doyle! Do not let him escape. You hear me? Get Scott to help you too."

"We're sorry, sir. We lost him when he refused to show up after we tailed them both from home to the exchange site," Frank informed Perez from his end of the line, loud enough for all to hear.

"What? What do you mean?"

"We would've stopped him, had we known—"

"Shit! Get his picture out, to every outlet possible. I want him found now!" Agent Perez yelled. "We can't lose Brett... Jacob, now." He hung up and then turned to Joel. "We need to head back to Phoenix, Joel. Your family needs you while we hunt that sneaky bastard down," he explained. "We will make sure that Petra gets proper medical assistance on the way. The other kids will be fine here too, as the paramedics are taking care of them already. Most of their parents have all been notified by now."

Joel had never been so happy in his life. He hadn't been the same man they knew, because his paternal instincts had transformed him into a man desperate for the truth.

While it had taken a toll on his sanity, and while he had been castigated as a monster, he didn't care. It had been worth it. His only desire all along had been to reveal the truth of things and to get his daughter back, even if it meant going through a literal hell.

He knew that they were watching him, believing that *he* was the culprit behind her disappearance, so he had to evade the authorities at all costs to keep track of the real criminals. Of course, some of his actions and decisions hadn't helped. And there was nothing he could do about that anymore.

"I am so sorry for everything, Petra!" Joel apologized, watching his frail daughter shed more tears as they headed into the black SUV provided to them for transport.

"You were right all along, *Papi*. I should've trusted you and not Brett... Jacob. Or whatever he heck his name is. The devil!"

"It's okay, baby girl."

"But yeah, it was his friends who took me after you dropped me off, while they spoke on the phone. I clearly heard Brett on the other line, *Papi*, because he was on speaker. It was him! This guy and his wife came to the house, supposedly looking for Brett, right after you dropped me off at home that night. But they grabbed me and took me into a van. They ripped my dress up and then they injected me with something."

"What guy? His wife? Who are you talking about?"

"You've met this guy, *Papi*, at a barbeque we had once. Lloyd. He came to our house regularly when you weren't with us, and is supposedly Brett's work colleague, or something," Petra explained. "He and his supposed wife always smell funny too. Like they are wearing the same cologne as Brett."

Then it hit Joel where he had smelled that cologne before. *That dirty bastard…*

"Joel, like I said, there are several things that I need to clarify, though," Agent Perez interrupted from the front seat. "For example, why was she bleeding in your car, on the night that you picked her up from the fair?"

"I didn't hurt her!" Joel promised.

"I had a bad nosebleed that night, after all the yelling and shouting at the restaurant and the drive. It happens to me sometimes. Especially with changes of weather," Petra explained. "I actually made a bloody mess in his car," she continued. "I got it all over my clothes, too."

"Huh. Interesting," the agent said. "I guess I can visualize it all now."

"Has Mom been notified?" Petra asked.

"She has," the agent replied. "But I figured you'd like to speak to her, and she definitely wants to speak with you. You can use my phone," he added as the driver sped off to the Ontario Airport, where the hunt for Brett—Jacob, the liar—would continue.

Soon the León family would be reunited.

And soon, they'd all hear the story from his and Petra's side.

# BROKEN

# EPILOGUE

THREE WEEKS HAVE PASSED, and a lot has happened during this time. I learned that my church and my school had organized a search for me during my disappearance. I also learned that my friends and family had been busy doing more than just crying during my absence; they were physically searching for me, including being proactive online for any clues. Especially Amanda and the girls. A party was even held in my honor to welcome me back.

I was interviewed by Genesis Gill of the *L.A. Chronicle*, and a piece was written about my ordeal. My entire story was published today, and it will hopefully bring about awareness of this cruel reality that exists.

But something else also happened during these past weeks. Dad made peace with the family, asking for our forgiveness. And we all did the same to him, for believing and having concluded with certainty that he was the devil himself, when in fact we'd let it into our home. It is evident now that we misinterpreted his jealousy. In reality, he was truly being a loving father this entire time, wishing nothing but to get me back unharmed.

Dad now owes money to the IRS, but his money in the wall all checked out. He had recently gotten paid for a big building project, and had wanted accessible cash for his investigation without drawing attention from the bank. So he stashed the money in the garage for safekeeping. The posters with pictures and information on the missing girls on his attic were from his own investigation, with the help of his friend Ricky, who does sleuth work like this for a living. Since no one had believed him, Dad felt like he would have to take matters into his own hands, until he went on the run after me. The clothes in his home were from a time James and I went to his place and used the community pool. The blood in his car had all been explained and cleared.

There is no doubt in anyone's minds that both my parents love James and me unconditionally. They both realize that having a healthy relationship between them is the best for us, and while it will take time, they are eager to continue a friendship like they did before Brett... Jacob... came into our lives. And that's all that James and I want anyway.

Mom is struggling with her own issues after discovering that she had brought a monster into our home and our lives, but she is getting help from a therapist. I'm glad she's also getting help, because I cannot imagine the guilt and regret she must have of bringing someone like that into her kids' life. Not to mention the personal sense of violation at being in a relationship with someone as evil as him.

I am doing well too. Well, better. It's a work in progress. My father's embrace and forgiveness when I was rescued were all that I needed to begin mending the broken pieces of my soul. It was in that moment that I felt complete again. And now, back home, the healing process is in full effect. I am taking it one day at a time. It's all I can do. I know that my healing will take time, but I am learning to not blame myself for any of this. Of course, my own therapist helps a lot.

Sometimes in the middle of the night I wake up shivering. The nightmares come and go. I still sleep in my mom's room at night. Sometimes during the day I cry for no apparent reason. But each time, my loved ones simply hug me and let me know that they are there for me.

I know that there are videos of me out there. And yes, I am still scared go to out anywhere by myself. Perhaps I will never be the same. However, I am reminded daily of who I am. I am Petra León. I am strong. I am resilient. And even though I was broken, I am being made whole again.

Interestingly, I do feel like I have matured since the incident. I appreciate every minute of my life. I am now enjoying better meals and the company of my loved ones, cherishing every moment of my freedom and loving family. I also try not to fight too much with James. He's changed, too. We all have been transformed by this experience.

Today, we are having a special meal after church. A celebration of life. Mateo is here with us too. He and I also made our peace. We agreed to take things slower. I sure am glad about that. I need to work on me first. And to be honest, I get scared of being kissed or touched. It triggers bad memories. Besides, I suddenly feel so young for all of this. Of course, he understands. Mateo and his sister will always be my cherished friends, no matter what, and I am thankful for that.

My relationship with Pastor John is also different. I now understand that this all stemmed from immaturity, and children should never be involved with adults in certain ways. The truth is that, whether I accept it or not, I know I am still a child. Pastor John is a good man, with a great family, and I believe he's learned a few lessons on how to interact with youth too.

Dad is over for lunch today. And I am so glad he came! I hope he visits more often. Jimbo and I certainly want to spend more time with him, and with his life changes, he says he'll make all the time in the world for us. I couldn't be happier about that.

After the meal, Dad read out loud from a tablet the piece about me in the *L.A. Chronicle*. The piece is titled "Little Barbies." At first, I didn't know what to think about it. I knew it was an investigative article about children who are being bought and sold for sex in the United States, and that it took Ms. Gill across international and state borders. I also think that it will bring awareness, and that my story needs to be told. However, as my dad begins to read, I start to shake. I grab on to my chair, feeling sweat dripping on my neck.

"Child sex trafficking is a big business, quickly becoming even more lucrative than illegal drugs and guns," he reads. "A pound of methamphetamine or a Glock can be retailed only once, but a young girl can be sold up to fifty times a day."

As memories of my captivity rise to my mind, I start breathing harder. James, who is sitting next to me, hugs me. I put my face on his shoulder and squeeze his arm.

"There were boys too," I say.

"What, my love?" Dad asks.

"It was both, girls and boys," I repeat. "Just go on."

Dad clears his throat as he continues reading to us. "It's happening everywhere, right under our noses, in suburbs, cities, and towns across the nation. Trafficked women and children are advertised on the internet, transported on the interstate, and bought and sold in motels, hotels, and even office spaces. They are kept in isolated warehouses, where they are tortured and starved, only to be taken out for 'jobs.' The value placed on human life takes a backseat to profit."

My cheeks are now wet. A combination of tears and cold sweat moisten my face.

"Do you want me to stop, baby?" Dad asks.

"No, *Papi*. It's okay. I want to hear it." I gather courage and sit up straight. "Please continue."

Mateo holds my right hand, and James, my left, as Dad continues.

"I got the chance to meet 'Mindy,' whose name has been changed to protect her. I also met her heroic father, who helped bring the kidnapping ring down. Mindy shared her story with the hopes of bringing awareness to this evil that is happening right under our noses."

I smile, thinking this is the third name given to me. Petra. Eve. Now Mindy.

"'Mindy', a straight-A, talented student who belonged to a close-knit community living in Scottsdale, Arizona, is an example of this trading of flesh. Only fifteen years old, when she was snatched from her own home by an acquaintance's friend and his wife. Forced into a car and held at gunpoint, Mindy was bound, stripped, drugged, and taken to an unknown location in a car trunk. At the location, she was r..." Dad suddenly stops. A tear roll down his cheek. "I am sorry," he says. "This is just... it's hard to read."

"I agree," Mom adds. "I think this might be too graphic to read out loud in front of a survivor, especially in the presence of a friend."

"I need this," I say. "I *want* to hear it. And others need to hear my story too."

My parents look at each other; it is obvious they don't know what to say.

"Are you sure?" James asks me.

"Yes." I am determined.

I reach out across the table and take the tablet. I clear my throat and quickly find where Dad stopped. I continue, "At the location, she was raped by multiple men and filmed. She was also put inside a small dog kennel and treated like a dog. Mindy was taken across state lines to California, where she was placed at a large storage facility with forty-seven other kids, all victims of sexual trafficking, several of them from other countries. Mindy's captors advertised their services online. The money that Mindy and the other children made for their services was kept by her kidnappers. At times, the children were forced to go without water, food, or sleep until meeting a quota of forty to fifty men. The raping, humiliation, and torture continued, until local and federal law enforcement, aided by Mindy's own father, were able to find and liberate her and the other children."

I pause, as my own face is flooded.

"It's okay, baby. You can stop," Mom tells me.

But I continue, "Her traumatic ordeal, a nightmare from beginning to end, lasted for twenty-five long days, but felt like a lifetime. Mindy was broken. However, Mindy's father heroics helped not only liberate all the children taken, but also aided in the apprehension of several of those responsible. I was there when..."

Suddenly, Dad's phone rings interrupting my reading.

"It's Agent Perez," he says, bringing an eerie silence to the room. He excuses himself from the table to take the call.

I put the tablet down.

We all look at each other, in unnerving silence. You can hear the clock on the wall as each second passes by.

As we wait, I think about how Ms. Gill told my story and how hard it is to listen and to read it. But I also feel proud in certain places, especially when she talks about me being a survivor and Dad being a hero.

A couple of minutes later, Dad returns with a grim-looking face. We all stare at him with worry.

"What happened? It has to do with Jacob, doesn't it?" I ask, anxious. "Please, we don't want any more bad news, *Papi*." Mateo squeezes my hand to comfort me.

"Just tell us, Joel," Mom demands.

Dad takes his seat again, still wearing the gloomy look, before suddenly bursting into a happy smile, revealing bright white teeth. "They caught him! They caught the bastard down at the border in Douglas, trying to escape to Mexico," he says, raising his hands in the air in victory.

We all shout in joy, relieved that justice will be served and that everyone is safer without him on the streets.

Dad looks around to each of us with a smile on his face. There is joy in our hearts. I hadn't seen James this happy since I got back. Mom can't contain her excitement, either. Mateo smiles. And I cry with joy.

My family went through hell. I was taken and broken. Dad was compared to the devil himself, and he himself suffered on my behalf. But he endured it all in order to come out on top, even when it seemed that God wasn't on his side.

However, as I look around the room, I see that the love my parents have for us surpasses everything, even understanding. It is evident to me now. They would have given their lives to save me, paid any amount of money, and never given up on me. And they would've done the same for James, if it had been him in the same situation.

"I guess Jacob couldn't be like you, *Papi*. He wasn't smart enough to get away, after all," Jimmy teases.

We all laugh.

"You know what?" I say, "Jacob *is* a better name for him. A deceiver. A liar who fooled us all. But in the end, all lies crumble and truth prevails."

"He never fooled *me!*" Dad replies with brows raised.

"True that," James says.

I don't recall ever being this happy as a family. And now, we all gather together in the middle of the living room after our meal and do a group hug. It is a long embrace. The unit is all back together as it used to be before.

"It's great to be home," I state with happy tears. "I just want to see you more often, *Papi*."

"Oh, you will, *mi amor*. That's a promise! You'll see me so much, you will get tired of my face," he teases.

"I doubt that!" I smile and hug him. "I love you, *Papi*."

"I love you too."

Yes, I was taken. I was broken. But my journey back to wholeness starts in the best place that it could happened—in the arms of my loving father.

All is well with my soul.

# BROKEN

## <u>Human Trafficking Statistics</u>

- Human trafficking generates $9.5 billion yearly in the United States alone (United Nations).
- The average age of entry into prostitution for a child victim in the US is 13 years old (U.S. Department of Justice).
- The average victim may be forced to have sex up to 20–48 times a day (Polaris Project).
- Fewer than 100 beds are available in the United States for underage victims (Health and Human Services).
- A pimp can make $150,000–$200,000 per child each year, and the average pimp has 4 to 6 girls (U.S. Department of National Center for Missing and Exploited Children).
- One in three teens on the street will be lured toward prostitution within 48 hours of leaving home (National Runaway Safeline).
- Nearly 800,000 children go missing every year; that is roughly 2,185 children a day (National Center for Missing and Exploited Children).
- Adults purchase children for sex at least 2.5 million times a year  in the United States (USA Today).
- Every two minutes, a child is exploited in the sex industry (Huffington Post).
- On average, a child might be raped by 6,000 men during a five-year period of servitude (Sun Sentinel).
- It is estimated that  at least 100,000 to 300,000 children – boys and girls – are bought and sold for sex in the U.S. every year; some of these children are forcefully abducted, others are runaways, and still others are sold into the system by relatives and acquaintances (U.S. Department of Justice).
- For every 10 women rescued, there are 50 to 100 more women who are brought in by the traffickers (CNN).
- Immigrants, runaways, foster youth, and children in youth shelters are usually the prime targets for sex traffickers (Herald Tribune).
- Those being sold for sex have an  average life expectancy of seven years, and those years are a living nightmare of endless rape, forced drugging, humiliation, degradation, threats, disease, pregnancies, abortions, miscarriages, torture, pain, and always the constant fear of being killed or, worse, having those you love being hurt or killed (National Center for Missing and Exploited Children).

# About the Author

Obed Olivarría was born in Mexicali, Mexico and spent his youth as a fully bicultural transnational citizen. He has a passion for writing both fiction and nonfiction, public speaking, composing, arranging, and performing music, as well as traveling around the world. He loves the thrill of adrenaline-pumping activities, but also the quiet reflection he gets from writing and creating.

His love for books started at an early age, as his parents were eager readers and owned thousands of books. His passion for writing was born after winning a city-wide short story competition while in high school in Arizona. The publication of this in a local journal inspired him to continue creating worlds and characters in print.

Obed has worked as a youth and young adult pastor, as a graphic designer, as a session musician, as a ministry consultant, as university dean, as school administrator, and school psychologist. Having worked at every level of the education system, from pre-k to university, has given him an expedition to the human psyche. He has a dynamic love of life and ministry, and he is a deep thinker, and an honest intellectual to the Christian gospel.

Obed lives in sunny Orange County, California with his charming wife and two energetic children. Obed hopes to continue writing inspiring books that entertain, but also challenge the status quo. Personally, he would like to visit every country in the world, drawing inspiration from these travels for another great story.